"Where's Silver?" shriek
my mind filled with panic, communicating at one
hundred times its normal rate.

I scoured the raging skies. There was no sign of him.
An instant later the cloud patterns changed and
great grey and white streamers poured upwards and
out of sight. Harmony screamed, suddenly and
loudly, and I looked and saw Silver, a small, dark
shape, totally at the mercy of the gravitational
vacuum. His limbs threshed, his body slowly twisted
as he rose and fell, fighting ineffectually with his
gravity belt. He vanished into cloud, re-appeared to
plummet down for a second, up for a second, round
and round, tossed and flung – plunging towards the
event!

"THERE!" cried a hundred voices. "SEE THERE!"

The clouds vanished in the centre of a whirlpool,
into an area of distorted imagery and vanishing
perspective. And at the very centre flared a brilliant
spot of intensely blue-white light.

The quantum black hole itself!

ROBERT HOLDSTOCK

In the Valley of the Statues

the Statues

and

Other Stories

VGSF

VGSF is an imprint of Victor Gollancz Ltd
14 Henrietta Street, London WC2E 8QJ

First published in Great Britain 1982
by Faber and Faber Limited

First VGSF edition 1988

British Library Cataloguing in Publication Data
Holdstock, Robert
 In the valley of the statues: a collection
 of short stories.
 I. Title
 823'.914[F]   PR6058.O442

 ISBN 0-575-04023-8

Printed and bound in Great Britain
by Richard Clay Ltd, Bungay, Suffolk

To Eric and Diane (and BJ too!)

Contents

Acknowledgements

I wish to express my thanks to both the Dublin Office of Public Works and to the archives of Trinity College for their patient and interested assistance during my location work on "Earth and Stone".

Earth and Stone

The sunshine is a glorious birth;
But yet I know, where'er I go,
That there hath past away a glory from the earth.
Wordsworth, *Intimations of Immortality*

Carrying loudly across the rolling grasslands the *crack* of transmission was almost indistinguishable from that *crack* which follows the splitting of the great boulders, the megaliths of the tomb-builders who had lived in this land for seven hundred years.

The man, riding on a stocky, black horse, appeared as if out of nowhere. He was well wrapped in skins and fur leggings, and wore his hair in tight, shoulder-length plaits. His beard and moustaches were curled and stiff with some reddish paste. His saddlebags were anachronistic in this third millennium before Christ, but were at least fashioned crudely out of leather; their geometrical bulkiness was unavoidable since the equipment they contained was essential for the man's ultimate return to his own age. Like the horse, the leather bags and what they contained would be destroyed as soon as they had served their purpose. Of that there was no doubt in the man's mind at all; but his conviction was for the wrong reason. He had no intention of ever returning to his own time. He was going to remain here, among the people of the Boyne valley with whom he had become so involved—in an academic sense —during the short span of his life.

His name was John Farrel. He was nearly thirty years old

and in this time of earth and stone he expected to be able to live another ten years.

As he came through the transmission field he turned his horse and peered into the blur that was the future. It started to fade and the last air of another time leaked five thousand years into its past, bringing with it a sour smell—the smell of machines, of artificial scent, of synthetic clothes; the odour, the stench, of successful adaptation.

Cold winds, the winter's last voice before the sudden warmth of spring, carried the smell of the future away, dispersed it across a land wider than Farrel had ever known. Machine, perfume, plastic, drained into the earth, were sucked down and away, lost from the grassy crispness of this age of rock and blood.

Farrel rode up the small hillock that lay immediately in front of the transmission field, turned again as he reached the summit, and peered down the valley. The river Boyne wound across the landscape, a silver thread meandering eccentrically between the low hills until it passed out of view. Farrel's mind's eye felt, for a moment, the lack of the sprawl of red brick dwellings that would one day supersede those ragged forestlands of the wider curve. For a moment he thought he saw a car flashing along a main road : sunlight on speeding chrome. The illusion was just the gleam of fragmentary sunlight on the spread wings of a gull, riding the winds above the river, back to the sea.

Where the transmission field was slowly dissolving the river was a blur, the land a green haze that came more and more into focus. Wind caught Farrel's hair, cooled the sweat on his cheeks and made him blink. The grass beneath him seemed to whisper; the wind itself talked an incoherent murmur. It droned, distantly. Grey clouds swept across the pale sun and shadows fled across the valley, were chased away by brightness. The transmission field finally faded and was gone.

For a moment, then, Farrel imagined he saw a woman's face, round and ageing; blonde hair perfectly styled, but eye-shadow blurred and smeared with tears and bitter, bitter anger. *Why you? Why you? Why you?*

Her remembered words were only the gusting winds and the animal sounds of his horse, restless and anxious to be given free rein across this wild land.

How loud the silence after hysteria, he thought. He had not known how haunting another's heartbreak could be. *You'll never come back! Don't lie to me, you'll never come back. I know you too well, John. This is your way out, your means of escape. My God, you must really hate me. You must really hate us all!*

Last words, lost in the roar of street traffic. The stairs had trembled beneath him. The outer door had slammed, an explosion finishing them forever.

I'm here now. I'm here. I got away from them, from all of them, and they think—most of them think—that I'm going back when my job is done. But I'm not! I'm not going back! I'm here and I got away from everything, and I'm not going back!

The ghosts of the future faded, then, following the transmission field forward across the centuries. The land about Farrel came sharply into focus. His mind cleared. He breathed deeply, and though for a second he felt the urge to cry, he stifled that urge and looked around him, stared at the unadulterated landscape.

Small mounds were scattered in clusters down the hillside and concentrated along the river itself (thus being nearer to the river goddess, or so Burton had implied in his last transmission). The oldest tumulus was possibly no more than two hundred years of age. The youngest? Farrel searched among them: four hundred yards away there was a mound, perhaps twice his height, perhaps fifty feet in diameter. It had a kerb of grey stones which separated the dull greenness of the hillside from the dark earth mound, not yet fully covered with its own field of grass. A grave, perhaps no more than half a year old; new, with the cremated remains inside it still heavy with the smell of burning.

He felt dizzy with excitement as he associated this new tomb with the low grassy bump that it would become during the next five thousand years, a tomb so crumbled and weathered that only the discovery of its fractured kerb-stones would identify it. A handful of carbon fragments, preserved in a natural cist between two of the chamber stones and identified as human remains, would raise a thousand questions in the minds of those who were fascinated by this enigmatic neolithic culture. And a year ago those splinters of charred bone might have been alive, walking this very countryside.

A flight of starlings wheeled above his head, spiralling at the mercy of the winds. A lone magpie darted among them until the starlings turned on it, and then the bigger bird dropped away down the hill to vanish against the sheen of the river. The shrill bird song was a brief symphony of panic and Farrel reined his horse around so that he could look towards the distant forest and the rolling downs of what would one day be his home county.

From behind a low, rain- and wind-smoothed boulder, a boy was watching him.

FIRST TRANSMISSION—SECOND DAY

I have arrived in early spring, and as far as I can determine, seven months later than anticipated rather than five months early. I don't blame Burton for not being here to meet me. He must have rapidly become tired of hanging about, especially with something "fantastic" in the offing. Whatever was about to happen that so excited him, there is no sign, now, of either him or the Tuthanach themselves. Correction: a single Tuthanach . . . a boy. This is the strange boy that Burton mentioned in his last transmission, and he is the only human life I have seen in these first few hours, apart from some invisible activity (in the form of smoke) from the direction of the hill of Tara. The boy was not overly curious about the horse, and has shown no interest in its disappearance. He ate some of its meat today and never commented on what must surely have been an unusual flavour. I'm very grateful to everyone who made me bring the horse, by the way. I'd never have caught any of the wild life, and I had to travel a good two miles to find a satisfactory hiding place. The village—I suppose I should say *crog Tutha*—is deserted and shows distinct signs of weathering. I confess that I am somewhat puzzled. The burial mound at Coffey's site K, by the way, is very new, something that Burton failed to report. I had a frightening thought earlier: could Burton be buried there? There is no sign yet of tombs on sites L or B, but there are so many others that are not detectable at all by the twenty-first century that I don't know where to begin. Burton hinted as much, didn't he? I wonder why he didn't go into specifics? The tumulus at site J is already well weathered, which suggests our dating was a little out—say by four hundred years? And as Burton reported, the site of the giant Newgrange mound is still barren. I actually came out of the transmission field on the very spot the great tumulus will occupy. I didn't realize it for quite a while, and then it made me feel very strange. Further details will follow in my second transmission. For the moment, since my fingers are aching: signing off.

For the first two nights Farrel and the boy slept in the spacious shelter afforded by a deep rock overhang and the entwined branches and roots of several stubby elms that surrounded the cave. By the third day Farrel's interest in the unexpectedly deserted crog began to outweigh his reluctance to actually camp in the decaying village. He remained uneasy. What if the Tuthanach returned during the night and took exception to a stranger setting himself down in their tents? Burton's report had not indicated that this particular Boyne people was in any way warlike or violent, but this period of the neolithic was a time of great movement, populations succeeding populations, and axe and spear-head used for drastic and final ends. The megalithic tomb-builders of Brittany, especially, were familiar with this part of the Irish coast. In their massive coracles they hugged the south coast of England until the confused currents around Land's End swept them round the Scillies and up into the warm flow of the Irish Sea. From there they up-oared and the shallow seas carried them automatically to the Irish coast north of Dublin, along just those picturesque beaches that had seen the original settlers putting into shore, seven or eight hundred years before.

In one of his transmissions, Burton had given a single, brief account of a small "rock-stealing" party that had raided a crog further south, near Fourknocks (crog-Ceinarc). The raiders had killed and been killed, not by the Ceinarc, but by wolves.

Wolves were what Farrel feared most. In his own time wolf packs were quite timid and easily scared. In this age, however, their behaviour was altogether different—they were fierce, persistent and deadly. Better, he thought, to believe in the non-hostility of the Tuthanach than risk the teeth of such wolf packs. Provided he kept clear of the rocks and stones in the territory of crog-Tutha, and in no way "stole" them by carving his own soul spirit upon them, he imagined he would be safe.

He explained his plan to the boy, whose name was Ennik-tig-en'cruig (Tig-never touch woman-never touch earth). The boy put a hand to his testicles and inclined his head to the right. Uncertainty? Yes, Farrel realized—a shrug, but a shrug overlain with anxiety.

"Would this Tig's people kill us if they returned?" he asked, hoping he had said what he meant to say. . . . (Man-woman this Tig and this Farrel on the wind—tomorrow, more tomorrow man-woman close to this Tig this Farrel?)

Tig darted to the entrance of the overhang, peered out across the windy downs, looked up to where the branches of the elms waved and weaved across the drifting clouds. He spat violently upwards, came back to Farrel grinning.

"Death (—wind—) has no room for this Tig. If this Farrel

14

stranger will be my friend (—lover?—earth-turner?—) death will spit at this Farrel too."

"Did death make room for that Burton?"

Tig sat upright and stared deeply into Farrel's eyes. For two days the boy had declined any knowledge of Burton, pretending (obviously pretending) not to understand. Now Farrel pushed his advantage home.

"Does this Tig want this Farrel stranger as a friend? Then this Tig must tell this Farrel where that Burton lives or dies."

Tig curled up into a ball, burying his head beneath his arms. He wailed loudly. Farrel was about to ask again when Tig spoke:

"That man-stranger Burton is touching earth. All Tuthanach are touching earth. Not this Tig. Not this Tig. Not this Tig."

Farrel considered this carefully, not wishing to distress Tig to the point where the boy would leave. He knew that "touching earth" was something immensely important to the Tuthanach, and he knew that Tig was forbidden his birthright of touching. He could not touch women, he could not touch earth. No love, no involvement with the land. No children for Tig, and no spring harvest as the result of his love for the earth. Poor Tig, denied the two most wonderful consummations of this early agricultural age. But why?

"Where does that Burton touch earth?" he asked.

The boy looked blank.

"Where?" pressed Farrel.

Tig again crawled to the cave entrance and spat into the wind. "This Tig is just a beast!" he yelled. "That man-stranger Burton said this Tig is just a beast!"

And with a loud and painful shriek he vanished, running across the downs, a small skin-clad figure, clay-dyed hair sticking stiffly outwards, fat-greased body shimmering in the weak sunlight.

THIRD TRANSMISSION—FIFTH DAY

Still no sign of the boy who ran off three days ago when I

questioned him about Burton. I suspect Burton upset him in some way, possibly as simply as calling him names. Burton is "touching earth" apparently, but I have a suspicion that he is dead and touching it from a few feet under. I hope I'm wrong. But Tig—the boy—has said that *all* his people are touching earth. What can it mean? I see few of the expected signs of agriculture in the area. My hunch is that they are either farming at some distance from the crog, or raiding other neolithic settlements. Time will tell. I confess that I am worried, however. There is no sign of any equipment or any message or record spools of Burton's. I shall continue to search for such things and also for Burton, whether or not he is alive.

I am now encamped in the crog itself. A pack of dogs terrorizes me, but they are sufficiently diffident at times that I suspect they belong to the village. They have one useful function—they help keep the wolves at bay. I have seen wolves prowling through the cemetery, near the river. They seem to scent something and occasionally excavate a shallow trench in the earth, but always they leave in apparent panic. They also prowl around the skin wall of the crog, but the bones and shrivelled carcasses of their own kind that hang suspended from tree limbs have some effect of discouraging their entry. The dogs chase them off which concludes the process, but they always return. I am not myself safe from the obviously starving mongrels that are sometimes my guardians. If only Tig were here, he might be able to control them.

My H.Q. is the largest hut, possibly the headman's house. The inner walls are daubed with eccentric symbols that are identical to the rock carvings in and around the many tumuli. These paintings are absent from other huts, and I may well be in the local shaman's hide-out.

I keep saying "hut". I should say tents. The material is deer skin, sewn together with leather thongs. No evidence of weaving, though mats, door edges and light-holes through the tents have been made out of leather threads interlinked in suspiciously familiar ways. Wigwam style, four or five shaped wooden poles hold the tent upright. Each tent has a fence of carved bone points standing around it, and in the centre of the crog is a group of four low tents, skin stretched over bowed wooden frames making four rooms not high enough to stand in. These have been separated from the rest of the community by a deep ditch. Carved boulders, showing circle patterns, stand both sides of a single earth bridge across the ditch. Is it a sacred enclosure? An empty grain store? I don't know. I've explored the tents thoroughly and there is nothing in them save for a few polished stone beads, some maul-shaped pendants, spirally carved, and a skin cloth containing five amphibolite pestle-hammers, unused I think. Maybe you can work it out. (Ironic, isn't it ... I'd normally jump to all sorts of conclusions!)

Imagination is the worst enemy still—I'd thought that particular frustration would have stayed behind when I left the future. Ah well. Incidentally—the ditch is probably that small enclosure between the trees at strip-site 20. We're in that sort of area, as I said in my second transmission. Other features along that strip are not in evidence, and may well not be neolithic. I am fairly convinced that this is the Newgrange settlement. There are no other communities in the area, and this one settlement will probably be responsible for all three major tumuli, even though several miles separate them. There's nothing but small burials on the Newgrange site as yet. I wonder when building will begin?

Artifacts? Thousands of drilled stones, pendants; axe and arrow heads; several bows, very short, very limited range; slings, leather of course—two tents used for pottery and some marvellous Carrowkeel pots all lined up ready for firing in small clay and stone kilns. Most of the weapons and stones are clustered inside the skin wall—ready for action? The skin wall itself is two layers of hide, suspended from wooden poles. Human heads have been sewn between the two layers and the outer skins have been drilled with holes so that the dead eyes look out. Although some of the heads are fairly recently severed (both sexes) I can't see Burton's. Hope still flickers.

Head hunting seems to have started even earlier than the pre-Celts, unless these are sacrifices. But no carvings of heads, so perhaps it's just a small part of the culture at the moment.

God, where *are* they all?

It's a marvellous spring. I've never seen so many birds in my life, and the insects!

At dawn of the day following his third transmission, sudden activity among the already noisy lark population of the deserted tents on the western side of the crog brought Farrel running. He recognized the darting grey shape as Tig and called to him. The boy furtively crept out from his hiding place and stared at Farrel, lips slack, eyes dull.

"Glad to see you," called the man. Tig smiled and slapped his hands together.

"This Tig hungry."

"This Farrel hungry too. Can this Tig use a sling?" He waved a leather sling he had been practising with. The boy rushed forward, lips wet, eyes wide, snatched the weapon and lovingly caressed the leather. He stared up at Farrel.

"Lark or hare?"

"Which is the tastiest?"

Tig grinned, slapped his stomach, then dropped to his knees and kissed the soil. Jumping to his feet again he ran off out of sight behind the wall of skins, and ultimately out of earshot down a tree-capped slope. He returned after half an hour, blood on his knees, dirt on his face, but carrying two fat white-chested hares. Farrel started a fire in the small outside hearth that seemed to serve as a fire-pit to all the tents in the vicinity. As the wood fire crackled and browned the pungent flesh, Tig threw tiny chips of stone onto the embers. Retrieving one of the fragments Farrel saw it had been scratched with zigzag lines. The patterning, which he recognized as a standard rock-carving of the Boyne Valley area suggested flame and Tig confirmed this. We take fire from the earth, he explained, so we must make the earth complete again with a small soul-carving.

"But this Farrel didn't carve this. Nor did this Tig. Is that the way it is done?"

Tig immediately became worried. He crawled away from the fire and sat distantly, staring at the smoke. Farrel drew out his mock bone knife, scratched a zigzagging line on the same piece of stone, and cast it onto the flames. Tig grinned and came back to the pit.

"This Tig can't carve. This Tig can't touch earth, or carve soul. But this Farrel is a good soul-carver." He pointed up into the air and Farrel noticed the smoke rising straight up since the wind had suddenly dropped. He didn't understand the significance, but soon forgot to question it as the meat cooked through. The fats sizzled loudly as they fell on the flame and rich odours brought both man and boy crowding to the tiny spit, eyes aglow with anticipation.

"Ee-Tig cranno argak ee-eikBurton en-en na-ig?" *You knew Burton?* (This Tig eye-felt wind-felt that Burton man-stranger?)

Tig spat a small bone onto the dying fire. He eyed Farrel suspiciously for a moment, then rose up on his haunches and passed wind noisily. He seemed to find the offensive action very funny. Farrel laughed too, rose up and repeated the action. Tig opened his mouth wide and shrieked with laughter. Farrel repeated his question and Tig spat onto the fire. The saliva hissed and steamed and Tig laughed. Farrel asked for the third time.

"Kok." *Yes.*

"Ee-eikBurton 'g-cruig tarn baag?" *Is Burton dead and buried?* (That Burton eats earth, skin cold?)

Tig hesitated. Then his hand touched his genitals, his head inclined. He didn't know, but he was uneasy.

"Ee-eikBurton pa-cruig pronok dag?" *Is he alive?* (That Burton kisses earth, urine warm?)

Tig said he didn't know.

"Ee-Tig ganaag ee-Farrel olo ee-eikBurton ee-Farrel ka'en-ka-en?" *Are you afraid of me because you think I was Burton's friend?* (This Tig afraid of this Farrel because that Burton this Farrel were not not-strangers?)

"Kok."

"Ee-Farrel cranno orgak ee-eikBurton. Ee-Farrel en-Burton. 'n nik Farrel." *I knew him but I didn't like him. I have a woman.* (This Farrel eye-felt wind-felt that Burton. This Farrel not touch/never touch that Burton. This Farrel close/touch woman Farrel).

What would she think, he wondered, of being used as a sex object to a twelve year-old moron? Joke. How many thousands of years would it be for the joke to be appreciated? To the Tuthanach, to all the Boyne peoples, denial of friendship to a man had to be coupled with a declaration of friendship with a woman. It seemed so unrealistically simple to believe that a man with a woman whose sexual appetite was high would not have a close male friend . . . (*nik*, woman, implied a sexually aggressive woman; a woman or man without any such desires was called *crum-kii*—stone legs.) It was a bizarre piece of nonsense and yet it appeased. Like the beast that presents its hindquarters to an attacker—submission. The name of the game.

Tig was much happier. He clapped his hands together repeatedly, pausing only to chew a ragged nail on his left index finger.

"Ee-Tig en-Burton. Ee-eikBurton en-Tig. Ee-Tig tarn ee-eikBurton baag na-yit." *I didn't like Burton either, and he didn't like me. But I killed him some time ago.* (This Tig never touch that Burton. That Burton never touch this Tig. This Tig skin Burton cold several yesterday.)

"A-Tig tarn ee-eikBurton baag?" *You killed him?*

"Ee-Tig . . ." eyes downcast, voice lowering. "Ka-kok." *I*

hope so/I wish to do so/I think so. Which was it? Farrel felt infuriated with himself. What *had* Tig said?

"Orga-mak ee-eikBurton m'rog?" *Where is Burton's body?* (In all the wind Burton's head?)

"Ee-Tig-ee-Farrel Tig cranno na'yok." *I'll show you now.* (This Tig this Farrel Tig eye feel high sun).

FOURTH TRANSMISSION—SIXTH DAY

The simplicity of the language is deceptive, I'm sure. I talk easily with Tig, but have an uncomfortable feeling that he is misunderstanding me in subtle ways. Nevertheless one thing seems sure—Burton is in trouble, and possibly dead, killed at the hands of the backward boy who is now so important to me (while he is in the crog the dogs don't come near). Everyone who should be here is "touching earth". You might dispense with that as something unimportant— tilling the ground somewhere? Planting seeds? Nothing of the sort.

Tig led the way across the hills, some miles from the river. The forest is patchy across the downs, never really managing to take a dominant hold on the land—trees in great dense clusters hang to the tops of some hills and the valleys of others so that as one walks across the country there appear to be bald knolls poking through the foliage on all sides. Tig himself is inordinately afraid of the woods and skirts them with such deliberation that I feel some dark memory must be lying within his poor, backward skull.

After about an hour we waded across a small stream and ran swiftly (Tig covering his head with his hands and wailing all the time) through a thinly populated woodland, emerging on the rising slope of one such bald hill that I had seen earlier. Boulders probed through the soil which was perhaps not deep enough to support the tree life. There were shallow carvings on many of the boulders and Tig touched some of these reverently. Most noticeable about this hill, and most puzzling—and indeed, most alarming—was the profusion of small earth mounds, overgrown with a sparse layer of grass and invisible from any substantial distance. Tig ran among these mounds, the highest of which was no more than four or five inches from the ground and vaguely cross-shaped, and eventually found a resting position on one of the least carved boulders. His stiffly crouched figure seemed overwhelmed by fear and regret, his hair sticking out from his head like some bizarre thorn growth, his thin limbs smeared with dirt and crusted with his own faeces. He stared at me with an expression of total confusion and I tried to put him at his ease but he turned half away from me and began to vocalize an imitation of the lark song that echoed around us from the vast early spring population.

I asked him about Burton and he merely clapped his hands together and shrilled all the louder.

You will have the picture—I appeared to be standing in a wide and irregularly laid-out cemetery. Crouching over the nearest mound I excavated a little of the earth away. A few inches below the surface my fingernails raked flesh and came away bloody!

I can't explain it but I panicked completely. Some terrible dread crept into my whole body, some inexplicable fear of what I was witnessing. I left Tig sitting there singing with the larks and starlings and ran back to the crog. I shook for hours and failed to sleep that night. The blood beneath my nails clotted and blackened and when I tried to wash it away it wouldn't come. In my frantic efforts to clean the stain I tore one of my nails right back to the quick and that sudden, appalling pain brought me back to my senses. I can't explain it. My reaction was panic. Something external possessed me for an instant and I was psychologically unready for the power of it. There is something in the ground of that hill, and I don't just mean a body.

I shall return tomorrow and report again.

Farrel left the crog at dawn. The grass was wet underfoot,

and across the valley a heavy mist hung silent and sombre. The birds seemed quieter today and what song he heard was often drowned by the murmur of the trees and the disturbing crying of the wind.

Strange, he thought, how mist seems to tangle itself in the forest, hanging in the branches like cotton.

He made his way back towards the strange cemetery on the hill, stopping occasionally to listen to the stillness, hoping to hear Tig crashing towards him, or calling him. When he emerged onto the hillside the mist had lifted and he could see, from the top of the knoll, the river Boyne and the scattered tumuli of the Tuthanach. He could see the hills where, in the next few years, work would begin on the massive sheer-fronted mounds of Newgrange. Who or what, he wondered, would be honoured by that vast structure? And who or what would be honoured by the second and third giant tumuli, built to the east and west of Newgrange at almost the same time (and not centuries earlier as the dating techniques of Farrel's time had suggested).

Of Tig there was no sign. The larks began to sing quite suddenly and sunlight pierced the early morning clouds, setting the forest alive with light and colour. As if—reflected Farrel—some force of night and cold had suddenly gone. Normal service being resumed . . .

Where he had dug in the soil of one of the human burial places yesterday, there was now no sign of interference. The earth was smooth and quite firmly packed. Tig, probably, had repaired the damage.

Farrel wasted no time in excavating down to the flesh again. He felt a cold unease as he cleared the soil from the naked back of the Tuthanach male, that same surge of panic, but today he controlled it. He scooped the earth out of the narrow trench until the man's body lay exposed from head to buttocks. Face down in the mud the man looked dead; his skin was cold and pale grey, the pallor of death. His arms were outstretched on either side and Farrel, on impulse, dug the soil away from one limb to discover the fingers, clenched firm into the earth as if gripping.

Turning the man's head over Farrel felt a jolt of disgust, a fleeting nausea. Open mouthed, open eyed, the earth was everywhere. It fell from the pale lips, a huge bolus of soil, dry, wormy. It fell from his nostrils and from his ears—it packed across his eyeballs, under the lids, like some obscene blindness.

Surely the man was dead; but the flesh was firm—cold, yet not in that rigidity associated with recent death, nor the moving liquefaction associated with decay. Easing the body down again Farrel put his ear to the naked back, listened for the heart.

For a long time he heard nothing. Minutes passed and he felt sure the heart was dead. Then . . .

A single powerful beat. Unmistakable!

Over the course of half an hour Farrel ascertained that the buried man's heart was beating once every four minutes, a powerful, unnaturally sustained contraction, as if the organ were forcing round some viscous fluid and not the easy liquid blood it was used to . . .

An unnerving thought occurred to Farrel and for a second he was ready to cut a vein in the man's hand—but, quite irrationally, fear of what he would find dripping from the body held him back until he recollected the blood under his fingernails and felt a strange relief.

He stood above the body, staring down at the un-dead corpse, then let his gaze wander across the countryside. The spring breeze irritated his scalp by catching the clay-stiffened strands of his hair and bending them at its will. As he stood on the knoll he grew irritated with his make-up and wished he could be clothed in denim shorts and a loose cotton shirt instead of being wrapped in skin that smelled of its previous owner and attracted flies.

Everything, bar this cemetery, was so normal.

The tumuli, the crog, the weapons and pottery, the hunting, the language—it was all just what he had expected, a new

24

stone age colony, conscious of religion, of its ancestry, its future and its agriculture, a colony just a few generations into its life in this green and bountiful land. Further north and south were other communities. Farrel had seen the signs of them, and had read reports about them from previous expeditions to this time. Some were larger than the Tuthanach, some already showing different cultural styles. They all seemed to mix and mingle together (so Tig said) to exchange ideas, to form joint hunting trips during the winter, to compare art forms and techniques of etching them into the rock. They were basically agricultural and peaceful. They feared the Moaning Ones from the earth, and the rock stealers from across the sea, some miles to the east. But for the most part they lived without fear, growing and maturing, becoming ready to accept the new Age of Bronze, still some eight hundred years in their future, at a time when the peacefulness of this country would be shattered by the new sounds of metal clashing with metal.

All those settlements had mixed together and had welcomed Burton—so he had reported—during his first four days in the valley. He had not told them from where he came (his arrival site, like Farrel's) for if the Ceinarc and the Tagda were passively afraid of the Moaning Ones and the Breton raiders, they held a healthy and active hostility for one other thing—crog-Tutha, and the insane settlers from beyond the forest. They would not float their coracles through the wide bend of the Boyne that took them round the foot of the Tuthanach hills, with their scattered mounds and shrieking women. It was a fearsome area, and one where no man could go and return unpossessed.

Reading the reports five thousand years away, Farrel had at first thought this to be a typical piece of forest-fearing, with the settlement on the wrong side of that forest being linked to those same dark forces. He had dismissed them aloud.

Now he realized he shouldn't have dismissed them at all.

There was something wholly unnatural about the people of

crog-Tutha. He had travelled more than five thousand years through time and expected surprises—but he had not anticipated being so totally mystified. This was not the simple life of a primitive people—it was something out of the dark corners of the supernatural!

No one up-time would believe him, he was sure of that.

FIFTH TRANSMISSION—SEVENTH DAY (EXTRACT)

... and as I filled the grave back in, Tig appeared at the edge of the wood. He ran up the hill and crouched over the mound, watching fascinated as I covered the body of the Tuthanach. I get the feeling that Tig, when he vanishes, is never far away. I always have an acutely uncomfortable feeling of being watched, and I suspect that wherever I go Tig is never far behind. What do I represent to him, I wonder? He is afraid of me still, and still refuses to show me where Burton is buried (if indeed he *is* buried). There are too many mounds on the knoll to excavate them all on an off-chance, so I really do need the boy to open up a little more.

I sat for an hour or so, on a boulder, looking across the forest to where the great crog on Tara was in evidence as a winding spiral of black smoke. The encampment there, Tig tells me, is surrounded by a wooden post-fence and seems to be more hostile than the other crogs. He says they are raising earthworks behind the wooden walls; does that suggest the first dun is being raised on the site? Fascinating. I have no idea how Tig knows this. Tara lies four days to the south. Would he wander that far?

While I watched Tara Tig sat quietly, chewing moodily on the remnants of one of those hares. I didn't ask him about Burton, or about anything. I hoped he would tell me of his own accord. His eyes suddenly grew wide and the bone dropped from his fingers. He was looking up at the knoll and I turned to see what had scared him. It gave me quite a turn too, and I don't blame Tig for scampering off.

One of the graves was moving, as if the body it contained was trying to force its way out. As if . . . ? First the man's hands poked through the ground, the fingers bloody and dirty. Then the earth fell away from where his head was raising up and his whole body followed. He stood upright, black with dirt, and earth fell from his ears and mouth. He spat violently and shook more vigorously, brushing soil from his chest and arms. I hid behind the boulder and watched as the strange apparition turned slowly round, looking upwards into the sky through eyes still caked with dirt. He was sexually aroused and the skin of his penis was lacerated and dripping blood profusely. I have the uncomfortable feeling that he had been copulating with the earth.

Several minutes of brushing and shaking exposed his skin again, cleared his eyes and nostrils and he seemed to get his bearings. He swept back his hair, which showed yellow through the mud, and ran off down the knoll, leaping the mounds and entering the woodlands with loud shrieks and painful crashes.

I followed him to a small stream, a tributary of the Boyne, and watched him crouching in the flow, washing and splashing, and emptying his bowels of a phenomenal amount of soil. He warbled bird song and laughed in abrupt, almost humourless bursts. He seemed to wash himself for hours, but finally crawled up onto the bank and sat quietly for a while, obviously sensing and enjoying the scenery around him. Then he rose to his feet, waded the stream, and vanished towards the crog.

That all occurred a few minutes ago and it means I shall not return there myself. I'm too puzzled and too frightened if you must know. I have my transmission equipment with me, but medication and field-link pack are still in the crog, which means I'm trapped here for a while, and must be careful not to injure myself.

When Farrel arrived back at the knoll Tig was crouched

over one of the mounds, the only one to show a good grassy overlay, and poking at it. He saw Farrel approaching and ran away, leapt onto a boulder and slapped his hands together.

Farrel stared at him for a moment, then at the grave, and an icy unease crept into his mind. Oh no, he thought. Oh God, this is the moment.

The boy gibbered something incoherent.

Farrel asked, "Ee-eikBurton 'n cruig pad-cruig?" *Is Burton buried here?* . . . (Touching earth, feet on earth?)

"Don't know."

Farrel sensed the lie. He dropped to his knees and scrabbled at the soil and after a moment he found himself staring at black hair, the back of Burton's head. "Thank God," cried Farrel, and grinned at the boy.

What should he do though? It might be dangerous to move the man—the best thing would be to leave Burton alone until the strange process had finished and he resurrected himself in the "natural" way.

But Farrel found he could not resist examining his colleague in the same way as he had examined the Tuthanach earlier. He scraped back the earth from Burton's head and shoulders.

A funny smell.

For a moment his hands hesitated; he stared silently and motionlessly at the body beneath him. The skin was grey, cold —that was, by all accounts, normal. But there was something wrong, something indefinable, something not quite right.

He reached down and turned Burton's head sideways. Earth poured from empty sockets, worms fell from the gaping, toothy mouth. Where skin remained it was taut and shrunken. Putrefaction rose from the rotting brains through the holes in the skull, driving Farrel to his feet with a terrible scream.

Sweeping back the earth from the torso he found the thigh bone fragment that had been driven into Burton's heart as he lay there, thrusting through the rib cage from behind, ripping skin and flesh and cracking bone. The clenched fists of his colleague took on a new significance. He had died in agony.

28

For a moment Farrel screamed abuse at Tig for what he had done, then his anger drained away. There was something in the boy's eyes, something in his expression. . . . Farrel felt instantly terrified. He reached out towards Tig and shook his head.

"I'm sorry, Tig. Burton called you a beast . . . I understand. . . ."

"Not once. Many times," said Tig. "I hated Burton. I gave Burton everything he had earned."

Tentatively Farrel touched the boy's shoulder and when Tig did not flinch he secured the grip and smiled. "Burton was not my friend . . . but he was known to me and he was important to me. I was upset to see him dead. Forgive me, Tig. I didn't mean what I said."

"I didn't understand what you said."

Farrel, guiltily, realized he had shouted in English. He laughed quietly, almost thankfully. He wouldn't have wanted the boy to hear what he had called him. He needed sleep too much and the boy was potentially very lethal.

He walked back to Burton's body and covered it over. A few feet away another mound began to move and Farrel and Tig ran out of sight and watched.

SIXTH TRANSMISSION—EIGHTH DAY
Burton is dead. Tig killed him, perhaps some months ago. I am terrified of Tig now and don't dare question him further about Burton. If only I knew where Burton's equipment was hidden. Tig knows, I'm sure of it. He has hidden it. I pray that in the same way that he indicated Burton's grave to me (uncompromisingly) he will lead me to Burton's records. Burton understood what I have been watching, he must have done—he participated.

Meanwhile I am back in the cave and Tig, now, is in full control. I sleep fitfully and in snatches—terrified of him striking when my defences are down. I woke, last night, to find him crouching over me, peering at my sleeping face. I dare not ask him to refrain from startling me like this. My head hurts and my heart is in pain, as if in anticipation of a long-bone shaft being driven through it.

I can't get my field-link equipment. The crog is active again. Over the last day many Tuthanach have risen from the earth and returned to their homes—men, women, children, they return with bountiful energy and begin to lead a life no different from the Ceinarc or the Tagda—what *were* they doing in the earth? What have they gained? What was the purpose of it all?

SEVENTH TRANSMISSION—TENTH DAY

The trickle of Tuthanach returning to their crog has ceased. They are all home. I remain in the cave, uncertain, insecure. Tig hunts on my behalf, but no longer eats with me. He has become very affectionate, but behind the kindness is a repressed anger that I truly fear. Sometimes he stands in the cave entrance and shrieks with laughter. The garble of words he yells refers to Burton and to me, and I hear "stone legs" and "twisting head", two favourite Tuthanach insults. He invariably ends his tirade of abuse by defecating in the cave mouth and elaborately holding his nose and backing away. And a few hours later he brings me a hare or a brace of fat doves, some gift, some appeasement for his show of fury. A bizarre boy and not—I now realize—backward at all, but in some way insane. Listen to me! Do I understand the meaning of my own words any more? What do I mean—*insane*? Is my behaviour sane? Tig is more than just a boy. I suspect he was chosen for his role—Tig-never-touch-woman-never-touch-earth; the only Tuthanach not to touch earth in the strange way I have described . . . why? Why Tig? Or should I ask, why *one Tuthanach*? What was he watching for? What are they asking of him now? What role does he fill?

Tig seems aware of some finality in his role. On his most recent visit he came with a large chunk of meat—deer, I think. Tears filled his eyes as he passed the joint to me and accepted a small portion back. We ate in silence. As he chewed he watched me, and tears flooded down his cheeks. "Farrel, my friend, my dear friend," he said, over and over. The warmth was immense. The Tuthanach have no way of expressing magnificent friendship and he struggled to voice his feelings and I eventually had to stop him. I had understood. "Farrel and Tig are the only ones not to touch earth," he said. "Tig can't, but Farrel . . ."

Time and time again he began that sentence, staring at me. Each time he said it I was filled with his intensity, and with my own anxiety. The thought is terrifying, truly terrifying.

Then the anger from the boy, the shrieking. He raced out into the dusk and vanished swiftly. I face another night alone, more than half afraid to close my eyes . . . not just Tig, though that is certainly a part of it, but the past . . . my past. I am haunted by memories and faces; they fill my dreams, and I can sense my own time in everything I smell or see here. It is insecurity that makes me rue the warmth of civilization, and I shall not bend to any great desire to return; but it hurts, sometimes. Sometimes it really hurts.

Three days after the seventh transmission two Tuthanach males came to the cave and crouched in its entrance watching Farrel. They were both middle-aged, dark-haired, and their skin was decorated with green and blue dye: circles around their eyes, lines across their cheeks, elaborate patterns on their breasts and bellies. They looked angry. Farrel remained quite still, trying to hide his fear.

Then Tig came slipping into the cave, boisterous and noisy as ever. Farrel tried to piece together something from the boy's excited gabble, but all he could make out were words for "woman" and the insult "stone legs".

A tension grew in the pit of Farrel's stomach and wild thoughts filled his mind. What was Tig up to?

The next thing he knew he was being chased from the cave

by the two men. Tig grinned at him, and winked elaborately. "Soul curers," he said, pointing to them. "Make soul good for this Farrel. Make this Farrel's soul ready for earth." And he patted his loins.

Farrel felt terrified.

They took him to the crog and led him inside the skin wall, past the fire pit and to a smaller circle of skins around which were grouped several women and children. He was led to a small tent and pushed to the ground. Making no attempt to speak to him, nor demonstrating any puzzlement over him, the men left. After a while one of the younger women got up and walked across to him.

By that time, realizing that his sexual need was far more intense than he had admitted to himself for the last few days, Farrel was lost in thoughts of his past.

He saw the Tuthanach woman through a blur of remembered faces, saturated bodies and irritatingly noisy beds. He smelled her through an imagined veil of perfumes, cigarette smoke and the salty and erotic smell of sweat. He felt pain as he remembered these things, a real pain, unlocalized. The woman had crouched before him, her wool skirt drawn up above her knees so that she displayed her white and grossly fat thighs to Farrel's casual gaze. He tried not to think too hard about what he saw.

Then she extended her hand and cocked her head to one side, smiling broadly, letting him see that only two of her teeth were missing.

Farrel took her hand, pressed the cool, firm fingers and noticed how the woman's palm was sweating like his. The past surged into his mind; agony:

A girl he had known for years as a friend. He had been taking his leave of her small, two-roomed apartment, conscious that his wife would start to worry soon. With his usual calculated shyness he had reached out and shaken her hand again, playing at being nervous. "I don't like all this hand shaking," she had said, in a way that made him realize that

32

*she had wanted to say it on previous occasions. "I'd much
rather have a cuddle." So he'd cuddled her, and she hadn't let
him draw away. She was tall and lean and felt awkward
against his stocky, muscular body. But it had been a long
moment, and a good one.*

He realized he was excited and the Tuthanach woman was
pleased. Her breath was sour as she leaned across him, her left
hand gripping him gently between the legs; she kissed each
cheek and then the tip of his nose. Then she rose and tugged
him to his feet, pulled him into the tent and slipped off her
clothes.

She picked up a stone chip, artificially smoothed by all
appearances, and made marks on it with a piece of flint. Farrel
watched her as he undressed. Her breasts were full and plump
at the ends, flat and sac-like where they grew from her body.
He hated that. She smelled of animal grease and smoke (as did
he) and of something else, something pungent and sexual and
offensive. Spitting on the stone she grinned at Farrel and passed
it to him, indicating that he should do the same. As he spat he
saw the crude phallus she'd drawn on the rock. With her
thumb she rubbed the spittle into the sandstone, and laughed
as she lay back on the skin-covered floor. She patted her belly
with the fragment. She still said nothing.

As Farrel climbed onto her recumbent body and tried to find
her he noticed that she popped the stone into her mouth and
swallowed it.

They made love for about ten minutes. At the end of it she
was obviously disappointed, and Farrel for no reason that he
could identify felt like crying.

EIGHTH TRANSMISSION—FIFTEENTH DAY

It has begun. Newgrange, I mean—the building has begun.
Yesterday I crept around the crog and went to the hills
overlooking the Boyne, where the cemetery is located. There
was much activity down by the river, men and women
gathering water-rolled granite boulders for the facing of the

mound; they carried these, one per person, in a great chain up the hillside and the piles grow large. Earth is being excavated from several sites ready for the tumulus. Several small tombs on the site have been demolished for the earth and rock they can offer. The past no longer matters. Only the great tumulus seems to concern them now. The first massive orthostats have been dragged to the site, and an artist is working on what can only be the small lintel that will lie above the passage entrance. The work, especially the art, will take many months. The air is filled with the sharp sounds of repeated picking blows as symbols and designs are carved on the dressed rocks, ready for incorporation into the tomb. The speed with which they work is fantastic, but the job they face is enormous. Who will be buried here? Who will be honoured?

I walked closer to the activity, managing to remain undetected behind some trees, and watched the artists at work. Imagine my surprise when I discovered Tig directing the symbol-carving operations! Some thirty men, all old, all frail, were crouched beside or above their slabs and each worked on specifications laid down by the darting, probing, shouting form of the boy.

I watched fascinated for a while, until the sun, beating bright and hot upon my naked back, drove me away to a shadier place. Tig must have caught sight of me because, as I crept down the hill towards the slopes rising to the unbuilt mound of Knowth, he came racing after me, calling my name.

"It will be a huge mound," he said, breathing heavily. "A great temple."

"A temple to who, Tig?"

But he just laughed and slapped his hands together. "They have all forgotten the symbols of the earth, and the wind, and fire and water," he babbled happily. "This is why I was left behind, to remember, to teach them. . . ." He was

34

obviously delighted about it. "Soon this Tig shall no longer be Tig-never-touch-woman."

"Will this Tig touch earth?" I asked him.

He fell moody, but brightened suddenly and grinned. "This Tig never touch earth always . . . but this Farrel . . . this Farrel will touch earth soon . . . this Farrel will understand and learn the symbols."

"This Tig might kill me," I said carefully. "Like he killed that Burton."

He slapped his genitals repeatedly, not hard, but apparently quite painfully for he winced visibly. "If this Tig kills this Farrel may legs turn to stone."

And at that moment . . . I felt the compulsion, the fascination to discover, the intrigue, filling me like some uncontrollable ecstasy, like a psychological magnet pulling me down towards the earth. Tig danced happily about . . . had he seen my possession? He ran off, then, shouting back over his shoulder, "This Farrel knows where to go."

I am torn between desire to know, and fear of knowing. I keep seeing Burton's rotted corpse, lying there, denied that same knowledge by a thin shaft of bone and a vengeful child. But I also remember the pull of the earth, the feel of magic and glory, the glimpse (for glimpse is what it was) of some great power lying beneath the grass. . . .

I will have to make my choice soon.

Farrel knew where to go all right. He thought about the knoll and its now empty burden of graves, and as the night wore on and a heavy rain began to drum across the countryside, sending icy rivulets across the uneven rock floor of his cave, so the knoll, dark and invisible in the night, seemed to beckon to him. Tig writhed before him, a boy at the mercy, the whim, of forces dying, but still far greater than any that man had ever conceived of, either now or in Farrel's own time, far in the future. And yet, perhaps that was wrong— perhaps the people of this time *had* conceived of the sons and daughters of the earth who somehow, inexplicably, were directing the destiny of the Tuthanach. Perhaps it was only with time and greater self awareness that man came to forget the spirits and guardians of all that he surveyed, the rock and stones, the trees and winds, the earth, the vast earth; mother . . .

She called to him and Farrel responded with fear. They had been with him for some time, directing his thoughts, but their touch was tenuous, uneasy. Farrel drew back into his cave and covered his head, blocked his ears and eyes and tried not to see or hear or feel what was coming to him : he tried not to think of it, but he could not empty his mind of their presence.

He screamed, confused and terrified by the strangeness of the contact. Dark-eyed, shivering with cold and terror, he cowered in his cave until morning, and dawnlight, and peace again.

He ran across the storm-threatened land, pacing heavily on the saturated turf, waiting for the next cloudburst. Tig scampered towards him and he felt a great sense of relief.

The boy saw his fear and laughed, jumped high in the air, then clapped his hands together in glee.

"What does it mean?" cried Farrel.

Tig-never-touch-woman-never-touch-earth dropped to his haunches and plunged his fingers between the tightly knotted grass mat.

"This Farrel is being prepared to touch earth," he said. "Don't be afraid."

"But this Farrel *is* afraid. This Farrel is terrified!"

"There is no need to be," said Tig, suddenly less childish. He watched Farrel through bright, deep brown eyes. Grease and paint were smeared about his cheeks and chin, a meaningless mosaic of colour and half formed design. The wind blew suddenly strong and Tig shivered. He rose to his feet and glanced up, wrapping his thin arms around his naked torso. Farrel too hunched up and followed the boy's gaze into the heavens, where dark clouds and lancing sunlight played confusing chase games across the valley.

"What is going to happen to this Farrel?" asked the man.

Tig smiled, almost patronizingly. "Wonderful things."

"What is underneath the grass? What is hidden there?"

"This Farrel will soon know. Fear is unnecessary. This Farrel will lose nothing he has not already lost."

Farrel stared at him, feeling suddenly old, suddenly alien. "What has this Farrel lost?"

Tig grinned. "His past, his people, his dreams, his strange images. This Tig never understood them, never understood the words. This has always been between us. When this Farrel has touched the earth they will be gone. We will build the temple together : we will build our dreams and our people together."

"It sounds magnificent," said Farrel. "But this Farrel is still afraid."

Tig laughed again. "Afraid of the earth?" He scuffed the ground with his bare feet. "Afraid of clouds? Afraid of sun?"

"Afraid of . . ." He stopped, unsure. "This Farrel doesn't know what of."

Tig slapped his hands together, shook his head. "This Farrel should go back to the cave. Wait there. When you are called, go to them. Go to them."

Unquestioningly, resigned to his bizarre fate, Farrel turned and walked back to the overhang.

By dusk it was raining again.

She called to him and again Farrel responded. He was still afraid, but Tig's words, his reassuring attitude, helped him overwhelm that fear and put it from his mind.

He walked through the driving rain, the clay in his hair running into his eyes and mouth, giving him a foretaste of the great oral consummation to come. He swallowed the clay, tasted its texture, wept as he ran through the rain, through the moaning woods. Behind him, high on a hill, torch light burned beneath a skin shelter where an artist worked on stone late into the night, anxious to express the earth symbols that he had relearned from the one boy who had not forgotten. He was an artist who added his soul to the rock and the rock to the temple . . . a temple to the earth gods, the Great Ones, the Moaning Ones, those who inhabited the boulders and the wind, the clouds, and the running mud, the grassy turf of uncountable acres of virgin earth.

Through the night and the rain Farrel ran, until he found himself, without thinking, on the knoll that rose above the woods, the great source of earth energy that he had tapped so briefly, so frighteningly, several days before. And here he lay down on the ground, in the trench left by one of the Tuthanach, and stretched out his arms—

Gripped the mother's flesh—

Penetrated the mother's fertile womb, ejaculated with the ecstasy of contact—

Ate her breast, drank the cold and grainy milk of her glands, felt it flood into his body, through the apertures of his prostrate corpse, driving the substances of his canals before it, replacing his warmth with its own loving cold. Earth closed over his back, the rain filtering through ran down his skin, drained deep into the tissues of the soil below. His lungs filled with mud—he breathed deeply and after a moment his heart stopped, his breathing stopped . . . suspended, touching the earth.

Almost immediately they were there, rising out of the deep rock, flowing through the earth and the pores of the soil, entering Farrel's body through the tips of finger and penis, down the earth bridge that extended along the convolutions of his gut. He was consumed by them, consumed them for his own part, welcomed them and heard their dying greeting, the words that had flowed through the minds of the Tuthanach during the weeks previous. . . .

I am earth, Farrell, I am the earth, I am of earth, the earth is within me and without me, I am soil and rock, diamond and jade, ruby and clay, mica and quartz, I am the litter of the dead who live in crystalline echo in the sediments of sea and lake, I am ground, I am woman who suckles the infant flesh of man and beast, I am womb and anus, mouth and nose and ear of the great world lover, I am cave and tunnel, bridge and haven, I am the sand that sucks, the field that flourishes, I am root and clay, I am man pre-carnate, I am dirt, who has been called Nooma and Shaan, and is Tutha and Cein, and will be Ga-Tum-Dug and Nisaba, I will be Geshtin and Tammuz and my branches will be earth against the sky and all will be one, I will be Faunus and I will be Consus, I will be Pellervoinen and Tapio, I will be Luonnotar who floats on white water and touches the wind, I will be Asia and Asia-Bussu, Lug and Jesus, I will be coal and ore and I have existed since a time of desolation and of thunder and of sterility—you, Farrel, who know all these things should know also that this is the moment of our great dying, the breath of wind passing out of the body of earth and into the memory of man. . . .

A second voice: I am wind, who has been called Godsinger by the Kalokki who were the first men, and is called Tag and Feng-po, and Huaillapenyi, I am breath and life, I am death, the rising odour of decay, I am storm and rage, light and dark, I am thunder and fear, I am the changing seasons of time, I am the urger of seas and the calmer of wings, I will be remembered as Taranis and Wotan, Thor and Zephyrus and Ga-oh and Hino and my thunder shall be heard until the final fire, but you, Farrel, who know all these things should know also that this is the moment of our great sorrow, where we abandon our domain and enter the minds of men, for only in the minds of man can we continue to survive. . . .

And others, then, crowding in, jostling to be heard: I am fire who is Tinedia, who will be Svarogich and Sun and Steropes . . . I am water who is Uisceg . . . I am sky . . . I am serpent. . . .

All these Farrel heard and consumed, and then they fell away, back into the rock, up into the wind, leaving just a fragment of each god, a morsel of each great being, settling in his crowded mind.

He rose from the earth, shaking his body and feeling the dirt and clay fall from his limbs and his mouth and his eyes. The day was cold; he was conscious of rain, of heavy cloud, of a dullness about the saturated countryside: he loved this. Some greater or lesser part of him was aware that a full two seasons must have passed while he lay in his intimate embrace with the earth. From this same greater or lesser part of him came an alien thought, a last tearful cry from his dead future: *truly a great and noble glory will have gone by my time of glass and steel.*

The new born child turned to regard the virgin land. Rain beat against him, washed him. He opened his mouth to drink it and his laughter joined the gentle sounds of the natural world.

I've found life, at last, at last. ...

The great gods were still there, he thought, as he blinked rain away and stared at the greenness all around him. They were dying, now, committing their great suicide, surviving only in the Tuthanach and their children, and their grand-children, and so on until they were spread everywhere ... this they were doing as a gesture of acquiescence to man, but just by staring through the rain, through the unspoiled distance, the man called Farrel could see those gods, could feel them and smell them and hear them.

As he ran down the knoll he could sense them, too, in the brightness of his mind. They were with him by inheritance when he came here, and now they had come direct and he was ecstatic at the greater awareness they had brought him of so many things ... over the centuries their presence would dilute and become weak and perhaps they had not reckoned on that.

There was plenty of time for them to explore him and

understand how things would be. As far as Farrel was concerned there were more important things to do than worry over a day and an age when he would be dust and ashes.

He was a part of the earth, now, a man of the earth, a Tuthanach. His people were building a temple to the earth, and he knew how magnificent that temple would be, for he had seen it. He would mark the rocks of the temple with his soul, raise the walls of the temple with his sweat, and fill the temple with his ecstasy. He ran faster across the rain-soaked land until he could hear the sounds of the stone being carved.

The earth went with him.

A Small Event

There was a great gathering by the banks of the Taim, and we were among the last to arrive.

We had left the gyro spinning silently and happily on the side of a hill, and indulged ourselves in a physical walk across the last few miles of naked moorlands. One of my great pleasures is to feel unfiltered wind on my face, the soft springiness of water-sodden turf beneath my feet; there is no sound quite as mournful and musical as the low moan of wind between hills; no colours can quite match the subtle shades of grey that streak a stormy sky.

And so I had insisted on walking although Harmony, the female of my current triad, soon tiring of this extravagant spending of energy had strapped on her warm-field and gravity belt; she whisked high into the dusk sky, where she bobbed and blew, a small yellow shape, hair and gown streaming in her wake.

I plodded across the low foothills around the Taim valley, examining every brand (no, species! They were natural) of hardy plant I saw.

By early evening we were within sight of the gathering of aesthetes; the MECH's huge machine towered into the sky, breaking the natural skyline with its sharp angles, sparkling with inner light. I too, then, strapped on my gravity belt and rose beside Harmony. She came close and smiled and we held hands so that her power pack was recharged from my own by way of our skin. I tingled when I touched her, and we laughed and flew swiftly down to the river.

We dropped to the ground a short way from the first of the glowing camp-fires, a small red box from which simulated flames cast light and heat in a circle twenty yards across. The noise of laughter and conversation was inviting and confusing; I imagined I could recognize the voices of old friends, but in the season of alteration it was impossible to say. The nicest, richest voices were never long with a single individual; bought at high prices they passed between two or three persons a year. My own voice had belonged to an actor now seven hundred years dead.

Walking into the area of the gathering I was greeted at once by several acquaintances. By the nearest fire was Helios Ice-Shaper of Polar South who greeted us in that most revolting of south polar ways; he spat in his hand and slapped the palm to my face. I recoiled and he grinned, turning to Harmony, waiting the return of the compliment. Harmony touched a finger to her nose and ran around the man, who turned back to me, surprise and anger in his face.

"Animal!" shouted Harmony. "Beast!"

I pushed past Ice-Shaper myself, a dramatic gesture received with dramatic silence.

I recognized others, notably Aragos from Isreel and Collector from Old Nor. With both of them we spent long minutes talking and exchanging news. Eventually I found Silver, seated more or less alone by the very edge of the river, his gaze fixed on the moonlit, firelit waves of water. Harmony saw him and ran to him, kissing and fondling the reticent youth while I, the "older" man, waited my turn with patience.

Silver had lately been the moody member of the triad, and he had left our home some fifteen days before the announcement of the coming event. Harmony had been hysterical at first; myself, approaching the problem practically, I could see no reason why, wherever our silver youth had hidden himself, he would not hear of the forthcoming excitement. And he was bound, I had reasoned, to make his way to the site and meet us there.

The accuracy of my prediction earned me much hugging and love from Harmony, who was suddenly as happy and excitable as the mental child she was. I put my arm around her and smiled at Silver, whose face broke into a wide and knowing grin; in the fragmentary moonlight, by the bright light of the fires, his silver skin was alive with glitter and the very act of blinking sent flashes of radiance from his face.

"Why did you flit off like that?" I asked him.

"We were worried," said Harmony severely. "You really should tell us when you plan to throw your moods."

"Yes, I'm sorry," said Silver, glancing at me with an indefinable expression on his smooth face. "I was thoughtless."

"So why go?" needled Harmony, stroking his white hair back from his forehead.

"Oh . . . pressure, I suppose . . . I don't know. . . ."

"Love pressure?" I asked. "Me pressure? Harmony pressure? City pressure? Art pressure? Pressure on its own doesn't tell us anything."

"Nothing at all," agreed Harmony. "What made you go? What *really* made you go?"

Silver shook his head, looked out across the flowing waters of the Taim. "I don't know. Just . . . just a feeling, a depressed feeling. I can't explain it."

We didn't push him further. We were both too glad to be a threesome again. We erected our tent and consummated the camp site for an hour or so, and if there was something troubling Silver deep down he certainly didn't show it.

Outside, then, for an evening investigation of the MECH.

I recognized the human component of the MECH immediately. He was a man in miniature, standing less than half my own height and further testimony to his complete eccentricity was the sparkle of wires across his close-cut hair—a vault-network worn *outside* the cranium. His dwarfdom, however, was a post-nat-tank choice on his part—somewhere in his home city the excess flesh remained, preserved, in case he should decide to return to normal size.

I had last met him seventeen years ago, at the site known locally as Stonehang, a primitive place of worship which had been long since swallowed into the earth leaving only one or two rounded, weathered boulders as evidence of the site's importance. The MECH, new to me then, with a very small machine component, had impressed us all with his prediction that the site—a focus of time every seventeen hundred years —would give us a five-minute view of the distant past, a shimmering image in the air of sacrifice and seduction, of warring brothers and the bestial feasting of our ancient ancestors. For the Midget's speciality was *time*, and the distortions in time that could be caused by physical effects. I felt an immediate anticipation, a twinge of excitement—time, that most fascinating of dimensions. We would soon witness its disruption, I was sure.

But what purpose was served by the huge bank of machinery?

And huge is no exaggeration. The bank of green- and red-faced screens towered high over the camp site, stretching up for at least twenty feet and lying along the ground fifty feet to the flowing waters themselves. The Midget operated controls along this entire length, concentrating frantically and using the information to send his thoughts racing back along the face of the machine to somewhere else, changing readings, settings, standing back and watching the vector plottings on the great screens above his head—we all looked up to see the glowing white lines, angles, moving dots, pulses, spinning and twisting shapes.

It was all quite unaesthetic, probably substantially meaningless, and yet because of its involvement with time and the consequences of time disruption the MECH probably had to work harder than others to predict the cosmic events that we, the elitist aesthetes, might find amusing. For this reason we were, as we approached, respectful of the man's light show—more than a little of it would be of real importance, and more than a little could go wrong in the event of hostile personal fields tampering with the delicately-tuned interior workings of the machine-man complex.

"Hi, MECH!" I shouted at a moment when the little man relaxed from his involvement with the battery of signals.

He turned, stared through huge blue eyes at his three visitors, looked from one to the other of us, recognized me, smiled, frowned, shouted: "I'm busy as *sky* and you come *chitter-chattering*! Can't you see how delicate everything is, how precise it all has to be? Go away, don't bother me for the moment...."

Harmony giggled at the little man's strange antics. Silver watched him expressionlessly, failing to observe any humour in the situation. I said, "But Midget ... what are we to see? What are you predicting?"

The Midget was furious. He shouted something incomprehensible and busied himself with the nearest console of the gigantic machine component. We all watched as certain of the displays went through ugly contortions.

Finally, with an audible screech of frustration, the little man pressed a hand-shaped plate at the very bottom of the machine and came across to us. He had put the whole thing on automatic.

"A human *is* necessary," he snapped, perhaps detecting my unvoiced thought. "Imagination for one thing. Check on the machine. Keep a positive life field interlinked with the *son of a bitch*."

"What sort of language is that?" asked Silver in irritation. His depression was showing at a bad time; it was important to keep the Midget favourably inclined towards us or we might never find ourselves invited by this MECH again.

But the Midget puffed up with pride and began to lecture us on the old languages of earth. That particular expression, he told us, was called *slang*, and it had been spoken by a mighty race who had once lived on a land mass west of Ireland.

It all sounded very improbable, and gently I returned the little man's interest and enthusiasm to the prediction at hand.

"It will hit the Earth at precisely eleven forty-three point three three seven tomorrow morning—we won't notice *that* of course, because it will have already sped through the atmosphere with noticeable and spectacular effect. It will hit the Earth seven feet from the northern shore of the Taim—you can see where the point has been marked with a light focus. I shall, of course, turn that off before the event."

Still a little confused as to what exactly we were about to see, I tried to keep him in conversation. He grew impatient.

"Look, there are the vectors, you can follow them all night if you wish, just don't bother me. By the time it reaches point 221, that's marked on screen five, I have to exert traction through the machine to alter its course very slightly so that it doesn't miss the earth. The precise effort on my part will cause it to strike at the co-ordinates I've already given you. Do you see? Will you go now? Will you stop annoying me?"

He bounded away. Silver left our group and went to sit by a camp fire near to our tent. I stood in the chill night, Harmony standing close by and projecting her sympathy for the depressive. She seemed less childish than usual, as if some deeper maturity within her was pushing through the mask she had adopted.

I turned back to the MECH and tried one last time. "Exactly *what* are we going to see colliding with the Earth?"

His voice, high with anger and excitement, sounded across the campsite, caused heads and bodies to turn. "A quantum black hole, you fool, a quantum black hole of course!"

What *is* a black hole?

Why, simply (it was explained to us by Robeard of Tunis) a point in time and space where matter has collapsed in upon itself until it is no longer there. A universal node which sucks light from the nether regions thus appearing black since the reverse of light is, of course, dark. A cosmic inaccessibility, a place where the power of a Galaxy is directed, a negative attraction into which whole worlds might easily vanish if the hole had not been properly screened.

At least (added Robeard) that's what I think it is.

Thus enlightened we waited out the night.

Entertainment by the banks of the river Taim :

Silver drew third in the lottery for entertainment during the long night. Harmony drew fourth, but lay just outside the circle around our campfire since her particular artform required some work beforehand. Myself, I drew nothing, which was as well since I had nothing to offer.

The Moon was a pleasant disc, low over the eastern horizon, watching our antics with something less than its full face. The zenith was cloudy, but a sprinkling of stars testified to the ever-present heavens. How, I wondered, as we waited for the entertainment to begin, would one spot a black hole against the black night sky? It seemed to me to be useless to try and distinguish the hole from where we sat, most of us gazing idly heavenwards.

For thirty minutes we watched Jarrol, from the southern land of Isreel, digesting a variety of living creatures; his stomach and belly walls were made of transparent bio-silicone, a closely knit sheet of living connective tissue and silica. He illuminated the proceedings internally, and had treated the animals with special dyes that were released with bizarre effects as Jarrol's ultra-powerful digestive juices stripped layer after layer from the struggling but swiftly motionless beasts.

I had never been convinced of the artistic value of Jarrol's creativity, but my companions applauded wildly. There was a market for anything, I supposed.

More to my taste were the death memories of a strange solitary man called Diabla, from the ancient fortress city of the eastern steppelands that had no name. Diabla had extended his very real telepathic abilities to the watching of the dead as they struggled out of the mortal sphere. We shared what he had seen, a series of edited clips from forty or fifty dying-dead. In the few minutes after life there were voices, shapes, colours, feelings—but they made no sense, and when some sort of familiar pattern did begin to emerge, that was the end of the clip—to have remained linked with a fleeing soul any longer would have been death for Diabla as well.

Then Silver was called into the circle. He was in no mood to be entertaining but he recognized the importance of etiquette at occasions such as this. As I urged him to the centre of the ring he shook me off, roughly, almost angrily, then turned and looked at me with an unvoiced apology in his eyes. He walked away from me to take up his position by the fire; I felt a great sadness, almost despair. Silver was growing away from me, and had been doing so for some weeks. Why he was distancing himself I didn't know, but it made me angry, and the anger was because of my unhappiness. I watched him by the fire, moody, solemn, and I knew that he was thinking of me, and of nothing else, and that I would hate to know what was in his mind.

Silver stripped off his clothes and pushed his silver cells to their full brilliance so that his body gleamed in the firelight like polished alloy. To attune his mind he stared at the nearest visitor to him, and gradually her shape was etched in black and silver upon his torso, the detail becoming sharp after a few seconds.

"How does he do it?" whispered a woman close to me. Her partners had no idea, and after a moment I felt the gentle tingle in my scalp that told of the mind probe she was directing, not only to me but probably to everyone else about the circle (with the exception of Silver, naturally). I allowed my knowledge of Silver's genetic peculiarity to filter three levels toward my conscious mind and felt each fact snipped away by the curious mind that sought enlightenment.

Silver's skin colour was the result of surface melanophores that could, at his will, expand to cover him completely and allow their silver or black pigments to give him his particular colouring. At will he could selectively depigment his body in lines and etchings to show whatever image he wished. Thus: a girl, her hair in artistically portrayed folds, her eyes, large, sparkling in the firelight, her lips moist, parted, ready to engage the sensitive skin of her lovers as soon as the night's enjoyment had become . . . tiresome.

Silver, excelling himself, was the focus of attention for nearly half an hour, depicting many of those in the circle engaged in erotic or hilarious activities. His *tour de force* was a scene from history, stretching across his torso from side to side, up to the lower part of his face and down his legs almost as far as his calves. The Great War of antiquity, a war fought between millions of men, with gunpowder and knife, with plane and ship. And what a spectacle Silver made of those events. In the frozen instant of war, in the depiction of a battle as it might have been seen from the air, there were literally thousands of individual shapes, figures, soldiers, engaged in their bloody exchange. Each figure was the controlled expansion of just a few cells!

Silver's final and most dramatic touch was the suffusion of his subcutaneous tissue with blood; through his translucent skin the deeper flesh shone brightly, redly, and the entire montage became awash with rivers of crimson—and there, beneath that wave of gore, those million men died, faded and were lost.

Silver sat quiet, and we were awed. What mental power had been required for that particular feat! What fantastic micro-control! Pride coursed through my body, pride at being the lover of so magnificent an artist. Harmony was almost crying, perhaps for the same reason. We hugged each other while Silver breathed hard, and listened to the resounding applause of his audience. True genius was measured not by the collision of asteroids but in the capability of handling a million body cells all at once.

And yet we all sensed that Harmony's aesthetic display would outshine even Silver's, and as she finally came into the circle, into the firelight, there was an almost tangible sense of anticipation. She kissed Silver, who walked to the edge of the circle and sat solemnly regarding the young woman. Harmony waved quiet the greeting round of chest-slapping and sat down upon the warm turf. She signalled that we should all remain silent for a few minutes, and we fell still. The aura of expectation in the air grew stronger.

Harmony sat with her eyes closed, cross-legged and motionless, concentrating; she had told me, in the past, of the sensations she experienced whilst pushing the biological process in her womb forward at an unnaturally fast rate: some pain, to begin with, then dizziness which had to be controlled (this was the result of wild hormone changes in her blood stream). Then a feeling of peace and a sense of communication—mind filling with the sound of the foetal heart beat, the surge of foetal blood, the multi-levelled waves of foetal awareness unbesmirched by the pollution of sensory input.

After a few minutes Harmony was ready. Distantly, from other fires, came the sound of cheering, of laughter, of singing —the entertainment of the elite took many forms, but our own circle had provided an evening of mainly anatomical amusement.

It was warm in the red light of the fire, with the waters of the Taim splashing gently a few yards away; behind Harmony the slopes of a hill rose to sombre heights, penetrating the lower of the scudding clouds. All was very relaxed.

She disrobed, to the accompaniment of whistles of appreciation; Harmony was slender and graceful, every womanly feature dainty and precise. No angle was too sharp, no curve too round. By looking carefully the slight swelling of her belly could be seen, but it was the only concession to biological deformity discernible by the unpractised eye.

She lay down, right by the fire, drew up her legs and closed her eyes.

"A cyclops!" cried Jarrol.

"With green hair, over all but its face." This from a girl called Hayzel.

"And a forked tail, threshing wildly!" A man named Helix.

"And a cry like a house-spider...." Jarrol again.

"And—"

"Enough!" I shouted, smiling to let them see I meant no disrespect. "There may be time for all your tastes."

We sat back and watched, then. Harmony began to whine as she directed the forces of her mind and imagination to the task at hand; her belly writhed as the life within went through its multifarious changes, and her hands clutched the distorted flesh to ease the pain and pressure.

Finally—only a few minutes had elapsed—she cried aloud and seemed to be exerting great effort. Her womb opened and a single eye regarded us, unblinking, neither hostile nor friendly, a neutral eye, in a pink bare face. The foetus slipped from its watery hiding place, green fur sticky and plastered in bizarre patterns about its eight-inch body. A tail—unforked I noticed—whipped this way, that way, striking the insides of Harmony's legs so that she yelled and sat up.

Stricken with panic the homunculus shrieked high and loud and began to run, ducking under legs and crawling over laps, pleading with cries and strange sounds as if sensing its impending doom. I touched it as it scampered past, and it turned and grasped my finger with two little hands, staring up at me imploringly with its huge single eye. Amused, I poked it away, trying not to hurt it, and it darted towards Silver who—with a flick of his hand—sent it reeling back towards the fire. Finally Harmony snared the tiny being in a neural web and carried it back through the air into her clutches.

It struggled in her grasp for a moment, its plaintive cry bringing sympathetic responses from some of the elite. Then swiftly she dug her thumb and forefinger into its neck, pinching until the soft bones parted. The homunculus kicked and squeaked, scrabbling at Harmony's fingers until its eye glazed over and it fell limp in her grasp; the monstrous head lolled as she tossed the pitiful corpse towards Jarrol, who snatched and scrutinized it, a satisfied expression upon his face.

"Any more?" begged Hayzel. Harmony shook her head apologetically.

"I'm exhausted. That creation was very difficult."

There were murmurs of disappointment, but no argument. Harmony probably had three or four more half-formed embryos in her womb, but would discard them rather than re-incorporate them into her strange germinal tissue. I smiled at her as she sat down beside me, pulling her flimsy robe about her body. Harmony was a true artist! There were no others in the world who could do what she could do, sculpting life itself, moulding the living flesh of her own body. And for that matter, there were few who could compete with Silver. How lucky I was, a non-artist, to be a part of a triad containing two such truly unique artists.

Time passed, minutes only, as the elite contemplated what they had seen, seated in silence, just the breeze and the river sounds drifting across the camp.

I was about to rise and go to our tent when I heard Harmony's unvoiced puzzlement beside me. I looked at her. She was staring beyond me, round the circle, and as I followed her gaze so there came a murmur of query from all the aesthetes around our fire.

I looked to see what was attracting their attention and my heart raced! Silver was standing, his naked form stretched out in a thin, rigid line with toes digging into the soft earth of the river bank and arms high above his head. His skin flashed as it silvered and a moan of anguish left his lips.

"Silver!" I cried, and ran towards him. In an instant his cry became anger as he opened his eyes and stared at me. "Leave me alone! Leave me alone, Walker! I don't need you! I don't want you! You're always in the way, Walker. *Go away!*"

Shattered, almost sick, I backed away from him and felt Harmony's arms slip around me, comforting.

"What have I done?" I begged.

Tears in her eyes she shook her head. "I don't know, Walker. I don't understand. . . ."

We both looked back at Silver, still stretched taut and rigid. On his chest a picture began to form, slowly at first, then more and more explicit as the detail filled in. It was a picture of me, facing a Silver who was armed and angry. In my clutches, looking to Silver for help, was a distressed and dishevelled Harmony.

"No, Silver!" I shouted, shocked at what he was insinuating. "No . . . she's happy! We're all happy!"

Harmony's hold on me became tighter, her small body transmitting her fear to me.

Silver began to shout. "None of us are happy, Walker! You've stolen her from me . . . you've come between us from the start! You're an old man and you've stolen her from me. Why don't you *go away!* GO AWAY!"

"Not old, Silver," I sobbed, unable to keep back tears. "Not old, just . . . just a passing physical form . . . not old; young! In love with you, with Harmony." I sat down and hugged my body . . . not old, just the old form I had adopted at the last season of alteration. Silver should know that . . . mature of look, mature of mood. We might reverse everything this coming season. Who knew? I felt a tremendous depression encompass me. Harmony was crying softly, her face in her hands. Depression. Everywhere depression, as if the prevailing mood of one member of the triad could reach out and infect the others.

Then I noticed, on Silver's chest . . .

"The figures are moving!"

Jarrol's cry convinced me that I was not seeing things, but

even so I could hardly believe it. I could hardly believe the evidence of my own eyes!

A great crowd was moving in to watch the display. On Silver's chest my figure was moving towards the figure of Silver, and suddenly—a knife, produced from Silver's imagination, appeared in his hand, and the figure on his chest sent the blade deep into my body, through the heart, deeply through the heart, and there I watched it, my murder, my assassination. And before my body had crumpled to the ground, becoming a shapeless mass of black and silver shadow and light, there was Silver moving into a love lock with Harmony.

The picture faded, but not the atmosphere. *Body mobiles*, the crowds murmured, naming the artform without hesitation. Silver had invented body mobiles.

And, by finally managing to express something he had, perhaps, been unable to express before, he had destroyed our triad!

A gain and a loss in just a few moments of time.

Silver collapsed to the camp floor and his unconscious form was swiftly carried into the security of our tent. I remained seated, bewildered.

A hand on my shoulder, warm lips on my ear. Harmony, tears in her soft, green eyes; she kissed me, caressed me.

"His last alteration was overdone," she whispered. "That's all it is, Walker. He opted for depression and they overdid it. In a few weeks he'll want to forget this as much as I do."

She was right, of course, and yet the wound had gone deep. Too deep. I shook my head. "He's envious, Harmony. He's jealous of me, and he's broken us up."

"Not us . . . not you and I, Walker. The three of us, perhaps, but . . ." she trailed off, the words catching in her throat. She no more wanted to break with Silver than she would want to break with me. She was comforting me because of my hurt, but I could detect her concern for Silver. As artists they had always had a special affection for each other, nothing unpermissible, but . . . special.

I kissed her hand. "Go and see if he's all right," I said. She smiled and ran towards the tent.

When I returned to the tent both Silver and Harmony were sleeping. I sat for a long while listening to the sound of their breathing, but the exhaustions of the day overtook me eventually.

I woke late in the morning. Harmony was still curled up, but Silver was gone, perhaps out exploring the terrain before the event hit. The day was still and fairly warm, although ominous grey clouds poured across the sky from the hills, and the air was filled with the signs of an approaching storm. But reassuringly the MECH predicted that the weather would be fine all morning, up until the moment when the tiny black hole caught up with the Earth.

I left the tent and indulged myself with a wash in the icy cold waters of the Taim. This high up in the hills the waters were clear and tasteless; I felt as if I was returning to nature.

Drying myself with a palm-dryer I watched the strange shapes and arrows on the MECH; one display, a summary display, showed me the shape of our Earth and the location of the river Taim, and the approach of the black hole. The singularity would penetrate the Earth almost vertically; at that time the planet would be moving away from the approaching event. The final velocity through the Earth would still be more than twenty miles per second. Yet for the instant the black hole was above the river the MECH would vastly slow our time sense so we would observe the passage of the hole across a time span of several seconds. The effect should be marvellous, I thought, as I made my way to the food mash.

The MECH had instructed us to tune our time-space shields to a very high level. The quantum hole, though only one hundredth the radius of a small atomic nucleus, would nevertheless exert a gravitational pull of over two gravities at a hundred-foot distance, and we would be sitting a little closer than that!

The depression of the previous evening had lifted but I still felt our triad was doomed. Silver's jealousy, I could accept, was the result of a badly tuned construction during the previous season of alteration. But the emotion had been so powerful that I felt there had to be an underlying rationality. Even without his terribly depressive state, he would still have felt jealousy.

Triads often broke up and reformed, two splitting from one, all splitting from each other—it was no new phenomenon. But I had thought this, my third triad, was stable for life. If it broke again I should have to shrug off my chosen façade of age and maturity and adopt a more youthful persona. This was the way things were done in my home city. I was convinced that any split would be between myself and Silver, with Harmony opting to stay with the youth.

I found Harmony as soon as I had eaten, and we sat by the river as the minutes ticked by. She had recovered her full strength after the exertions of the night before, and now she sat and contemplated the spot indicated by the light focus above the river.

"You're very thoughtful, Harmony. Tired?"

"No. Not tired. A little down, that's all. I talked with Silver last night. We talked a lot."

"About me?"

"Partly. You don't bother him anywhere near as much as he made out last night. That was just anger, and the anger was just . . . frustration."

"Frustration over what?"

"Over . . ." she searched for the words and the silence was long and strained. Her hand found mine, her head shook, her gaze never left the water. "I suppose it's what I've felt for a long time, and Silver has felt it too. It's a lack of . . . of significance!"

"Significant art?" I laughed. "Art is for enjoyment, for relaxation. It was never meant to be significant!"

"Wasn't it? We play a watching game, Walker. We watch

each other creating in different ways, we create for others to watch. But we're idle. We lack compassion, too . . . oh we *do* Walker!"

"We do not!" I cried. "You're taking the myths of Legend Week too seriously. Those times were primitive, irrational. What is shown during that week are the petty attempts of morons to create art—compassion, yes, they had compassion, but what does that mean? Their art was meaningless, compassion or no. Our art is meaningful—even if not all of us have a conception of compassion."

"You're wrong, Walker," she said simply. "Idleness, self-centredness, indulgence . . . they've all perverted art in our hands. I'm sure of it. We've lost that very valuable sense of the primitive that just now you held to be something worthless. Without it our art is totally . . . empty!"

I argued no further. If a sense of the past, of the primitive, was really important then it was beyond my ability to see why. But if contact with the past was important then Harmony might find some relevance in the artistic indulgence scheduled for just a few minutes' time—I couldn't believe this particular MECH would advertize a new physical toy unless there was a very real time-contact predicted as well.

Other elite were joining us by the river. I checked the hour and saw no more than ten minutes remained before the arrival of our small event. I ran back to the tent, paged Silver several times without success, and carried the force field generators back to where Harmony was still sitting. Suitably protected in our shells of distorted space-time we were invulnerable to the collision of galaxies.

The MECH was going wild, the Midget frantic.

Where *was* Silver?

We searched the crowds for him, scanned the landscape, the skies. He was nowhere to be seen.

Then:

The wind began to shriek. Above our heads the clouds

ceased their graceful flow and became, in an instant, a grey and white confusion of swirling mist. . . .

Time slowed.

There was grace in the heavenly motion, the clouds forming a spiral as they spun towards the unexpected gravitational upset—the wind growled, the river oozed past us, a viscous, sparkling stream.

"Where's Silver?" shrieked Harmony, her voice in my mind filled with panic and unnatural tone; she was communicating at one hundred times her normal rate.

I scoured the raging skies. There was no sign of him. An instant later the cloud patterns changed and great grey and white streamers poured upwards and out of sight; as we watched so the streams of cloud changed direction, lowering their focus as the black hole dropped through the atmosphere.

Even the waters of the Taim were violent; the surface broke and jumped, great strands of fluid darting upwards, ten, twenty feet from the main flow before shattering and dispersing under the conflicting forces around them.

Harmony screamed, suddenly and loudly, and I looked from the water to the sky and saw Silver, a small, dark shape, totally at the mercy of the gravitational vacuum. His limbs threshed, his body slowly twisted as he rose and fell, fighting ineffectually with his gravity belt but at the mercy of the upward current. He vanished into cloud, re-appeared to plummet down for a second, up for a second, round and round, tossed and flung—plunging towards the event!

Harmony sobbed, but remained motionless, resigning herself to the inevitable death of her lover. I watched in horror as Silver surged along a streamer of cloud towards . . .

"THERE!" cried a hundred voices. "SEE THERE!"

The clouds vanished in the centre of a whirlpool, into an area of distorted imagery and vanishing perspective. And at the very centre flared a brilliant spot of intensely blue-white light.

The quantum black hole itself!

The motionless body of Silver slipped down the gravity gradient followed by a surge of water as the river itself rose in a thrashing sheet and was sucked into the holocaust. Rocks, turf, fragments of mountain followed as the singularity descended toward the dry river bed, sucking water downstream in a miniature *tsunami*.

At the instant of his death Silver had felt at peace. I had felt it and Harmony had felt it. He had wanted to die, and he had died in a fashion that would never be forgotten. Perhaps he had seen death as the only honourable way to apologize to me; perhaps in some peculiar, unfathomable way he had seen it as an answer to his feelings of futility. Perhaps the act of death itself was creative, and he had forever stolen the field for creative death!

We continued to watch, solemnly, numbly, as the area of distortion passed through the wide, bare river bed. A great cascade of rock and coloured fragments rose slowly, beautifully, up into the air, seeming to rise forever until finally turning to tumble back down to the surrounding countryside, here and there spinning harmlessly away from an onlooker's invulnerable force shield.

At that same moment the time distortions began—in the air, thirty feet above the impacting black hole, I saw the first shape struggling into existence: a huge, black-skinned man, dressed in flowing green and yellow robes—he came into our time only to fall slowly and dreamily into the gaping crater below. But even as he fell, others were bursting out of the past.

Men and women, children of all ages—flaxen haired, black haired, naked, clothed in the most diverse of garments—they came tumbling gracefully out of nowhere, some to die instantly as they hit the ground, others recovering to begin running in exaggerated slowness away from the source of the distortion.

The MECH reverted our time sense to normal.

It was bitterly cold as we came from our protective shields, the howl of the wind mingling with the screams of the time relics and the roars and cries of beasts too, for all manner of animals were also pouring from the rent in space-time. One great grey beast towered above everything else, rearing up on hind legs that were huge pillars of flexing muscle; its forearms were tiny and useless, its teeth gleamed in the daylight as the great mouth opened and closed on a fleeing man. After a moment the beast lumbered away from the river, chewing its prey. A large band of the elite set off in hysterical, delighted pursuit.

The time-effect ceased and the outpouring from the past was cut off. Most of the relics were already dead, but a good thirty or forty had survived and were scattering in all directions; men dressed in furs, waving huge metallic weapons (but running just the same), women in brief garments standing and shrieking at the tops of their voices as they were taken by members of the elite. . . .

The web of a historian reached out from behind me and froze specimen after specimen, and the angry voice of the Collector roared in my ears as he cursed the slaughter of the relics. He managed to secure five of the creatures before they had all dispersed, and set about their examination still grumbling his fury at the waste.

All the rest were in the hills, fleeing, the elite in hot and noisy pursuit.

Harmony ran along the river bank towards a figure that lay writhing and screaming upon a bare rock overhang.

"Walker!" she shouted, by voice and by mind, and I raced after her, attention half on her and half on the scene of confusion and carnage that was spreading in a widening circle around the crater, itself now beginning to fill with the waters of the Taim.

Harmony was crouched over a woman who was, even to my inexperienced eye, obviously in the final stages of a natural childbirth. Her garments were rough and seemed cut straight from the fur of some shaggy beast. She wore metal bracelets and a necklace of polished stone. Her hair was gathered back in a double plait. Her face was unpainted and contorted with pain as she screamed and sobbed, hands clutching at her swollen belly.

Harmony immersed herself and the woman in a warm-field and tore the garments from the threshing body, exploring the distended belly with its network of blue surface-veins. It was the first time either of us had seen such a sight, except on the medi-grid, and I thought how rich it was in aesthetic qualities.

"Oh Walker!" cried Harmony, delighted with her find. "What a beautiful sight."

She pressed her face to the woman's belly and immediately the woman began to fight her, beating futilely with small clenched fists and whimpering in a language as incomprehensible to my ears as the howling of the wind.

"Hold her, Walker!" cried my mate (had she forgotten Silver so soon? Beneath her delight and enthusiasm did there remain any shred of grief for our lost mate?). I entered the warm field and grasped the arms of the struggling mother-to-be. Again Harmony's head descended to listen to the sound of the unborn child. "Oh it's so beautiful!" she raved. "I've never heard anything like it! It's nothing at all like the sounds *I* hear." She was quiet, then, for a long, long moment, examining with her mind, and then she looked up at me, eyes wide with excited realization.

"Walker . . . Walker I've got a chance to *really* use my power. Oh Walker what an opportunity, what a moment to be *truly* creative!"

I looked from her to the straining flesh beneath which lay the unborn child, then to the mother's huge blue eyes that looked up at me, not understanding, but . . . trusting, strangely trusting. Back to Harmony.

"It seems a pity, somehow . . ."

"Oh Walker, silence! You don't understand. I can—I can *really* put my powers to the test. Help me. *Hold her.* Hold her secure and don't argue with me."

And I obeyed; I held the woman's arms tightly and watched as Harmony placed her hands on the huge belly and closed her eyes to work her mental magic. After a moment the woman began to scream, but my grip only tightened still further. For now Harmony was possessed totally, and as the minutes passed so the sweat began to drip from her face, and her cheeks lost all their colour.

I wondered what was happening in the womb.

Ten minutes went by and still Harmony had not moved. She broke concentration with startling suddenness, stared down at the unsuspecting woman, then at me. "I did it, Walker. I did it! Walker—*I did it!*"

And there beneath the threatening skies, by the bank of the river Taim, she induced labour in the woman and delivered her of . . . perfect twins!

I stared at them—two perfect and identical boy children, each screeching its head off, each head slick with moist black hair, each tiny face a picture of panic, and Harmony soothed them.

"There's not even a mark," she said, showing me the back of each child's head. "They were joined halfway down their heads and down to mid-spine. Isn't that fantastic? Such things used to happen a lot in the dark ages."

"Fantastic," I said, and took a child into my arms, then passed it to the waiting mother who accepted the sobbing infant with great happiness.

I felt humble, and very proud of Harmony. I had failed to comprehend her disillusionment with art when we had talked earlier, but now fully realized what she had been seeking for. I rose and walked to fetch the gyro, passing the celebrating elite and the broken bodies of the time-relics as I did so. Its function over, the silent mournful shape of the MECH loomed over us and its human operator sullenly regarding the exhibition he had wrought.

In the Valley of the Statues

I

High clouds and the threat of rain later in the spring day made the arrival of dawn an affair of diffuse light, growing in intensity, rather than that particularly romantic vision of a sudden golden brilliance breaking low across the hills.

Watching from his open window, cool yet comfortable in his night robe, Alexander Arden found that he could not decide with certainty the precise moment at which night had fled and day had come. The land, the valley across which his room gazed, had seemed first to become an area of shadow; those shadows had continuously given way to further shadow, each lighter, each less stark and formidable than that preceding until—without being consciously aware of the subtle process of change—Arden observed that the valley was in colour, and the landscape appreciable in all its remote magnificence.

A thousand statues, each carved from some gleaming white stone, seemed to jut and probe from the sides of the valley; some rested gently upon the flatter land above the winding river; others appeared to move across the higher ground, the legs and arms of the figures given subtle life by the play of light and shade upon their facets. It was, Arden reflected, as if some giant yet sensitive celestial hand had scattered these human artifacts across the valley, and they had lain where they had fallen, untouched by humankind or by the eroding fingers of rain and wind.

Wherever he looked, for as far as he could see down the steep-walled valley, the white faces of stone gleamed between the complex colours of tree and grass and the lichen-covered grey stone of the area, a thousand shades of grey, sheltered by a thousand shades of green.

With dawn came the smell of the unspoiled land, heady, fragrant, something of the wild flower about it, something grassy, something of the pungent odour of woodland and undergrowth; a little something of decay. Arden shrugged off his robe and walked naked through the french windows to stand on the corroding concrete balcony. His hands, on the cold, dark-tinged metal of the safety rail, found the contact of the iron a delight, a sensory extravagance. He turned his back on the deep, rich valley and leaned against the rail, staring up at the sculpted façade of his host's mansion, the ornate and complex designs upon the windows and walls a testimonial to the frantic desire of a single man to outdo nature in the carving of rock into bizarre and beautiful shapes.

At dinner the evening before, the sculptor, Peter Stavanda, had raised his goblet at the conclusion of the simple meal and leaned forward heavily upon the unpolished oak table. "The beauty, Mr Arden, the magnificence of nature," he had said, with no hint of the Eastern European accent that Arden had anticipated, "is its wildness, its irregularity—unpredictable of form, made jagged and free by the disorderly erosion of time."

He had leaned back, staring at Arden through those intense blue eyes that disturbed the young Englishman so much. Arden guessed that Stavanda was some thirty years older than himself; his thick white hair and crinkled, wind-tanned skin gave him the look of a medieval sorcerer, perhaps of a man of wealth who has hidden within his private cosmos for more years than he can remember.

And yet the woman who dined with them, not his wife, nor even hinted at as being his mistress, was younger even than Arden.

Karina was slender, serene, her black hair tied formally and perfectly into a style that kept her neck free. Her shoulders, bare above her translucent black gown, seemed never to rise with her breathing, or fall when Stavanda's conversation reached its depths of grossness. She smiled only thinly at the Englishman, a cold expression that might have symbolized an English coldness of the heart so prevalent among Arden's countrymen. And yet she, this serene woman, knew that Arden was not a man lacking in passion: her eyes, dark, depthless, a Mediterranean warmth about them, an anger, a sexual hunger for the Englishman in every amber corner, her eyes seemed to linger on him, filling him with that same earnest desire to be alone with her that he had felt at their first meeting, in Paris three weeks before.

"And yet," the sculptor again leaned forward, reaching for the decanter of wine, allowing his goblet to spill over onto the table before he ceased to pour; Arden was uneasy for a second, imagining that he sensed, in Stavanda's half-smile, some awareness of his own passion for Karina. "And yet Man, most particularly as woman, is beautiful *because* of this contrast with nature!" Stavanda punctuated the statement with the edge, then the flat of his hand, pressed against the table, near to the glistening spill of wine. It was his most familiar mannerism, and Arden had found himself adopting it during the long evening and the simple, but drawn out, meal.

Stavanda had talked of his art for hours during the afternoon when they had sat so still, so formal after Arden's arrival, into the evening when they had faced each other across the coarse wood of the table. Arden was anxious to see the statues in the valley, for it was these that had brought him searching for Stavanda in Paris: doggedly, the hunter chasing through the reports from paper and magazine, trying to locate the elusive artist, ultimately locating him through the discreet promiscuity of his beautiful companion.

As his eyes lingered on Karina's lips and neck, remembering the taste of them, the smoothness of them, Stavanda was saying, "Man is smooth, and rounded, he is regular and patterned.

Man, most particularly as woman, stands apart from nature, arrogant, upright, different in every aspect from the jagged pinnacles of granite and sandstone that time has sculpted. Nature condenses into a myriad forms of life, all ordered and regular, microcosms of pattern in the chaos of the Universe. Man is the greatest of these, and to carve the pattern of man, and of woman, in this cold crystal stone, the primal clay, is to fuse the elements of order and disorder, to bridge the Universe of animate and inanimate."

He was silent, then, staring moodily, reflectively, at the remains of the roast duck that were such an ugly exception to what he had been saying. Karina politely sipped her wine, watching Stavanda with some embarrassment. Arden had watched her while thinking of the old man's words. Simple, perhaps even narrow, the words expressed that which had driven Stavanda through all the years of his life, fashioning pattern in rock, sculpting from his mind, through his hands, into the—what had he called it?—the primal clay!

"Man thinks and dies," said Stavanda quietly, glancing up at Arden with suddenly alert eyes, narrowed, penetrating. Was he looking for some response, some furtherance of the philosophy from his youthful guest? "The stone of the earth exists for all time without consciousness. What must the fusion, then, represent? What occurs when I shape the pattern of life in the crystal rock?"

"I have no idea," said Arden gently. "A permanence of form, but not of life. . . ."

"Not immortality?" said Stavanda with a thin smile. "Not immortality," he repeated, almost despondently. "Perhaps a persistence of memory?"

"The memory of form," said Arden.

"But not of life; is that what you're saying?"

"Memory of life while those who remember the human who has been depicted in the stone are living."

Stavanda laughed, then shook his head. "But what of my life? No memory of that? The artist?"

Uneasy, Arden met Karina's steady gaze. She was regarding him coolly yet passionately, as she always did. She rarely spoke. In fact, when she spoke it was always in whispers, as if she were afraid for her voice to rise above the barely audible.

"When one carves so realistically," said Arden, "it is always easier to see the life represented in the stone, rather than the life that shaped the stone."

Stavanda shook his head, not in disagreement, but almost fatalistically. "We still talk of a persistence of memory, an echo, a representation of some energy that has transiently involved itself with the stone. Is there nothing more?" Again he fixed his gaze upon the younger man, and Arden reached for his wine to hide the nervousness he felt. He had wanted to talk to Stavanda, to see his work, to record his thoughts, to profit by them. . . . Stavanda knew this, and had known it all along. Surely he wasn't in some way trying to punish him for doing his job!

Arden was out of his depth, not because he felt the argument was beyond him, but simply because he did not care as much for the sort of talk that Stavanda wanted as he did for the sort of talk that Karina wanted, the quiet talk of night, of love. He knew the woman would come to him or, at least, that she would make it easy for him to come to her. Stavanda would, surely, be so often in his valley, among his statues, that there would be time in abundance to know this woman's body again, and her mind, and thus certain facets of Stavanda himself that the artist would not supply. In this way, then, in the way he thought, Arden was as much a sculptor as Stavanda himself, planning the manipulation and usage of his material in order to produce something that would be memorable.

'To fuse the animate and the inanimate . . ." Stavanda said slowly, almost soberly, staring at the Englishman with an expression Arden thought might have been contempt, "must be to create something . . . something *more* than memory. Surely."

"Some creature of stone? Of primal clay?" said Arden, and smiled. His face was flushed and he felt hot. "A golem?"

"Some force of energy, of life," said the sculptor. "Something that is neither flesh nor stone, something . . . something that is neither, and yet is both. . . ."

Arden said, "A golem. You've created a golem, is that what you're saying?"

But Stavanda laughed. "You speak, my young friend, as if nothing that could emerge from the union could be beautiful. But then, you've not yet seen my statues. You speak of golems, but I always thought such things were forces of evil, without true direction of their own. That you talk of animated life at all amuses me. I speak of something more than just the solid photography of human life. I cannot believe that a sculpture in living rock is no more, no less, than a photograph. One is putting too much into the shaping of the stone. There is a vision there; surely there must be a vision, a creation *beyond* what we think of as creation."

Arden raised his glass, drained the sweet wine. "I regret," he said, "but I really do not understand what you mean. I feel that I should. I sense that you are aware of something which I, for my ignorant part, cannot grasp. Our perspectives are different. I am sure it will not diminish my pleasure at surveying your work."

2

The clouds broke towards midday, as Arden walked through the valley of statues some way behind the silent, moody form of Stavanda.

"They are quite magnificent!" called the Englishman, overwhelmed by the power of the sculptures. "Magnificent," he repeated, and smiled as Stavanda stopped and turned.

"Is there not a life to them?" said the old man.

"Indeed!" said Arden. "I begin to understand what you meant."

He looked about him, cool in the brisk wind which accompanied the sporadic flashes of sun through the high clouds. He wore only his windcheater and jeans, but Stavanda himself was in a thin white shirt and loose flannels and must have been quite cool.

The sculptor didn't show it, manifested only a slight irritation with the wind that insisted on blowing his hair about his face. They looked back along the valley to where the house seemed to grow from the rock face of what might have once been a quarry, or a cliff too sheer for any plant to find a perch upon it.

"Yes, a quarry," said Stavanda when Arden queried the site. "Very old, very old indeed. Running through the rock is a wide vein of the stone I use for my carvings. White stone, crystalline; I could have told you the name of it years ago, but names matter less these days. I built the house myself. I carved the façades myself. I *am* the house, Mister Arden; if you like, I am the valley, I am these statues. I am my work, which is why I found it so frightening that you failed to grasp how an artist's life is represented in whatever lifeform he carves."

He laughed suddenly, staring sideways at Arden, who was agreeing thoughtfully. The Englishman reached out to touch the porcelain-smooth surface of one statue that showed a man, crouching, staring into the distance. The sculptor said, "Do you see any golems, Mister Arden?"

Arden laughed. "I apologize for my naïveté."

"No need to apologize," said Stavanda as they continued along a winding path. They were several hundred yards from the river, but not hidden from it, for the trees appeared to have been cleared along a stretch of shoreline and Arden watched the cool waters enviously. He loved to swim in rivers, even in cold weather, and this river was as clean and crystal fresh as glass. Stavanda suddenly turned, blocking the pathway so that Arden was forced to stop, thrusting his hands into the pockets of his windcheater. The old man said, "No need to apologize, because if you think about it . . . *I* am a golem."

"Oh yes? You seem very fleshy to me." Arden laughed nervously. There was something disconcertingly intense about Stavanda's expression and attitude.

"But a golem I nevertheless am, Mister Arden. Look around you. Look at the house, look at the valley, my valley. I shaped it, I shaped everything in it. I am an artist. I work in stone, in the fabric of the earth, the floor upon which you stand. I am a shaper, towards an end that instils life into the cold stone. I am in this valley, Mister Arden; I am in the rock that lies beneath your feet, and the white stone that graces your eyes as you look around. And that stone is in me, I am inseparable from my work; it and I are closer than two adjacent drops of water in that river down there. I am stone, Mister Arden; I am the golem that for a second, last night, you feared to see stalking through the valley."

"Metaphorically," said Arden, unsure of himself again, nervous beneath Stavanda's intense scrutiny. He felt he was being tested, an appalling sensation. He didn't know what to do or say to impress this old man whose co-operation he needed both in supplying an article and in supplying the time for his interest in Karina.

"Metaphorically what?" said Stavanda. "Metaphorically stalking?"

"Metaphorically a golem," said Arden.

"As my statues are metaphorically life?"

"Indeed."

They walked on, Arden growing restless with thoughts of Karina. He had hoped she would come on this walk with them so that he could at least look at her, smell her, have an excuse —occasionally—to touch her. She had not appeared at breakfast and, though by nature Arden was impolite enough to ask where she might have been, he had not, somehow, found the words to phrase the question without advertising his more subtle intentions.

Wherever he looked in the valley he saw the human shapes of Stavanda's life work. Naked figures, and couples, animals and abstracts, all smooth, all detailed in that precise and irregular way that tells of a truly remarkable eye for accuracy.

Here, a woman bathed her face, leaning above an unseen bowl; the sun on her flanks brought white life to the cold stone, and as Arden watched her so she seemed to move slightly. When he looked at Stavanda the old sculptor was half amused; Arden felt that he understood something of the old man's fixation with the frozen life of his art, a life not human, yet something beyond his own conception of human life. Further along the valley he came across a montage of lovers, legs and arms entwined in the early embrace of potential love; Arden walked about the carving, amazed at the detail, the sensuousness of the white stone as it fashioned the commerce of the unknown couple. Elsewhere a middle-aged man petted a dog, the age depicted upon him as it had hung, loose and awful, upon his living body. The dog was on its hind feet, paws within human hand, mouth open in that anthropomorphic smile that makes a canine such a pleasant companion.

An empty pedestal appeared between high heather; purple-fringed and unnaturally precise, it seemed out of place in the valley and Arden was puzzled to know what might have once stood upon it.

Stavanda, as if in answer to the unspoken question, jumped upon the white stone cube and turned about to face Arden, his arms extended.

"Here stands the artist, alive."

"A self portrait?" asked Arden, and as he spoke his eyes found the thin markings of the chisel that spelled, in faint relief, the name Stavanda upon the base. "A self portrait," he repeated. "Is it finished?"

"Years ago," said Stavanda, descending to the earth again. "I'm polishing the stone, touching it up a little. You shall see it tomorrow."

"Thank you. I'd like to. Tell me, is there. . . .?"

He caught the flow of words in time, managed to appear distracted by some movement further up the valley.

Stavanda glanced at him, frowning for a second, perhaps angry for a second. "Is there what? Karina? Is there a statue of Karina?"

Angry with himself, annoyed that his simple question, his simple inability to complete the question, must have sounded intensely suspicious, Arden quickly said, with a surprised smile, "You've sculpted Karina? That's interesting. No, I was about to ask if there was a possibility of photographing some of your work."

"Absolutely not!" snapped the old man. "But believe me," he added more gently, as he led the way down towards the river, slipping on the fern growth and steadying himself with his hand. "Believe me, you will never forget my statues. They have an effect upon you. What you remember will remain with you always. Far better than cheap photographs."

"The persistence of memory," thought Arden with a smile as he slipped after Stavanda with only slightly more deftness; and, as he walked, so Stavanda sent a chill through him with his next words: "I wonder, Mr Arden, just what you will make of your article and me. I wonder what a man like you will do with what he learns."

"A man like me? What sort of man is that?"

Stavanda turned to look back across his shoulder for a moment; there was amusement on his face, mischief in his bright eyes. "A man who pretends to know so much and comprehends so little." He looked away from Arden. "Or perhaps you know the value of my name, if not my art."

Before Arden could answer they had reached the river. Here they stood and surveyed the statues that were half hidden by low-hanging tree branches and high-growing fronds of fern near the water. "She is there," said Stavanda, pointing to the right. "I know you find her very beautiful. I should be a depressed man if you did not. That, after all, is why I share my love with her."

For a second Arden was perplexed by the implication of spiritual shallowness in Stavanda's relationship with the woman evinced in his last statement. Then, his face burning, unable to look back at the old man, he walked towards the nude statue of Karina and stood before it.

She was seated, her legs tucked under her; she was leaning on one hand while her other seemed to brush back stray curls of hair. She looked across the water, serene, cool, as if she watched herself in the distorting ripples of the current. She seemed thoughtful, almost sad. Arden looked at that perfect body, the small breasts, the slender thighs, remembering them, remembering how they had been beneath his fingers, beneath his lips.

Love stirred him, made him redden and he turned away. He stooped and splashed his hand in the cold water, and, when Stavanda came up to him, he apologized.

"It's seeing her like this and knowing I must face her across dinner tonight. It's childish, but I do feel a slight embarrassment."

The old man laughed. "What an excellent liar you are," he said, and when Arden met his gaze he felt as if he himself had been turned to stone.

They returned to the house, Arden quite weary from the extensive walk and frequent scrambling. Almost as soon as they passed up the shallow steps to enter the area of lawned fore-garden, Stavanda excused himself and slipped away, around the side of the house and presumably to his studio, for soon after there came the distant, almost shrill, sound of a chisel working on stone.

Arden amused himself by walking through the shrubbery, past several greenhouses, and through an overgrown and obviously unplanted garden. A scattering of cabbages and potato plants told of previous years of cultivation, but now it was weeds and thistles that dominated the patch of ground behind the house.

He saw no obvious signs of the studio where Stavanda worked, although the sound of chipping continued, apparently coming from within the house itself. After a few minutes

Arden arrived back on the front lawn, where he located an easy chair and watched the advance of the afternoon.

After ten minutes or so of quiet contemplation he became suddenly uneasy. He turned on the chair to look back at the house, and for a moment he thought he saw Stavanda watching him from the balcony of his own room. Strangely, the figure moved away abruptly; the sound of stone-working had not ceased; and Arden relaxed slightly, supposing that he had been deceived by the reddening light and the fleetingness of the observation.

But he now found himself thinking almost obsessively about Stavanda, concerned not with the nature of his work but with thoughts of Stavanda's suspicions, or awarenesses, in relation to his guest and Karina. Surely Stavanda had not discovered about the affair in Paris . . . the man had spent most of the days walking alone in the streets and along the river, absorbing atmosphere and vision. His invitation to Arden to come to the valley had been warm and enthusiastic, the most noticeable moment of friendliness that Arden had observed from this insular old man.

His thoughts drifted away as the day vanished. Slightly perturbed at being left to his own devices he rose and walked through the french windows into the extensive drawing-room that faced the terrace. He located the drinks cabinet and returned to his chair with a half bottle of scotch and a glass. More relaxed, he consumed several shots of whisky while the lowering Sun set the scattered statues to all sorts of fire.

As dusk covered the valley, and the statues became invisible against the universal grey, he became aware that the sounds of work had finished. He rose, slightly unsteadily, and returned to the drawing room. He walked through the hallway to the dining-room, and here found Stavanda already eating. A place was set for him. Karina was not there, nor was the table set for her.

"Forgive me for starting," said the sculptor, waving a fork

by way of greeting, "but I was reluctant to interrupt your reflections."

"Not at all. I was quite relaxed."

"And I was too damned hungry to wait."

Arden seated himself, reached for the half-full decanter of claret and changed his mind. The scotch was repeating on him, and he felt dizzy and slightly nauseous. Roast beef had been served and he sliced a liberal portion, eating it alone, ungarnished. Stavanda finished his own meal, wiped his mouth and rose from the table.

"Forgive me," he said, "but I have work to do."

And as abruptly and as rudely as that, he was gone.

Arden finished his slight meal and decided on a glass of wine. Eventually he decided on the whole decanter and took this to his room where he lay down on the bed and soon slept.

He woke at a little after midnight and felt quite refreshed. The decanter of wine had spilled onto the counterpane of his bed and he guiltily stripped the covering and piled it in a corner. Combing his hair, removing his jacket in favour of a fresh shirt, he stepped from his room into the dimly lit corridor outside. Pausing at the farther end, by the room he knew to be Stavanda's, he listened hard for breathing. He heard none. Opening the door slightly he peered in, but the bed was made up, unspoiled, and the room had something of a stale, unused air about it.

He closed the door as gently as he had opened it, despite this being rather pointless caution. Walking into the right wing of the sprawling house he paused by Karina's room, listened here as well before gently opening the door and satisfying himself that her room, also, was unoccupied.

"What are you doing, Mr Arden?"

He was startled as Stavanda came up behind him, watching him suspiciously. Embarrassed, Arden smiled and said, "I felt like some company. I do apologize. . . ."

Stavanda smiled thinly. "I apologize for deserting you," he said, taking Arden's arm and leading him back to his own room. "I understand the need for talk in a strange place, and I promise not to abuse your patience again. Karina will be here tomorrow. Goodnight, Mr Arden."

"Goodnight."

"Sleep well."

3

In the morning, after a somewhat restless night, Arden arrived in the breakfast-room quite breathless from running down the stairs; he imagined Karina would be there, waiting for him, but to his disappointment he faced an empty room. The table was set for one.

The food was hot, smoked meats, eggs and toast. He was very hungry—the drink and his small evening meal had seen to that. Thus he soon forgot his irritation at again eating alone and filled himself with eggs, bacon and coffee.

It was only as he finished, and was rising with the intention of seeking someone out, that he saw the small white envelope propped up between two silver serving dishes. Opening the note he found it to be from Karina, asking him to come and find her near the river.

Smiling, he pocketed the paper and left the house.

It was a fine day, still slightly cloudy, but the sun was much more in evidence and there was about the valley that heavy warmth that characterizes summer; perhaps, even during the preceding night, spring had been nudged aside and the new season admitted.

As if to confirm the point he saw a butterfly, huge and speckled with brown and red colouring; it bobbed and weaved above the heather and the gnarled hawthorn until abruptly it stopped, apparently in mid-air, fluttering frantically. Arden walked closer and saw that it was trapped against an immense silvery spider's web spun between the branches of two small thorn trees. The gleaming body of the spider was suspended halfway between its lair and the prey, as if the creature were unsure quite how to approach this immense and violently struggling meal. Arden reached out to rescue the butterfly, but before he could touch it the creature had pulled free by its own efforts. The spider scurried back to its hidey-hole underneath the branch; Arden could see its trembling shape between the shiny and still life-like husks of its previous insect prey.

Walking on, Arden felt totally relaxed in the warmth. Even the statues seemed more alive, and he reappraised them with an eye far more sympathetic for the honesty of their appearance. They were, he acknowledged, masterpieces of sculpture. It was hard to believe that one man, one mortal pair of hands, had fashioned such beauty from the stone. A god, even two gods, would have been hard put to achieve so much.

As he passed the pedestal which the day before had been empty he found himself gazing at the canny, penetrating stare of Stavanda : perfectly formed in the white marble-like stone, the nude figure was crouched, hands clasped before it, watching him. There, in detail, were the deep lines, the facial sculpture that was the skilled work of time, rather than the chisel, but which was here chiselled in stone in such a perfect copy that Arden stopped and was amazed. He stared at the paunchy figure, the member dangling low between the thighs, the flesh of the legs and arms still firm, but beginning to show signs of deterioration. This was the Stavanda of yesterday, not yesteryear, and now Arden understood why the artist had been so keen to get away, so urgent to be alone. He imagined that this statue, this self portrait, was made to age along with the artist himself. When Arden had arrived, a stranger in the valley, a rare visitor, the ego of the artist had been such that he could not bear for the Englishman to see a sculpture that was not wholly and exactly representative of the lifeform that had inspired it.

While Arden had amused himself with whisky and idle thoughts of the beautiful Spanish girl, Stavanda had been etching into the stone portrait those features of the past few years which time had painted upon his own wind-tanned flesh.

Truly, a magnificent feat, and a wonderful piece of art. Living art. Art that transcended the life implicit in the flesh and the time implicit in the stone, the primal clay that formed the image. Stavanda was right. The stone *did* live, in a way beyond the simple understanding of any man but he who was *in* the stone, and in whom the stone itself resided.

His name was called from a distance—a woman's voice that he recognized as Karina's. He scrambled down the slope to where the land levelled until it reached the river. He saw her; she was sitting on a boulder, in the shade of an old and wind-battered silver ash. She was wearing a wide, knee-length dress with an off-the-shoulder bodice—white of course—that flattered her in every way possible. He walked towards her, glancing, as he passed the spot, at the statue of her nude form that he had scrutinized the day before.

For a second he thought he was looking in the wrong place, for the pedestal he could see there was empty. But Karina called, "Stavanda has it up at the house, putting a few touches to it. Always the perfectionist."

Arden laughed. He greeted Karina with a light kiss on the cheek, then took her right hand in both of his and lifted the fingers to his lips. "Not ageing the statue," he said. "There is no need for that."

"Thank you."

Unable to prevent the impulsive action, Arden drew the girl to his body and kissed her hard. She melted to him, entwining her arms around him and returning the kiss with all the fierceness of one who has waited, impatient, for too many hours. Breathless, they laughed as they drew apart, and then walked to the river, to sit upon the empty stone pedestal and watch the water.

"Stavanda's talent is quite formidable," said Arden. "He must have worked every moment of his life to produce so many beautiful statues. He must produce them with staggering speed."

Karina squeezed his hand and smiled. "Stavanda never

worked fast. The life of the statues grows slowly, almost agonizingly."

"But there are so many!" Arden looked about him, seeing little more than tree and undergrowth, but knowing that more than a thousand statues—a figure that Stavanda had himself supplied the day before—were scattered throughout the valley. "Are you implying that he didn't work alone? He had help?" Suspicious, intrigued, Arden caught the girl's attention, tried to pierce the coolness of her gaze so that he might discern Stavanda's dark secret. But Karina reflected back his suspicion as a millpond reflects sunlight.

"Does any artist work alone? Ever?"

More word games, thought Arden. She's referring to his talent, to that innate energy that drives him and which only he possesses in that particular form.

He said as much aloud.

Karina looked away, looked down. Arden found himself fascinated by the smoothness, the soft tanned skin of her face and neck, the full rise of her breasts, much revealed in the lacy bodice. The love in him stirred angrily, restlessly.

She said, "When he was still an eternally young man—perhaps no older than you—the stone possessed him, became him, and he it. Since that time he has created almost in concert with the valley itself." She glanced at him and Arden noticed that she seemed troubled, some dark thought, perhaps, shadowing the brightness of her face. "It's as if the valley *is* the sculptor, working through his hands, and he is the white stone from the quarry embodied in the dextrous form of the old man."

"Have you seen him work? Have you watched him?"

Karina shook her head and smiled, her moment of trouble gone as swiftly as it had come. "Never. Stavanda sculpts from experience, using people he knows or has met as models. Everything he does is part of a design; every action, every movement, every word he speaks, every drop of blood he sheds, all are for the sculpture upon which he is working, upon which the valley is working through him. But I have never watched him in the final work, and I suppose I never shall."

As if tired of this idle talk, perhaps remembering—as Arden was remembering—their stolen nights in Paris, those several weeks ago, Karina turned and kissed the Englishman, hard and with passion. She reached for his shirt and deftly slipped open the buttons. The sun was hot and summery, the pedestal beneath them warm to the touch, if hard to their flesh.

They slipped off their clothes as quickly and quietly as if they loved in a private house and were behaving with silent discretion. She touched him, gently and expertly, and as his weight came down upon her, easily, feeling with his skin the contours of her body, so they matched and melded, so he sank into her, every part of him, in the warm sex in her where he knew he belonged. Her legs entwined about him, trapping him, and her arms wrapped so tightly about his neck and waist that he thought their bodies would fuse. She allowed him no movement save that of his hips, which he moved quietly, gently, lingering over each deep approach so that they could both feel the power of the other in the drawn-out seconds of pleasure that accompanied each completion of his entry.

They kissed, and when their tongues met her teeth clamped playfully upon him, nipping the soft flesh and trapping him, so that he laughed, caught in this enjoyable fashion, trapped like an insect in a particularly lovely fly trap.

Abruptly she pushed him away, untwined her legs and shifted her body so that he was forced to withdraw.

Arden felt a moment's panic, his heart racing as he glanced about at the trees and river, and at the slopes of the hill. "Have you heard something? What is it? Stavanda?"

"He's watching us." Her face was pallid beneath the tan— her eyes wide with fear. She suddenly shivered, drew her blouse about her shoulders. "I should have told you."

"Told me what? Where is he?" Arden stared through the shrubs and undergrowth, seeing only statues and the dancing patterns of Sun on white stone. "I can't see him."

Karina laughed, and Arden thought it sounded almost cruel, almost pitying. "Of course you can. Didn't I explain to you? He's everywhere, Alexander. He has watched you every moment since you came here. He has been watching patiently, waiting to trap you. Oh God!" She had stopped and suddenly winced with pain, her eyes closed, her hands touching her face. "It's too late . . . too late for you, too late for him . . . for me. . . ." She suddenly laughed again, this time with a tone of irony behind the sound. She looked at Arden and shook her head. "It had to come to this . . . it had to happen that one day I'd love somebody. I'm sorry. . . ."

Not sure of why he was so afraid, Arden dressed quickly and stood by the pedestal, looking at the semi-naked girl.

"Is he going to kill me?"

She shrugged. "He's inhuman, Alexander. Quite inhuman. His art is all there is, and the valley is all there is, but the valley *is* his art—it misses only life, real life. He feeds on life, on my life, on your life, on the lives of all who come to the valley. He drinks their souls and shapes the stone perfectly because of it. People leave here as shadows, the shadows of statues. He uses me because of what I am—"

"An insect trap."

"A life trap. You, more than any man, I think he would like to suck quite dry, to suck your very vitality."

Arden felt cold sweat break from his skin as he looked anxiously around. "To suck me dry . . . to kill me . . . my God, how long has he known about us?"

Karina looked puzzled. "About us? He's known from the beginning."

Shocked, Arden found himself staring at her, shaking his head. "He's always known? Then why—then why has he waited so long to confront me?"

"He doesn't want to kill you because of your affair with me," said the girl quietly, speaking as if she addressed a child. "He wants to kill you because you are sordid in his eyes . . . and not just sordid, but shallow. Your writing is motivated not by inner turmoil, by some energy of imagination, but by material needs. He will never carve you in stone, but I think he wishes to suck you dry so that he can carve some darkness into the white stone, some imperfection into his perfect creations—" Again she winced with pain, twisted slightly on the stone pedestal, and touched a hand delicately to her naked belly. Her eyes, when she met Arden's concerned gaze, were filled with longing. "Alex . . . kiss me. . . ." Her body seemed rigid, almost stiff. Slowly she reached for him, her desperation communicating itself through every forced gesture. "Make love to me, Alex . . . love me . . . no, *no!* . . . swim, swim . . . quickly!"

He took a step towards her, drawn to her beauty, desiring her, longing to complete their lovemaking. She cried out, the sound of one dying. Arden turned and ran to the river, plunged in and surfaced out where the flow was fastest. He swam strongly, despite his sodden clothes, and found time to glance back, to the pedestal and that private place among the trees. Karina seemed to be waving to him, her skin quite white at this distance.

The river swept him fast, out of the valley and away from the danger that, in one sense, he had been aware of all along. He smiled to think that perhaps his escape had been a narrow one. He would have found it difficult to comment in depth upon Stavanda's highly personal view of his art and his life, and in all likelihood the article would have been worthless. Facing a cold and wet reality as he struggled against the current, tired now and seeking a place to come ashore, Arden came to terms with the fact that his real interest in Stavanda had always been a part of trying to impress the woman in his life. That brief affair had been worth the wasted effort of coming so far in search of such an unsatisfying art. And he was forewarned, now, against any future recklessness such as pursuing his dream of passion into the very home of the man he was deceiving. He felt pleased with his escape, although it grew bitterly cold in the water and the river swept him faster between the slippery banks.

Ahead of him, then, he saw a place on the shore where he might come aground and strip off his freezing clothes, to warm himself in the bright Sun. He swam towards the river bank where it jutted out into the water and was fleetingly aware of the Sun reflecting on something white upon the shore.

It was a statue of Karina, her body reclining, her arm outstretched as if waving, or reaching. The shock of seeing it made Arden lose his rhythm as he swam. He was swept past the place among the trees, and onwards into deeper water, where the river flowed faster, and grew colder, and colder.

And as he swam on, desperate now, struggling to find the strength to keep himself afloat, he heard the unmistakable sound of hammering . . . the sound of chisel working stone, with such excitement and energy that the ringing strikes were run together into a single passionate tone.

Ashes

Ash, ash—
You poke and stir.
Flesh, bone, there is nothing there—
> Sylvia Plath, "Lady Lazarus"

I am Joseph Questel: killer. Have you heard of me? I hope so. Not for any satisfaction of my over-rated ego, but because if you *haven't* heard of Joseph Questel you are probably the only person in our wonderful Galaxy who hasn't.

Some people call me "The Animal". I prefer Questel. I especially dislike the name "sadist". But I have been called "The Sadist Questel" and it makes me feel a little angry inside.

My name is Kevin Karr. It is a superficial disguise, concealing the killer beneath. I often wear false hair, eye-catching clothes. A flamboyant attire takes the roving eye away from the face.

How many people who catch your eye on a walkway, in a tube, catch your eye because of their facial characteristics? Virtually none? Of course. The human race is a collection of artificial fibres animated by shapeless blobs of pink flesh.

Which is lucky for me.

There are twenty-three Galactic news-sheets. Some are dailies, some are weeklies, some appear but rarely, depending on news content.

And I am news content. I feature on every front page, every day, every month, every year.

Me, Questel, killer of innocent and helpless children. My photograph, my movements, my sadism, my guilt. It's all there

in black, red and white; fuzzy photographs, clear-cut carica-
tures.

So don't tell me you haven't heard of me, don't tell me you
haven't seen me. I'm a way of life. And Rainer, he too is a way
of life, and Lazlo. And Queron, and Boor-Badalwi. And Jones,
and the Galactic nonentity called Major Findik.

Killers all, hated all . . . running all. News.

We all have a job to do. Mine is to be hated. Never mind me,
I'm just a two-dimensional adventure and my screen time is
running out.

And I run, and run, and I am hounded and wherever I go I
am found. And there is no escape.

May I bask for a moment in self pity? Will you forgive me
if I attempt to justify my hatred for everyone and everything?
Go ahead, take my words and digest them, feed them to your
hate, file them with the pictures and the stories of what I,
Questel, did during my war-time career in the 'Eighteen
Twenty-seven war.

I don't mind. It's my job. Take me or leave me.

Does it surprise you, perhaps, to know that I eat, I sleep, I
love . . . yes, *love*. Is there such a thing?

I love darkness. True love. My truest love was a small attic
in a dusty and dingy house on Cone-world. A rat shared that
darkness with me. Snug as bugs we lived in our dark corner,
sharing our food, sharing our love.

Rats in an attic. When the rat died I moved. The darkness is
still there, waiting for me.

If I walk in the street I am rarely recognized. My face has
changed, my disguise is effective. I pass unnoticed. And yet
always I am found. Explain that!

Women seem to find me fascinating. I believe it is because
of a certain youthfulness in my approach.

Forty years ago, when a youth, I fascinated women for a
different reason. It was because of a certain maturity in my
approach.

The women I fascinated were the same type.

Explain *that*!

I feast on flesh as the films and documents say I feasted on flesh during the war. Only in those days I killed, and now I merely savour. One day it will be taken from me, the right to taste a woman's flesh.

I shan't miss it. Meat is meat. I shall lick my arm and pretend.

Pretence, after all, is my trade. It is what keeps me a free man.

Free in all but mind.

I never married and now I never shall. I shall never do anything that is the right of a man, because I have no rights left. No rights, that is, except the right to run for my life. And I'm good at that, oh yes.

Except I'm always found. Explain it, someone.

To be truthful I don't need it explained and eventually I'll tell you why. In the meantime, pause a moment and think of a sun, a blue-white sun, slowly and gracefully billowing out into space as it begins its journey towards nova. Think of that star, and think of me.

When I was on Timeslow, a small and backward planet in the Dragonfire cluster, I was happier than I have ever been.

I found Joni on Timeslow, and a wonderful sense of isolation. The wind storms that ravished the planet's surface were kin to me, the hail that flung itself through the small city in which I lived was mother and father to me. Fog and sand, they were my most comfortable clothes.

In obscurity I walked, in comfort I lived. On Timeslow I was Kevin Karr, and Joseph Questel was the ghoul who lived within my shadow. And on Timeslow shadows rarely appear.

Once upon a time I slaughtered a billion innocent people. The details aren't necessary. I slaughtered them horribly, many at my own hands. Old men I garrotted. There are pictures of me doing just that. I am not smiling as I wrench the life from their squirming bodies. When it is done I let the bodies slip to the cold ground and I just stand there, and for a moment, before the film is cut, one would almost think I was unaware of what I did.

And I will swear the dead man breathes, but then dead men often do; don't they?

On the news-screen I have my own show.

It is called the "Search for Joseph Questel". It occupies the eleven to eleven fifteen pm slot and it has a musical introduction that I recognize as a concerto by Frederick Darzel as interpreted by the contemporary electroharpist David Forbes. I enjoy Forbes's music, his interpretation of early twenty-first century harp music rather than his own compositions. I once heard him play at a concert. He played his interpretation of Minuet in G. That is a piece of music written centuries ago. It was terrible, but then the music of centuries ago is coarse, and vulgar, and tuneless.

When the concert was finished, he was called back for an encore.

"Thank you, ladies and gentlemen," he said. I smiled from my seat in the back row. I held my hands ready to applaud for I had enjoyed his musical evening. "Thank you, thank you very much. You have been a wonderful audience. I shall play an encore with the greatest of pleasure. It is a piece of music I have adapted from a concerto by Darzel, and I call it 'The Mind of Questel' because it is hateful and arrogant, superficially beautiful and yet with viciously ugly undertones."

The news-screen always plays that piece of music before the show starts. Then a wizened little man with sparse grey hair appears on camera and in a racy, excited voice proceeds to outline where the search for me has extended itself in the last twenty-four hours. Then they show film of the bodies on the planet that I used as a dumping ground for the men and women I killed. Then that same bit of film of me dispatching an old man, and looking as if I'm not aware of anything, just before the film cuts off.

The commentary goes like this: "The hunt for Joseph

Questel, the sick man who personally organized and personally helped with the death, by the most gruesome methods, of over one thousand million innocent women and children has today been extended here to Timeslow. This is the first time Time-slow has been the foxhole of Joseph Questel. Throughout the day agents of the League of Hunters have been infiltrating the major cities and towns of the planet in an attempt to take Questel by surprise, an attempt that failed. Just to remind you of the sort of man the league is hunting, here is some film taken by an agent on Trona, the concentration-planet where the innocents met their grisly demise. . . ."

By the time the news of the hunters reaching Timeslow was being given its second airing, I was in deep space, light years away from the planet.

I was desperately lonely. Joni was still on Timeslow and I should never see her again.

Within the space of just a few hours my happy seclusion had been broken, and again, with just memories to carry me through the tortuous days and nights, I found myself looking for somewhere to hide.

Even then I was acutely aware of the inconsistencies, of the strange things that repeatedly occurred.

Things like the expression on my face as I killed the old man. . . .

The way the dead man breathed—or seemed to.

The morning of my hasty departure from Timeslow started badly, and continued as it had started.

First there was the nightmare. I always have nightmares when I awaken before dawn and drift off to sleep again. The nightmare comes then as if it is lingering on the borders between consciousness and unconsciousness, and only in my semi-asleep state can it come through. . . .

It is a nightmare in which I kill three people. It goes like this: there is a dark and expansive garden and a huge hound running towards me. Its mouth opens and shuts as if it is barking but there is no sound. As it leaps at me, mouth open to tear my throat, I shoot it with a small hand gun and it falls limply to the ground.

The two moons are high and I can see the house, a large, palatial house. There is a single light in one of the upstairs rooms. Tall pines sway and creak in the wind. One pine has recently fallen and it sprawls across the lawn, slowly dying. I run up to the house and my heart is thumping. I push open a window, creep inside, and find my way to the stairs; up the stairs, heart racing, jumping at every shadow, every noise, and then I come to a room where the door is slightly ajar.

I push the door open and creep inside—there are two beds, one has been recently occupied, and in the other a naked woman is sitting bolt upright and staring at me. Then I swing round and there is the man, dressed in pyjamas—he is holding a metal rod with which he lunges at my face. I shoot him through the chest and he gags and vomits a considerable amount of blood. The woman is screaming. As the man falls he strikes again and the rod glances off my forehead and smashes down to break the gun I hold.

The woman is still screaming. I rush across to her and slap her, but she keeps screaming. I panic and I draw my knife and cut her throat quickly. She collapses backwards.

Somebody comes through the door and, in panic, I throw the knife, not really looking to see who is there. As I jump to the window I glance back and there is a small girl slowly collapsing to the floor, the shaft of my knife sticking out of her chest.

I wake up screaming at that point for I fall from the window in the dream and the sensation of falling is the final straw. . . .

I have that dream many times, but only when I'm in the half sleep of early morning. Usually my nightmares are worse, much worse. I see great lines of people walking slowly towards me and I select one here, one there, and they are taken away to my own house. The rest are herded into execution pits elsewhere and slaughtered according to the whims of the officers in charge. The few I have selected, mostly young women and old men, I kill myself; I feel the bones snap, listen to the gagging cries as their life squeezes desperately past their congested lips.

I have *that* nightmare many times as well. It was no less a nightmare when it was fact, when it was reality.

Why does a man slaughter a thousand million innocent people? You would think that any man capable of such an act would be capable of answering that question. Yet I have no answer. I am unable to supply an answer to that question, even though I have searched my mind for an answer for many long years.

That is another of the inconsistencies.

And Joni . . .

My last morning on Timeslow I awoke screaming. Joni was there, holding me, and slowly I became aware that I had been dreaming.

I mouthed an obscenity, climbed out of bed and walked to the window, shaking.

Joni brought me in some coffee and the news-sheet. "Come back to bed."

I looked at her. She was very lovely, plump and dark. She was the right height for a woman, and dressed in her black housecoat she looked very homely. That appealed to me more than anything.

I climbed onto the bed and glanced at the paper.

"Oh God . . ."

"What is it?" She was sipping her coffee and reading the back page. On the front page was a small headline: "Hunt for Questel extended to sector fifteen, in particular to Timeslow and Timequick, the two innermost planets of Caprion."

"Nothing," I said. And she crawled up the bed and rested her head on my chest.

"There *must* be something. You never blaspheme and you just blasphemed. Now what is it?"

"Timeslow is being invaded by the authorities."

"But they're not after you!" She sat up and stared at me. "Kevin, don't *worry* so much. Nobody is after you on Timeslow. They're after that bastard Questel. They have no time for small crims like you."

Small criminals! If only she knew.

I suppose something of my thoughts expressed itself on my face. She asked. "Did you have that nightmare again? The one about killing a little girl?"

"Yes," I said. I had told her about the nightmare and I had convinced her that the reason I was on the run was because I *had* killed a little girl, by accident of course, but that hadn't been the way it had looked.

She understood, but I'm sure it was her instinct to mother me that had drowned out her revulsion.

"But it happened *so* long ago, Kevin. Surely you can't think the police are still after you."

"I don't know what to think," I said. She sat up and shook her head, slightly angry.

"I don't know. Anybody would think you were Joseph Questel, instead of Kevin Karr . . . hey . . ."

I was off the bed in a flash and at the window, clutching the sill as if my life depended on it. I can remember now how my mind was reeling and screaming. Outside, the city was immersed in grey fog. Hovercars zipped across the rooftops, faces peered from windows, blurred pinkness through the fog. And above them all, a hundred feet above the concrete roadway, I stared out across the morning and felt myself slip backwards towards insanity.

It was always the same! As if the expression was a trigger for my relaxing mind to double its efforts at horrifying me. *Anybody would think you were Joseph Questel* . . . and when it was said, for a long time I *was* Joseph Questel again, with memories as vivid as they would have been if they had happened yesterday. An expression that was now almost household, a nasty, sarcastic remark that could bring yesterday in violent and uncompromising visions.

Another strangeness . . .

Later, on the ship bound away from Timeslow, I sat in the lounge and watched in confusion as Joni appeared in the hatchway and smiling crossed to sit with me. For a long while I just sat and stared at her, not hearing the words I could see she was speaking.

Beyond her, reflected in the window that peered out across the depthless void of deep space, I could see an old man, a man with hair tinged grey all over, face drawn and haggard. A shadow of a man who had once been very striking to look at. When I turned my head away the man in the window looked away also, and it took a moment for me to realize who it was I regarded with such intensity.

I closed my eyes, then. When on Timeslow I had never seen my shadow. Now I knew why—I had become my own shadow, my body was as dead as if it had never been born.

"Kevin . . . listen to me. . . ."

I was listening to a concerto by Darzel. It was playing in my mind and I could see the eyes of the player. He was stroking the wires of his electroharp and singing. Between the notes that drifted across the audio-chamber I could hear snatches of his song: *the mind of Questel . . . an evil mind . . . beautiful to regard . . . filthy beneath.*

"Why did you follow me?" I asked Joni.

"I knew you would try and get away. But I couldn't let you go."

I laughed. "I've gone."

"From Timeslow, yes. But not from me." She reached over to hold my right hand. "I don't ever want you to go from me. I love you Kevin, don't you even know *that?*"

I nodded, vaguely. The grey haired man in the window watched me impassively. I thought to myself: You've killed whole nations. How do you feel?

The man in the window said : I feel like it never happened.

But it did happen. Because I can remember it.

I can't remember being born. Does that mean it didn't happen?

I don't believe I was born. No man as evil as I could have been born of woman's flesh.

The man in the window seemed to die a little.

Joni said, "Kevin, tell me why you're so afraid. Nothing is going to stop me staying with you, now, and I *must* know why you are so terrified of everyone. Why do you react so crazily when I say certain things. *Why*, Kevin?"

It might have been an hour later that I let her hand drop from mine and turned away from where she sat on the couch, watching me.

During that hour I had come to a decision. I had decided to destroy everything I had ever cared for. I would tell Joni who I was. I would tell her and thus she would be destroyed. But there was no other way.

I cannot remember anything of that agonizing speech when, for the first time since the war, I admitted to another human being that I was Joseph Questel. I can remember that when I had told Joni as much as I could bring myself to tell her, I sat back and waited.

Joni laughed.

If she had screamed, vomited, died . . . that I could have understood, that I could have borne. If she had shot me straight through the head I should have been a happy man.

She laughed.

"You fool, you silly fool." She was angry. "Do you think me so stupid that I would accept that . . . *story*? Oh Kevin, you annoy me!"

"I don't see what there is to laugh at," I said angrily. "I've just told you that I'm the man you most hate in this Galaxy. I expected you to be revolted. At the least I expected you to walk away, quietly. And you laugh!"

She looked at me long and hard. I met her gaze, but I broke

first. In the window I imagined I could see Forbes playing an electroharp. The notes formed rain patterns on the glass and trickled downwards to form the shapes of dead people. Behind him a grey-haired man, with sagging shoulders, gazed at nothing. Behind the grey-haired man sat a plump stranger, watching him distractedly.

Joni said to me, "I believe you really think you *are* Joseph Questel."

I smiled. "Keep your voice down—please."

"Kevin . . ." she composed her thoughts. "Questel, Joseph Questel—let me make this quite clear . . . Joseph Questel is not a *real* person. He's imaginary. I swear to you, Kevin. Questel and all the others—Jones, and Lazlo, and Rainer . . . they're imaginary people." She paused a moment to let her words seep into my mind. She finished with : "There is no such person as Joseph Questel. *Everybody* knows that!"

Once, when I was very young, before I began killing people and hating our wonderful Galaxy, I had a hero. I walked like him, talked like him, dressed like him and behaved like him. I even began to think like him. Thinking with his peculiar logic was what made my passage through the junior grades so easy. I was indebted to that man.

Then someone told me he didn't really exist, that he was a fictional character, and really I had known all along, but I'd been blind through choice.

I felt very bad for weeks.

On a ship speeding away from sector fifteen I had just been told that I didn't exist, that I was an imaginary character. Imaginary characters live, of course, in their own minds, their own imaginary worlds . . . but this was reality, and I had just been told I was not a part of that reality.

I felt deeply sick, but inconsistencies came back to me, strangenesses . . . things that shouldn't have been strange.

And strangest of all, why should Joni believe so sincerely that Joseph Questel was not a real person? Who was right, she or I?

I said, "Joni, the man on the half-hour spot on the video—
the Hunt for Joseph Questel spot. That's me! Look at me,
Joni, recognize me!"

Joni laughed. "Nothing like you. Oh really, Kevin! You're
only imagining things—I don't know what has happened but
you certainly seem to have flipped a little bit."

I could hear the Darzel concerto, the soft voice of Forbes:
The mind of Questel—arrogant, hideous.

I could hear the concerto reach forte, the strains of the harp
multiplying in the cavernous space of the concert hall, ringing
their message from the walls, the ceiling.

Allegro—angry!

"Flipped? Christ! I know when I see myself on the video.
I know when I see myself being hounded from planet to
planet . . . everywhere I've stopped they've found me. . . ."

"But never caught you . . ."

"Not yet. But one day the odds are all in favour of them
hitting lucky."

She shook her head. "You are *not* Joseph Questel. The man
on video is nothing like you. Why do you persist that he is?"

"I can recognize myself on the video!" And the man on the
video was me.

"The man on the video doesn't look anything like you.
Look, Kevin. Let me explain as far as I understand it. Joseph
Questel is an imaginary character, invented for the populace
of our expanding Galaxy to focus their emotions upon
Questel, and all the others—channels for our hate, if you like.
It works! That is why it happens. Front pages filled with news
of the hated few, video crammed with newsflashes about them
—and the billions of intelligent people strung through a
hundred billion stars can identify with those creatures and
hate them. And they can play the guessing game; where will
Questel turn up next? And so on. A profit-making sideline.
But mainly, Kevin, mainly a channel for our emotions. Fiction,
but through the media of our minds given flesh, given existence.

"But not existence like this . . ." she patted my hand. "Not *reality*. Are you saying that you are some hideous not-quite-human that our collective consciousness has brought into being?"

I didn't answer that. I could see the flicker of uncertainty in her eyes, felt her hand pull away momentarily.

The possibility was horrifying.

Horrifying.

There must be times in every man's life when he doubts any sense in his existence. A pointlessness of just *being* gets to us all eventually—with some it stays, a minority who seem to vacuolate and vanish into their own reclusion.

I had never experienced any sense of pointlessness. I went one better.

On a ship bound away from Timeslow and heading . . . somewhere . . . in the lounge of that ship I began to doubt my own existence.

Pianissimo. Fade away.

Joni was gone. I could see the plump stranger in the reflection of the lounge, his head hovering above the back of my chair as he, like me, gazed at the blackness of the void. Suddenly he smiled.

"You're Questel," he called across the empty lounge. "You don't look like the Questel on the video, but I recognize you. That woman was talking nonsense."

Fortissimo. Heart beats fast. I could see Forbes as he moved with the increasing volume of his playing, thinking perhaps: This is where Questel's heart beats as he sees the masses of the dead shovelled into a pit somewhere. . . . Allegro, vivace. Ugly mood.

I said, to the round-faced man, "I don't know who I am."

He laughed. I can see him now, throwing back his head and forcing the laugh from his throat. Then he was solemn again. "Questel. The Killer. I recognize you."

I crossed the room to where he was sprawled in a couch. He

watched me come, his eyes small and narrowed, his face round and moist. His jumpsuit was loosened around his middle.

"Don't worry Questel. I'm no nark. There's something I know about you that I know because I know it about me too. Follow that? Or shall I repeat it? I know *what* you are, because I'm one too. Christ, you must have done something really vicious to be a War Crim."

"Vicious," I said, nodding. "A million vicious things. I killed and loved it."

"You danced with the Devil!"

I didn't understand. He could see my blankness and explained. "You no more killed a million people than you danced with Satan . . . forget it. Don't you recognize me? Think, Questel. Think. A spot on the vid, about eleven in the evening."

I didn't recognize him.

"Rainer," he said. I could see he wasn't—at least, not the Rainer I knew. "Rainer, himself. That's who I am. We have a lot in common. Questel. . . ."

"We do," I said. "Your crime was as foul as mine but a hundred times more perverted."

He nodded, still smirking. "Perverted? Sure. I'm as perverted as they come . . . strangely, I don't *feel* perverted any more. Isn't that strange Questel? I was a pervert—they say—for thirty years and suddenly I'm not a pervert any more . . . does that ring a bell Joseph?"

The bell was ringing. I thought again of the question. Why does a man kill a billion innocent people? I remembered my inability to answer that question, my revulsion at the idea of committing the crime I had committed.

My focus returned to Rainer, the fat man with the cheeky grin. He was staring past me through the port. I turned to look. A star was approaching. A beautiful blue-white star, shimmering and gleaming in blue-tinged fire as the ship drew energy from it during a close-pass.

A star at the end of its life, but still to rise as the fabled phoenix in a brief and splendid moments's fire, sending its arms across the void in a sphere of intense radiation and light . . . to die in splendour and fade into grey, dead, ash.

I was blue. The phoenix stirred.

Rainer said, "No nightmares, Questel?"

"Nightmares . . . ? Yes, I have nightmares." I told him (I don't know why I bothered but I told him) of my day-night-mare.

He shrugged. "That's it, then. A nasty crime, a very nasty crime. Almost assassination. It happened. Questel. It really happened."

I shook my head. "It's just a nightmare. My crime involved the killing of many more than three people."

Rainer sneered. "You killed *three*. That's why you're being punished with war crimes."

I didn't follow. He said, "You've been caught, Questel. A long time ago . . . you were caught."

"I was never caught. That's why I run. That's why I've been running for the past seven years. That's why I'll go *on* running." *Allegro. Forte.* "That's why I can never settle, never find peace. That's why my nights are filled with horror, with sights of death, with smells of decay, and the screams of the not-quite-dead-but-being-incinerated-anyway. That's why I left Timeslow, why the video puts out a regular show on me, making people hate me, loathe me, search for me . . . You say I was caught? Christ—my body would be scattered over the Universe if I'd been caught. What they'd give to *catch* me, Rainer, what they'd *give*."

"They caught you," said Rainer disinterestedly. "Seven years ago. Take my word for it. Look, Questel, I'm only doing this for your own good, only telling you so that at least *one* guy like me can be given a chance not to waste his life being the goose in a wild, wild chase." He was so calm, so sure. I felt tears in my eyes, my reason spinning, slipping. Just as with Joni, there was an unmistakable ring of truth to his words, and yet I could not, could *not*, accept what he was saying.

"How could I have been caught?"

I was shouting and as I shouted he sat up and shouted back, pointing a pudgy finger at me. "They caught you, Questel, and erased your past, and made you into Questel, the War Crim. A man with terrible memories—memories to punish you for what you'd done to three people. And now you *are* a War Crim, but little memories creep back through, vague recollections of your previous life, memories that slip through when you least expect them. And me, Joseph . . . have some pity for me. I'm not a perverted killer. But I think I am—or rather, thought I was up until a few days ago. I believed I was a fugitive, on the run for committing a diabolical crime—as diabolical as yours, in its own way. It's the way, Questel, the way of punishment now. Big bad boys like you and me, committed to an eternity of running. The worse the crime, the worse the crime you *think* you've committed, and have to live with as you run.

"Do you know, Questel, that if a man runs from the law for three years he is as emotionally and physically and psychologically damaged and punished as if he'd served eighty years in the pens on Mars or Trega. Do you know that? And how long have you been running? Seven years? You've been punished, Joseph, punished you have *been*. But there'll be no end, Questel, not yet there won't. Perhaps not until you die! Always you'll think they're after you, and why? Because your name will be in the papers, on the vid, everywhere. And every time you see the unknown face that is Questel you will see your own, because that's the way you have been conditioned. And every time you and the two, three thousand other Questels that exist, all running, each time they come to a planet the bulletins go out. You're all scattered, all of you, like all the Rainers, all the Lazlos, all the Findiks. Scattered across the Universe . . . but you're observed, and everywhere each one of you goes there are faceless men, with many jobs, one of which is following you and your namesakes; they will see you and the planet you have come to and will then report 'Questel is here'.

"And you'll move on."

He was quiet for a moment. The ship's engines thrummed into life for a brief moment and died away below perception. "Time and time again. An eternity of running. For a crime you didn't commit, a crime that is worse than that which you *did* commit and for which you are being punished."

He sat back suddenly. His eyes glazed over. "I've been running for thirty years. And suddenly it's as if a veil had been ripped away, and there . . . I can see how it used to be, and the whole reason for my running I see is just an illusion. It's an accident . . . this lifting of the veil. It shouldn't have happened, I'm sure. But it has and now I feel sick, Questel, I feel really sick to think that I've been running from nothing *for* nothing. That's why I'm telling you all this, Joseph. Maybe I can prevent you wasting your life . . . maybe . . ." He shook his head. "But in all likelihood you've been given a conditioned reflex to reject such data as I'm giving you now. But one day you'll feel the same as I feel now because I don't suppose you'll run forever. Some day the veil will be lifted for you, the punishment ended. But by then you will never be the same again."

He never said another word, just sat back and stared at nothing. I wanted so much to believe him and yet, as he had said, my mind could not accept what he had told me. Even so, a part of my mind was studying his story and one overriding feeling came pouring out of that darkness : surely there was more point to my existence than just being punished? And the longer I thought about it the more I knew that there *had* to be something more, something that Rainer, for all his investigating and snooping, had been unable to come up with. Something . . . meaningful!

I was right. Looking back on that day when we sat in the lounge, the light from the unstable sun casting flickering shadows about the walls, I can see now how even then things were being framed ready for my final decision.

I didn't tell Joni what I had learned. Not because I was unsure whether or not I believed it but simply because . . . why should I tell her? I played along with what she had said, and convinced her that I was nervous and cracking, and needed rest, and *that* was why I had said I was Questel. She believed me.

"We will hide at the farthest reach of the Galaxy, on a backward, barren planet, with nothing and nobody but each other," and she hugged me, ruffling my hair and smiling. "My grey-haired convict, my beautiful, wonderful middle-aged frightened man. Just remember that I love you."

Eyes closed, smile so happy, lips full and moist as they pressed against mine, bodies clutched together as we sought for each other and fought against the currents of present time and were lost, out of time, out of the world, lost as only lovers *can* be lost, floating in a dimension as distant from the Universe as that state called Heaven is distant from me.

The next morning, as she slept, I gently pressed a needle into her jugular vein and administered a fatal dose of poison. She jerked in her death sleep, and I kissed her mouth until her body froze and her eyes ran with tears as if she dreamed in death of the life I had prevented her from experiencing.

Now, as my existence slowly comes to an end, there are fires in my mind.

I have immense sympathy for that blue star, somewhere in the void, a star that was visited briefly by a fragmental piece of machinery from another world as it stole an infinitesimally small amount of that dying energy. That sun and I are brothers, on the descending curve of the graph that is life.

Strangely, the descending curve is, at the moment, angled sharply upwards. But the crest is ahead, and beyond the crest there is just darkness.

Ash.

A new "spot" has appeared on the video.

A smart young man, dressed in the robes of a Senior Galactic Servant, sits before the camera and reads from what are obviously blank sheets. He has memorized already the terrible facts he has to report.

"The mystery assassin has struck at Valliant, a small world in the Yellow Suns cluster. Law officials numbering several hundred were senselessly killed by *tafrin* poisoning and their bodies defiled. This makes over a thousand killings by the man who signs himself 'K.K.'

"Information is now available on the identity of the killer who is believed to be Joseph Questel, a hunted man, wanted for his crimes of perversion and inhumanity during the Spiral War of 'Eighteen Twenty-Seven.'"

It went on. And on.

I had to laugh. I didn't mind that they had now revealed my identity. I didn't mind that now I would be snapped into confinement with the ease of an insect caught in a mesh cage.

I had revenged myself for my senseless running, for my broken life. Oh yes, I believed Rainer—with each passing day I believed him more. I had *made* myself believe. And with each passing day the feeling of some deeper, undefined meaning to my life grew stronger.

Fires burning, reaching. Rushing, tearing towards the crest. . . .

And strangely I no longer thought of a musician with an electroharp, strumming and insulting me with the elegant motions of his sensitive fingers as he rendered music to describe a monster.

I mourned a sun which, from my room, I could see as a glowing healthy sun, years away from the nova that would now be consuming a volume of space greater than the solar system that was my hiding place.

There is an urge within me. I had not noticed it until I embarked upon my spree of killing. And, I might add, the defiling of the bodies was not something I enjoyed, merely something I threw in for the sake of my Galactic viewership.

The hate must be maintained. We all have our jobs to do.

I think of Rainer, sometimes. With his grin, and his tears. A happy man, in the prime of his grief. A soul lost, and wandering. Looking about me at our wonderful Galaxy, at the planets and peoples, and chugging freighters, at the crews and passengers, at the suns and the men who walk upon them (for we walk upon suns in our advanced and wonderful Galaxy) I can see only drawn faces.

It is said that the shape of man is changing. In that ancient era we know of as the Dark Ages a man was tall if he rose above five feet five. In the twenty-first century a tall man was six feet six.

But it is not in physical dimensions that the man of the thirtieth century is changing from his predecessors. I have a photograph of my great-great-great-grandfather. He has a wonderful moustache, and his clothes are nonexistent as was the habit in those days.

He is sitting with his wife. They are both captured on the 3-D gloss in the prime of their life, seventy-six . . . they are both smiling.

Looking about me as I walk through moving streets and jump skyscrapers with the hop-over commuters, I cannot find any smiling faces.

Only shadows, dark lines . . . and disguised fears.

Perhaps, I think more often than not, perhaps I am a very commonplace specimen. I, Questel, who has been hounded across a Galaxy, without ever having been chased. Perhaps there are many, many like me. Joni, too, would have one day become a haunted figure.

I saved her from that. I hope.

Mankind has lost the forty muscles that enabled him to smile. He still has the sixty that enable him to frown. Once upon a time it was less exhausting on bodily energy to smile than scowl. Now a man has no choice.

The blue sun, yellow seen twenty years in its past, has no choice either.

Ash.

The urge within me grows. I try to fight it but I have been conditioned. Knowing this is no weapon to control it. Knowing it is just frustration.

I am ready for the final kill, the final burst of fury (expansion, fires reaching into the coldness) that will encompass a climax, the destructive furies of a nova. And then die . . . ash dead, grey dead. Cold and burned out.

Sprawled on a concrete pathway, neck broken. Except in the past.

Isn't it true that the past is the most important part of a man's life? In the past he is always alive. But the further into the future the world moves, the shorter his remembered span becomes, until eventually there remains just his death that is important about him.

A star is dying in the Galaxy and I wish I was out there to die with it. It will die at the same time as I, and yet, from my hideout, it will not appear to die for twenty more years.

From a million light years away that star is immortal. Practically.

Tomorrow night I will accomplish the fulfilment of my conditioned programme, the job that my whole life has been about.

The false memories, the hunting, the desperation . . . the revelation, the realization that was inevitable, all were leading to one thing.

The killing.

The killing by Kevin Karr, alias Joseph Questel, the assassination of a family.

The plan of the Programmers has worked almost to the minute. I still cannot believe that Rainer was just the final driving cog, the voice of the Programmer as he set my wheels into motion exactly on cue.

I still cannot understand ·why I was made to believe in Joseph Questel. What purpose did the deception serve, unless, perhaps, to make me totally a pawn in God-like hands, the faceless gamepiece at the edge of the board, unobtrusive, waiting, manipulated with ease, for it is easy to manipulate a mind already comprised of fictional images and false fears.

I have made three visits to the home of my victim. Each time I have tried to go in, to explain that I will kill him soon, but each time I have failed. Until the final time when I shall accomplish the deed.

Will it be as I have dreamed it?

Have I been dreaming the vision of a future-seer, a clairvoyant's picture implanted in my mind so I may read the motions as the lines of a play, or the notes of a musical score?

By Darzel perhaps?

The house is big, the alsatian is fierce. The man within is hard, but his wife and daughter are soft, happy. They alone, perhaps have the forty smiling-muscles in their faces.

For this they will die.

And in our Wonderful Galaxy, faceless men will move a chess piece towards a box at the edge of the board—and drop it in, with the other taken players.

Travellers

When we finally reached the outskirts of the city the time-node was well advanced. In a sense this meant I had lost valuable hours for searching but as yet, we were told, the visiting forms from the past and future were tenuous and unstable, flitting into vision and out again as fast as they realized they could not find a positive hold in this alien era.

In all likelihood, if Margaretta *was* in the node I would find her again after all these years. But what a frightening number of obstacles stood in the path of that achievement! Had she been alive when this sequence of inconsistency in time reached the fourth millennium? Had she been able to find the node and penetrate it? Was she looking for me as I would be looking for her? And my conscious dreams of her—no, *our*—daughter . . . were they just imaginative fantasy? Or had she indeed conceived a child, and thus, inexplicably, secured our brief contact across a thousand years?

Too many obstacles, too many uncertainties . . .

"Wake up, Jaim."

My travelling companion, Herok, was shaking my arm. I snapped out of my drifting dream and followed him towards the first of the gate-checks. As we walked, burdened by our packs and the necessary implements of survival, he looked round at me and shook his head. "Still thinking of her? You're going to lose us the chance of a smooth entry."

"I'm sorry, Herok," I said. "I just feel very . . . anxious."

"I know."

"And anxiety is a great distraction."

"It's all right, Jaim. I'll keep an eye on you."

Herok was a grand fellow. He was younger than me by ten years. We were both in middle grade, but in two years' time, when I reached forty, I would rise to the next level of the student ladder, the senior grade. My degree would follow within the decade; and a junior lectureship, with luck, within the decade following that. Now, however, we were travelling companions, bronzed and burned by the sun of Southern Asia, and hardened by our adventures in North Africa, where every day had been a test of our fitness to survive.

Over the years I had come to regard Herok as both peer and brother, and if we looked dissimilar—he being tall and thin, and covered with a fine blond down, myself being of shorter, stockier stature, with burnt-umber hair and a fashionable beard—this did not discourage us from pretending a family relationship when it suited us, or when it was convenient.

"I can see the gate up ahead," said Herok suddenly; I craned to see above the heads of the travelling crowds, and saw it, a primitive barbed and armed barrier to progression, through which a trickle of visitors was being permitted.

We were watched from houses and offices on every side. Here, at the outskirts of the city, the streets were wide, and we joined the queue of travellers, finding ourselves buried in a mass of silken, silky bodies, all pushing and jostling as they waited, impatiently, to try and talk their ways into the time-node. They would fail, of course, but there were always the thousands who believed that persuasion was a powerful weapon.

We jostled, bustled, edged towards the barrier.

"You are approaching the zone of observation," said a loud and indifferent voice, speaking apparently from mid air. "Red and green passes only."

We both had green passes, which would take us through to the node itself. The passes had arrived a few weeks before, shortly after the first signs of the impending node had been spotted. The allocation was based partly on the particular fields of research with which Herok and I were concerned, and partly upon the Psychoscan that had preceded our successful entry into a similar node, ten years before.

We were among the luckiest men on Earth, and I was thankful for the fact.

At the gate we were assigned to one of the many armed guards who took us aside and scrutinized our cards carefully; no doubt he was looking for evidence of forgery, but he found none, naturally, and passed us on.

We were now in the zone of observation and from here much of the node itself could be seen. The whole area appeared normal—if a trifle crowded—and the great mass of human beings that sprawled on walls and rooftops, staring and scanning down the mile or so to the edge of the node, seemed well content with their lot. Looking downhill towards the centre of the city (for the node had risen across most of the city centre and a fraction of the western sector) we saw the tenuous white ghosts of future travellers trying to break through into this time, and failing, although Herok stated positively that he could see the ludicrous garb of men from the next millennium, a time with which we were both well versed, naturally, having secured a great many friends in many future ages.

At the edge of the observation zone a force field of some considerable strength had been erected to prevent any unlawful penetration into the strange time flow beyond, and here we came to the final barrier through which we would have to pass. We were surrounded by men and women of all races and all ages, each and every one of them waving thick wadges of bank notes, or great clusters of sparkling jewellery. Why? The rich, the poor alike were begging us for our entrance passes, and in truth we could have made ourselves among the richest men on Earth that day, for the richest men on Earth were there, begging our favour. Money, wealth, possession, power . . . these were not the ways to acquire the green passes into the time field. The unseen men who commanded such entry, who imposed the rules upon society during the duration of a node, were interested only in natural attributes, it seemed —perhaps imagination, perhaps intellectual honesty; most of us who found ourselves together beyond this final wall shared something in common—a desire for knowledge for its own sake.

The pitiful creatures who clustered around us during that last walk towards the final gate were wasting their efforts. Communication with other times could far too easily take the form of torment and torture, and the sick and bestial elements of humankind were kept at bay. Even if their bribing succeeded, the passes they would have so obtained would have been useless to them!

A glittering diamond was thrust into my hand by a man who smelled of hyacinth and grinned in his fatty face, plucked nervously at the spun silver cloth he wore. The jewel, I was sure, would have bought me a city, or taken me on an endless cruise of our solar system; a treasure indeed. But beyond the barrier, in the zone of inconsistent time, there was a greater treasure. Margaretta.

I pushed the jewel back and mumbled my apology, but the man followed me, weeping, clutching at my sleeve. I tried to shake him off but his grip moved to my arm, became almost desperate.

Herok was being pestered by two women, both well past their prime, but both splendidly dressed and devastatingly beautiful. They were—I could be certain—offering far more than themselves, and I sympathized with Herok for his predicament.

We were silent and depressed by the time we were facing the armoured guards who stood between the zone of Observation and the huge Examination Hall at the edge of the time node itself. My arms were bruised from the attentions of the beggars; there were tears in Herok's eyes, but I recognized the after-effects of SymPathyn, a drug no doubt worn by many of the women in this zone.

The guards were satisfied with our credentials and passed us on and we walked into the cool, white-walled building, and stood for a moment getting our bearings. There were two queues of people, shuffling slowly forwards. The largest queue was for those with one-day passes, and movement was slow because each person bearing such an entry permit was being fitted with a recall-stud, just below their skin. The other queue was shorter, but the Examiners looked far more intense.

Apprehensive, excited, we joined this queue and within ten minutes were being interrogated as to our purposes and aims for the next few months. As students we had ready answers to most of the questions; Herok, as a trained Security Man, could answer truthfully that he would become such during the stay in the node, and could fit in his study between-times.

Everybody during their stay in the time node was expected to contribute to the maintenance of the enclosed environment.

I, as a trained mental therapist, could truthfully answer that my assistance could be called upon to help badly disoriented travellers from times when security was less stringent than in our own, or in the next few hundred millennia.

The toughest question came last. "Do you swear that you have no emotional involvement with travellers from any other age?"

"I so swear," said Herok quietly, and I could almost feel his anxiety. Would the guards notice? They could hardly fail to detect our feelings of worry, but with luck by now their senses would be dulled by repetition.

I could not, I knew, get away with denying my involvement if the minds of the guards were fully tuned, and searching for the tell-tale signs of a lie. Margaretta's importance to me was too great, the love I felt too deep for me to have replied an outright affirmative. I knew this, and Herok knew this, but in the course of our journey across the world from Penang, to Africa, and then to Western Europe, we had rarely discussed either the girl from the next millennium, or the obstacle that she presented to us gaining entrance into this node, the second node we had visited and probably the last that would manifest during our lifetimes.

Now : the crunch.

"No emotional involvement," I said quickly, and before there was time for any reaction, went on, "As part of my project I hope to re-contact several people from the next millennium and gain an idea of their time's developments during the intervening years."

Immediate suspicion. "Male or female?"

"Both sexes," I said quickly. I was feeling cooler, now, but the fixed stare from the nearest Examiner, a tall, sour-looking man, with piercing grey eyes, made my heart stutter and the electrical conductivity of my skin seemed to short-circuit all over my face.

"What's your project?" asked this emotionless figure.

"Social dynamism," I replied obscurely. He frowned briefly, then glanced at his companion, an equally sour man, shorter, possibly an inferior. Behind them four guards stood rigidly to attention, eight eyes fixed upon my face.

"Sounds feasible," said the shorter Examiner. "You can hardly re-contact people without *some* anticipation . . ." He glanced at Herok, then back at me. There was a long tense moment. Then the Examiner nodded, "Let them pass."

Herok and I bowed low, and smiled at each other. We gathered up our packs and strode out into the daylight on the time node side of the Examination Hall.

"We've done it," Herok murmured as we walked through the streets, getting faster with every pace. "Jaim, we've *done* it! We're in again!"

He began to run, and I followed. He began to laugh, and his laughter was infectious. In the cover of a ramshackle red-brick building we stood, leaning heavily against each other, and yelled our delight, forgetting completely how near we had come to being refused entrance!

We walked through crowded streets and listened to the rising pitch of excitement, the laughing and shouting of men and women hardly able to restrain their enthusiasm for the days to come. Around us ghosts appeared for brief moments and vanished again, some so quickly that there was not even time to turn and look to see from what era of time they had come. I nudged Herok and pointed to where a semi-naked man stood in the shadow of an office block and stared up the glass facing and bulging transparent walls. "Fifth millennium," I said, and Herok give it a moment's consideration before nodding. "Possibly. Margaretta was from the fourth, wasn't she?"

"Late third, early fourth, yes. I wish you had known her, Herok."

Although ten years ago we had been together in the previous time node we had led separate lives therein and separate adventures. Afterwards I had refused to talk about her for several months, and when I did talk of Margaretta I suppose it had been the ramblings of a lovelorn fool. I had wanted it to be that Herok knew her, had met her, and could therefore appreciate my love for her, but she was a stranger to him, an image created by my inadequate descriptions.

We found lodgings in a huge and draughty hostel and took bunks and meal seats in the wing devoted to men and women from all ages. The wing reserved for third and fourth millennia visitors was already full, and within a couple of weeks visitors would find themselves slotted into any available space, in very mixed company indeed!

The only man already in our wing was a fourth-millennium student-type, a middle-aged man with deep brown eyes who gazed at us nervously as we unpacked and unrolled, and discussed our plans.

"Are you from the third?" he asked abruptly, speaking with the nasal slant to his words that characterizes fourth-millennium interLing. It was the same accent that Margaretta had, and it was instantly warming.

"Yes," I replied, seating myself by him. I extended my hand

after a moment and he gripped it happily, shaking my arm with great gusto. His clothes were sparse and not very warm; a neck and waist band, joined by thin strips of cloth; a pouch to contain and support his genitals, and thick leather bindings down his legs. I felt overdressed in my mock mid-second-millennium kaftan.

"Garri D'rath," he said. "My name. Last time I was in a node I found out that I was descended from a family line called Rathbone. Interesting. I'm fascinated by your era . . . that's why I've come here. You probably think it's a bit unusual to stay in only one millennium . . ." He was smiling, almost self-consciously. There was a splash of soup on his chin and I wiped it off for him; he tensed, but laughed when I held up my green-stained finger. Slightly embarrassed, he wiped his mouth and chin with a small red tissue.

"Not unusual at all," I replied. "I'm Jaim Barron, by the way. This is Herok Vuutgenstein. We're both social dynamism students."

"There are enough of them about," laughed Garri. "But this coincidence makes it a valuable field of study, I suppose."

"You mean the two nodes so close together?"

He nodded. I grew tense. It was estimated there were just fifty of the node sequences, all spanning the greater part of time and along each of which a lucky few could travel. And for two of these sequences to have stopping points within the space of a man's lifetime was coincidence and gift indeed!

I was worried, however. Just because there had been one thousand and ten years separating the nodes of that first sequence, when I had met Margaretta, didn't mean that in this second, unrelated sequence the time between the nodes had to be the same. If eleven hundred years separated us, Margaretta would be long since dead.

"How long ago was the last node you visited?"

"How long?" He frowned, sought to remember. "About twelve years. Yes, twelve years."

She would have aged two years more than I, only two

years! It was ten years since we had met, ten years of wandering and remembering. For Margaretta, a twelve-year wait. But was she here? Had she gained entry? Had she even *heard* of this sequence of time nodes?

Garri was saying, "Myself, I'm a time engineer. That's really all I can tell you at the moment. As you know, there are strict controls about the acquisition of information. Until something is actually discovered, or realized, or worked out, it doesn't become general information to people from earlier times."

Herok nodded soberly. As a security junior whilst in the node he worked, part of the time, to ensure that that rule was enforced, without knowing what information he was himself restricting. He said, "Is this node of some importance, then?"

Garri looked thoughtful for a moment, then glanced around, a grossly theatrical concession to secrecy. Looking at us both for a second he nodded slowly. "You bet," he said with a wink. "You just wait and see."

A loudspeaker blared through the dormitory, summoning all new arrivals to the nearest Control and Allocation Centre. Herok slapped his hands together and called to me. I shook Garri by the hand again. "We'll see you later. This is where the hard work starts."

He chuckled. "Okay. I'll be here."

As we walked swiftly along the broad streets, through people in amorphous throngs, through seated circles of contemporaries busily discussing what they would do with their three-month liberation in time, so we saw the first signs of more ambitious journeys. A figure, a woman, a beautifully robed woman, shimmered into existence before us, suspended fractionally above the ground; she couldn't see us, of course, as she tried to move into our time, but we watched her for the few seconds that she tried to break across the barrier of years. She was a sixth-millennium visitor and had obviously broken as far back as the fourth millennium, but couldn't summon the mental energy to push back here, to the third. Her limbs waved as she lost control of her body with the pressure of her mind-direction, and for a few seconds she was a silent image of frustrated beauty, threshing in an age a thousand years removed, before finally fading back into future reality, to wait for the node to advance further and facilitate the extra movement required.

Herok laughed as we walked through the space where her image had been, and then a thought struck him and he glanced at me; I caught the unvoiced suggestion and grinned and he shouted, "Come on!" and gripped me by the hand. He dragged me into a breathtaking run. "Now!" he yelled, and we directed our minds into the future, and felt the surge of blood as our bodies followed, and the swirling colours of scattering third-millennium denizens left us to be replaced by the sober movement of people a thousand years hence.

We were in a vast square, green and white pavement stones beneath our feet and tall, impossibly tall, sparkling buildings at each of four corners.

As we came into the present, so we turned. She was behind us, watching us (we had arrived still shrieking our excitement) and we stopped, staring at her face and at her body, full and exciting beneath the white translucent material of her robe. Then Herok took the initiative and ran across to her. She seemed startled, and her hands clutched at the folds of her gown as she regarded first the breathless form of Herok, then my own grinning features. Herok said, "We witnessed your attempts to move into our time, my lady, and when you finally succeed I shall be delighted to act as escort."

She smiled, then, and bowed to Herok. "Thank you," she said. "I'd like that very much. Your era is my final destination, and if I can return the favour, I have a large apartment in this city—in the sixth millennium—of which you may avail yourself."

Herok bowed again and behind his back his hand was waving excitedly, the fingers spread wide in a sign of success. She gave him her address on a small blue card, and turned to walk away. Herok and I ran across the square and vaulted back into the past, moving through two walls (strange sense of cold and dark) and returning to the open roadway.

Back in our own time Herok stopped and wiped his face, his hands shaking. "What a magnificent body," he said. "And they say sixth-millennium women are animals . . . animals!"

"Filthy dog!" I shouted, and he laughed. "Remember your age, Herok. You're not a child any more."

"Oh but I feel it, Jaim. I feel—rejuvenated! Excited!" He was grinning all over his face.

"Your exuberance is nauseating," I pointed out, looking round to see if his noisiness was being observed.

And I saw her!

"Margaretta!" I shouted as she vanished behind a house. Herok grabbed my arm as I started to run. "The signing on, Jaim. You have to sign on."

He was right, I shouldn't delay registering but I had seen Margaretta, she was here. And even now was perhaps losing herself in the crowded streets closer to the centre of the city.

I thrust my green identity card into Herok's hand. "Explain that an important part of my project began prematurely, and that I'll be sure to show my face later."

I began to run towards the squat, ugly building with its sharply angular corners and gruesome air-vents behind which Margaretta had vanished. Herok called, "You'll need this in case you're stopped."

Running, I shouted back, "I'll take that chance." Then Herok was out of sight and I was facing a long, narrow street, and there was no sign of Margaretta.

As I ran I prayed to God that I hadn't been mistaken, that the slim girl in the trousers and red blouse who had flitted so briefly through my field of vision had indeed been my fourth-millennium lover.

At the end of the street I faced five ways to go, streets, alleys, entrances. There were people milling about, mostly contemporary with just a smattering of the multifarious types from the next millennium.

For a moment I panicked, and then, again seen from a distance and from behind, I spotted her; she was walking down a roadway beneath a sign that, in many different time languages, said "City Centre". As she was about to vanish from sight she looked round, seemed to look right at me. . . .

Margaretta! Without any shadow of doubt, it was Margaretta. I became ecstatic, raced after her, my heart pounding with joy. But when I reached the end of the road there was no sign of her. I jumped to the next millennium, but she was not visible there either. For a moment I felt anxiety, and for a second moment despair, but if I knew Margaretta she would be moving towards the centre of the node, drawn by curiosity and the thought—I hoped—of perhaps finding me in the greater crowds who gathered there.

Back in my own time I pressed on, down side streets and across plazas, pushing through the drifting crowds, avoiding the white and grey forms that filled the air, some successfully breaking through into this time, others fading back into the future (or the past?) to wait a few hours longer.

At length I came to the centre of the node. There was, as I had expected, a huge crowd of sightseers, formed in a vast, excited ring several hundred feet deep. At the centre of the ring was the enigma, and though I had seen it before I felt an urge, a great temptation, to push through the ranks of visitors and natives and view it again. . . .

A white shape shimmered momentarily before me, but faded quickly when it realized its mistake. Time travel was not permitted this close to the centre. It was too dangerous by far.

I began to push through the crowds; some, inspired by my positive motion, followed in my wake or began to stir up the motionless mob themselves, insinuating their bodies into every crack and gap in the circle of human forms. I kept an eye for Margaretta, and every woman with a babe in arms caused me to stop and stare, even though I had already seen Margaretta without a child, and even though that child, our mutual daughter, would be twelve . . . no, eleven years of age and certainly not in her mother's arms.

After a few moments, a smattering of minutes, I reached the innermost ring of the group of humans and found myself pressed against the unseen but impenetrable wall of force that would always protect the enigma from the curious touch of we mortals.

In a small clear space, perhaps eight feet across, surrounded by a wall of silent humanity, was the Traveller. He, she, it . . . what was appropriate?

It squatted on the ground and not a fibre, not a muscle moved. It was totally, absolutely black. Not black because of its skin or its clothes, but black because of the total absence of light or shade. The features of the Traveller were distinguishable only by the swelling and rippling of its surface and when one looked closely, when one focused carefully upon those unbroken black surfaces one could see eyes, a nose, organs and organelles upon the body that did not really relate to anything terrestrial. It appeared to be clad in armour plate, and clutched in its two broad hands an all-black machine, a box with black featureless buttons, and it never moved to switch or press a knob, and it never seemed to breathe. Its closed eyes never opened to show us a moment of its black, depthless mind.

It squatted there, the absolute centre of the time node, protected by its force shield, oblivious of its curiosity value. And we stared and did not fully comprehend, except to realize that the figure was a Traveller through space-time moving across our frame of reference for a few brief months.

I pulled away from the enigma and bustled out through the crowds, into the clear plaza beyond. There I stood for a moment catching my breath and searching the environs. Margaretta had well and truly vanished.

Sadly I walked back to the hostel. If only . . . if only my

mind link had remained after the birth of the girl. And what strangeness was contained within that single moment of regret! A *mind* link . . . across a thousand years . . .

Sounds and sights vanished during those next few minutes, as I walked heavily through streets that could have been paved with burning coals and I'd not have noticed. I was experiencing a vivid reliving of the months following the decline of the previous node, the gathering place of ages when I had first met Margaretta. As the node had faded, as the people around me had faded over the days into ghost forms, as more and more of my contemporaries had arrived back, reluctantly, from farflung millennia, unable to maintain their space-time distortion, so I had watched Margaretta fade from me, slip into the sea of time, her hand outstretched, her eyes filled with tears. It had been a matter of seconds between the kiss and the loss, and I carried the memory of that last touch for many hours before a biting wind had chafed my lips to numbness and the moisture in my eyes had begun to sparkle and crack.

Sank into depression.

Months. Three months.

Waking during a night, during a dream, during a kiss, a moment's excited touch of Margaretta's body. Awoke and felt heart beat, warm rush of blood, sonorous shift of muscle . . .

Room swam. Lay back and stared at . . .

Listened to . . .

My daughter. My daughter. In fluid womb, floating in warm liquid, basking in Margaretta's awareness.

My daughter?

Our daughter, Jaim.

Margaretta I love you.

Always, Jaim, always. I visit your grave and love you more every moment. . . .

Shifting, blood runs faster, heart beats harder, across a thousand years.

Fully awake. Vision goes. Dream?

Oh Margaretta . . . visiting my grave, cracked gravestone,

crumbled bones, but loving me as I live, united through her womb, through the sparkling embryo, the squirming tadpole, the fusion of two ages in the bloody wall of future.

A touch across a thousand years; a vanished hand, holding me close.

Back in the dormitory I found Herok pulling the final piece of his new uniform on to his tall, spare frame. He looked very smart in the green and white outfit of the Security Force, for which he would have to work four hours every day. As I strolled into the long room he turned and smiled.

"When's your first shift?" I asked.

"Right now," he said ruefully, picking up a sheet of names and jabbing his own name with a gloved finger. "Right now. But fortunately there are a fair number of faces and figures to memorize...." He picked up a sheaf of mug shots and flipped through them. "So shift number one is memory work. Ugly bunch," he went on. "Most of them will be making the Big Run, which should mean some action."

"The *big run*," I repeated, chuckling. "I wonder who first called it that?"

Herok shrugged, continued to study one of the faces in his file of illegal node-entrants.

There were two Big Runs: one was into the distant future, and one was into the distant past. The most usual avenue of attempted escape by those criminal types who managed to get into the node in the first place was to move to the distant future and hope to escape the time field that way. The future was more secure than the past, which was a difficult place to survive in and not only because of the flesh-eating Saurians that prevailed at that almost unreachable end of the node sequence. The atmosphere back then was stinkingly rich in toxic gases.

With Herok, the previous time we had ventured into a time node (our first and, so we had thought, our last) we had attempted to move back to the Age of Dinosaurs. We had almost made it, but it had been too difficult. The peak of that node had already passed and there were only a few seconds, a few moments, when the full range of travelling time, which always ended in the mid-Cretaceous, was available for the smallest of mental efforts; it was rumoured that only at that moment, at the peak of the node, could escape from the confines of the pocket of time be effected. Was there truth in such rumours? It was difficult to know, but enough denizens of future ages believed the rumour sufficiently to try and beach themselves at the ends of time, to escape whatever oppression they had been born to.

"Oh by the way," said Herok suddenly, "you have to report to Control and Allocation tomorrow, early."

"Oh."

Herok grinned and passed me back my identity card. "Don't worry. I've spun a good yarn on your behalf. I think they fell for it."

More visitors were arriving and taking bunks in the dormitory. We lingered for a while making their acquaintance and searching for people of specific interest, but found no-one whom we would have wanted to stick with. Most of the arrivals were early fourth millennium; a few were contemporary and there were a few from the second millennium who stood, nervously, watching their confident dormitory mates. Their clothes looked hideously uncomfortable, and their expressions quite moronic, but this was almost certainly due to Time Shock.

Part of my job, whilst in the node, would be to help "earlier" visitors adjust to later eras, and so we—Herok and I—moved ourselves into conversations with the small band of seconds.

There were the usual questions, the usual anxieties, from those entering their first node, experiencing the strangeness for the first time. We explained, over and over, how it would become easier to move through time as the node advanced, and how they were in no danger of impacting with objects because of the sense of getting frozen and the ease with which one could move away to a safe spot. How time, *in all nodes*, was moving forward, and no-one could ever move to a moment before the moment they had left. Detailed accounts of how paradoxes were impossible because of the Security Force (Herok took a bow), the information embargo, which was imposed on the first four or five millennia after their own (stopping things being known before they were discovered) and the unseen Surveillance Corps, always watching the activities in the nodes. No-one knew who the Surveillance Corps were, but they had absolute authority: yet despite their vigilance the nodes had given rise to all manner of legend and myths, visitations and strange phenomena in times before the second millennium.

Most of the questions concerned the Traveller, and here we had to be careful, remembering that only a certain amount of detail had been ascertained that thousand years past. We told them what we thought was safe to tell, and sent them to their own Control for any extra allowable information. Thus they learned more or less what we ourselves knew, that the enigma was a time traveller, from when to when we didn't know with certainty, or at least, whether travelling forwards or backwards we didn't know; the ends of its run, certainly, were in the middle Cretaceous and at a time in the future nearly five million years removed from the present. The view most often expressed by third-millennium people was that in the distant future, Earth—at that time deserted, we knew—was being used as a Way Station by aliens, exploring the Galaxy (perhaps just the Earth) of the Saurian Age. It was frustrating not knowing, when virtually everyone else in the node *did* know.

Garri arrived back looking thoughtful. He was pleased to see us and we went out into the city for a drink together, Herok deciding to shirk his first shift. Garri's thoughtfulness developed into excitement; he was obviously burning to tell us something, but when we pressed for him to open up he shook his head, looked worried.

"I don't know if I dare, but . . ."

"What? Come on, Garri, tell us what you know!"

"The information restriction, though . . ."

We huddled closer together. Finally Garri said, "This node represents a great step forward, anyway, and the information will be declassified before the end, so I suppose it doesn't matter if I tell you."

We waited. Finally Garri said, "One of your third-millennium mathematicians is—even now—making observations that permit almost full understanding of the time nodes. What he works out, what he *is* working out, will lead directly to the establishment of the Surveillance Corps, and to many experiments with time. We are living at a turning point . . . history, which most of us have known for all our lives, is being made!"

"Without the sums . . . what's he discovered?"

Garri ordered more drinks. We'd drunk too much already and my head was swimming, but we sipped the bitter concoction that he favoured and listened.

"The cause of the nodes," he said. "The time traveller theory is right, of course. In the distant future on this world there is an alien installation sending individuals back to the Cretaceous. If the Surveillance Corps know why, they're not telling. Each of the Travellers, though, travels through time in a series of jumps, stopping for infinitely small fractions of his subjective seconds in order to *pull power from the Earth's magnetic field*. They fuel themselves during transit."

"Wonderful," murmured Herok. Perhaps he had been expecting something a little more exciting. Myself, I felt quite emotionally moved by what Garri was telling us.

He went on, "The jumps are very frequent to begin with, which is why there are only half-millennia separating the nodes uptime; they get more and more infrequent as the Traveller builds his time momentum, so that by the Cretaceous there are thousands of years between nodes."

"Has he worked out—this mathematician—how the nodes get linked?" Herok asked.

"Yes he has, and it's sound maths, too. Practically speaking, each momentary stop by the Traveller distorts the time matrix, and during the few seconds of his time trip those distortions are accumulated and released at the moment of his landing, back in the past. The astronomically small time spans of these distortions and releases actually measure several months—on *our* time scale. The effect is that for several months at the time of each stop for power there is a narrow vein of captured time stretching from the past to the future, and this is what we are riding."

"Mumbo jumbo," commented Herok. "I didn't understand a word."

"Garri laughed. "I know how you feel. Social science is poles apart from time maths . . . but we don't have to let our professional differences spoil a good time, do we?"

Herok, happier, raised his glass and grinned. "Certainly not, my good fellow." He knocked the lot back, signalled for more.

For my part I declined a refill but pressed Garri for information about himself. I felt the tingle of static that said a member of the Surveillance Corps had, at some time during the last few minutes, tuned in on our conversation and decided we should be watched, and was now coming close enough to intervene.

Phrasing his words carefully, also aware of our observer, Garri said, "I'm quite a junior researcher, really, at an Institute for Sub-Quantum Physics. I'm involved with time theory, and am involved with certain practical developments from the maths being turned out at this instant. In fact, there are several tests and experiments being carried out along this node sequence . . ." he broke off, looking uncomfortable. After a moment the sense of being watched went away. He said, "I think you'd better steer clear of me, for a while. . . ."

Over the days I searched for Margaretta, between my compulsory service and the necessary work for my project. She had vanished, however, utterly and completely, and I never saw any sign of her. Herok was no help. He had never seen the woman and my description was too sentimental for him to obtain a clear mind's view of her.

I began to feel panic. My excursions through time became thoughtless and reckless; twice in the far future I nearly drowned when I came into a time when the node had opened over the sea; once, in the distant past, when it had opened across the mouth of a volcano, I nearly crisped.

The node advanced, and time flowed easier into the future and the past; other ages arrived and departed, many in groups with a single interpreter; the first of the real aliens showed its face, and all at once a mood of festivity and total excitement burst upon the city, not just in my natural time but in all times. The peak was approaching.

I watched part of the ninth Roman Legion, bedraggled and muddy, pace across rain-logged, marshy European landscape; fifty or sixty men, weary from battle—clattering beneath their equipment, pacing north to join their garrison. They would never arrive. I searched the crowds who watched them, knowing that Margaretta had a fascination for that greatest of European empires, but there was no sign of her. She could not have failed to have heard the Site-watcher's announcement in every time that the legionaires were passing; she must have declined the temptation to stand, with the hundreds of others behind an Invisibility Seal, and watch their progress.

I went into the distant future and watched the building of huge ships; and further still to see the strange life forms that crawled across the Earth after man had deserted his home world. I talked with a Dhorr, from the Sirian empire that was still, in his time, subservient to the Earth Empire in the Galaxy. He told me, through an interpreter (which itself had nearly as many air-holes as the Dhorr, but which could manifest Earth sound through each one of them rather than speaking different pitches with each set of lips) that he had talked with his own kind of the millennia beyond the extinction of the human race, and they had despatched and received unmanned vessels between the galaxies. There was a great race in Andromeda who were trying to cross the gulf between the star cities, and the Dhorri had a strong feeling that their intentions were not particularly friendly.

We stood, the tubular alien and I, and stared at the black and enigmatic structure of the Traveller, and we wondered. . . .

"If they had conquered time," said the Dhorr, "and crossed the gulf in deep sleep, and thus travelled naturally many millions of years into their own futures, they might use a planet such as this to return, once their journey was finished, to their own time."

"It's an intriguing thought," I said.

"And a happy one," said the Dhorr. "If they want to conquer the Galaxy of three hundred million years ago, they are very welcome. Neither your race nor mine were around at that time."

"And if they *did* spread throughout this Galaxy, their conquest has been forgotten. Their leavings dissolved in the natural span of centuries."

A happy thought indeed!

I searched for Margaretta in her own millennium, stood in the middle of that vast plaza and felt the wind blowing cold against my flesh; shouted her name, searched the crowds.

The beautiful white-robed woman came towards me and remembered me, and asked wistfully after Herok. We talked, and she left.

The node was approaching its peak. Half-way done and I had not found Margaretta. Half-way wasted!

I went back to my own time and found it was night, and I walked through the streets towards the hostel, my soft bunk and a depressed period of sleep. I was nearly home when she called to me from the shadows, and when I stopped she moved into the light and stared at me.

"Jaim?"

"Margaretta!" I cried; ran to her; and for a long time I just hugged her to me and wept with joy.

"I thought I'd never find you, Margaretta."

"I've been searching for you too," she said, and stood back to examine me closely. She was still as I remembered her, and age had left little mark; a few more lines around her eyes, a slightly more tired expression; her hair was cut short and her clothes were styled more youthfully. But it was Margaretta in every way, and I thought my heart would burst!

We still had six weeks. Six weeks together until time separated us again, almost certainly for good.

"Where is . . . ?"

"Jayameeka?"

Jayameeka! She had been called after me! (Well, almost).

"Yes. Our daughter."

She looked sad. Her arms unwound from me. "She's safe, Jaim. But I couldn't bring her. I'm sorry, Jaim, but they . . . they wouldn't let me bring her."

Stunned!

"Who wouldn't let you?"

She shrugged. "Whoever's in control. The Time Authorities."

"But why? Why such a restriction?"

"Jaim . . . she was conceived in your time—this time; but born in mine, a thousand years hence. She belongs to two times, Jaim, and the authorities are terrified of her. . . ." She was hiding something; in her voice, in her manner, in her words were the hints of a deception, advanced, perhaps, to protect my feelings.

"Margaretta," I said, as we stood in the darkened city. "Tell me."

When Jayameeka had been born (Margaretta told me) the story, the facts, of our relationship had been made known. Jayameeka had been taken away from her, and brought up in an Institute devoted to obscure scientific studies; Margaretta had had full access to the child, and had spent much time with her, but she had become the object of study; a child of two times might—they had said—give a clue to the nature of time travel. She was too important to waste. And for all those years she had been the centre of interest for a small group of researchers, working in the field of temporal dynamics.

I would never see my daughter!

I had waited eleven years to see the offspring of our love, a desire that had been drowned, certainly, beneath my anxiety, my desire to see Margaretta herself; now that the truth was known, I felt a great emptiness, a substantial and painful sense of loss.

And anger! My daughter, an experimental animal! Why, if they had wanted such children for their studies they could easily have arranged such consummations!

A shiver down my spine; an uneasy glance at Margaretta as we walked through the night streets. Perhaps . . .

Had she too thought of the shocking possibility?

Surely, though, such an experiment would not have been undertaken without the awareness of the participating bodies?

Creeping into the dormitory we slipped silently into my bunk and vanished beneath the sheets. She was nervous at first, almost hesitant, a span of so many years causing her desire to be drowned by apprehension; at least, this is what I assumed, since it was happening to me as well.

But after a few minutes of hugging and warming, of gentle touching and featherlight kissing, we became bolder, more confident, and Margaretta returned with passion. If Herok heard, or felt, our joyous reunion he said nothing from the upper bunk.

Strangely the sensation of basking in each other's awarenesses, the slight empathy that had linked us through time (for however brief a span of time) never returned as it had those eleven years back. I didn't comment on it; it would come in a few days, no doubt.

In the morning . . .

I opened my eyes and found myself staring at the floor. During the night I had slipped out of the bunk, possibly pushed by Margaretta's sleeping form, and was now draped across the edge of the bed, my right cheek dented and sore from its contact with the rough wooden underfoot.

Margaretta was gone, and for a moment I just sat on the edge of the bunk and rubbed my eyes; then I felt a great panic! If she had left, perhaps too upset by the thought of eventually parting for ever . . . how would I ever find her again? It had taken so long, would take too long to repeat the search. . . .

"Herok!" I shouted and stood up to rouse him out of bed. He too was gone, his night-shift folded neatly across the pillow, the bunk highly presentable. He had been gone some while, probably about his part-time duties as a Security man.

At that moment the door at the end of the dormitory burst open and Herok arrived, running frantically, and breathing like he would burst.

"Where've you been?" I demanded. He waved me quiet.

"Where's that mug file? Ah . . ." he found his folder of criminal faces and was leafing through the pages rapidly, excitement in his face, nervousness in his fingers.

"Who are you looking for?"

"I'm sure I've just seen . . . ah, yes . . . it was! Can't stop, Jaim. I'm about to make my first arrest." He uttered a little yell of pleasure and raced out of the dormitory, drawing his gun from its pouch on his hip.

I smiled and shook my head at his exuberance, and turned the open folder towards me to see whom he had seen.

Margaretta!

MARGARETTA!

I nearly collapsed, but somehow kept my suddenly useless legs in a straight position and I stared at the picture of Margaretta. He must have seen her as she left. . . .

My eyes picked out the words below the picture. Wanted . . . Time criminal . . . illegal entry into node . . . Jayameeka Strahn . . .

Jayameeka.

My world collapsed. I remember hitting the floor with a deafening crash and feeling all sensation leave me.

I came round to the sound of Herok's urgent voice. He was bending over me and looking very anxious. When I recovered consciousness he smiled and helped me up. "What happened?" he asked. Garri was crouched beside me and holding out a glass of blue liquid; I suspected something very potent and decided that I needed it; sipping the drink I nearly choked, then looked at Herok.

Careful, I thought. Very careful.

"I got out of bed too fast," I said. "Fainted." He grinned; he knew I'd been drinking fairly heavily for the previous few days, and no doubt was imagining pains and unco-ordinations in my head that were not, in fact, there. "Did you get who you were after?" I asked.

They helped me up.

"No," said Herok, disappointed. "No, she gave me the slip. But I've alerted the Security forces up and down time. We'll get her."

Garri said, "I expect she'll be trying to make the Big Run. It's not long before that will be possible."

Not long at all, I reflected. It couldn't be pin-pointed with total accuracy, but it would begin sometime this afternoon, the peak of the node, a mere twenty seconds!

If Jayameeka—Jayameeka! My daughter! Where had I miscalculated?—if she could locate that moment and avoid the gathering of Security men, she could slip away into the past or future and, if God was on her side, "beach" herself on the real world at whichever extreme of the node sequence she was planning on heading for. When—if—time slipped away from her, she would be free of whatever oppression had driven her to such despair. And she would be free of me, lost to me for ever. . . .

Herok left.

"Don't go away," said Garri, cryptically, and he made to follow Herok. I grabbed his arm.

"Garri . . . what went wrong?"

He looked blank. "I don't understand."

"The nodes . . . you told me twelve years . . . twelve years since your last entry into a node sequence!"

He looked uncomfortable, glanced at the dormitory door, then back at me. "I'm sorry, Jaim. I wasn't thinking at the time. Yes, I see the problem. I was never in the first node-sequence that you visited. My first entry was twelve years ago —a sequence that missed your own time, it arose earlier than you were born, and out over the ocean as well, which is why it was missed. It's thirty years since the first node sequence occurred . . . thirty years."

He walked to the door, checked to see if anyone was outside and then called back softly, "I have a message for you, Jaim, so don't go away. I mean it. If you want to find her again, stay put for a few minutes."

Before I could do or say a thing, he was gone. I stood slowly and stared after him. I was reluctant to remain in the dormitory, but something about Garri aroused my interest, and my suspicions. That he knew something was too apparent, but that he was more than he seemed to be was a subtle insinuation that I was only now beginning to notice. Who was our fourth-millennium friend, I wondered?

Things were happening just a little too fast for my constitution, I decided. I wanted to be out in the city, shirking my therapist's duties, searching for Jayameeka; but all I would do,

I knew, would be to run around aimlessly, and possibly attract the sort of attention I could well do without.

Herok's attention, for example.

Oh Herok! I felt so bitter; not at him, not even at what he represented. He could not have known that my daughter would become one of his prey . . . and it would, I had to convince myself, be unfair and unwise to tell him so.

I was not bitter at him, no; but at fate . . . at fate I was angry, at the twist, the cruelty of the orderly universe, at that was I furious! They could have spared me the agony . . . it was for so few weeks, so insignificant a number of days in the span of the world . . . I could have been spared such grief.

I looked at Jayameeka's picture. She was truly beautiful, and looked so like Margaretta that it was almost difficult to believe they were two people. But the differences were there, and I should have seen them. The wider nose, the slightly darker green of her eyes. Her youthfulness. How blind I had been; how susceptible to my dreams, that I should have believed Margaretta would not have aged at all!

If I stood in that fourth-millennium plaza I would be standing in the same time as Margaretta, but she was outside of my grasp, beyond me. Perhaps dead. Perhaps herself locked away. Perhaps hiding behind that wall of twenty years, the difference between us now.

I wept, of course. If I was maudlin, I make no excuses, nor any apology. It was right to weep, and very necessary, and after a few minutes I was calm again.

A chill went through me, then, as I remembered the night. The reconsummation of our love, the virginal tightness of Margaretta/Jayameeka . . . the nervousness . . . the look in her eyes. . . .

Oh God. It was not quite an unbearable thought. I dared not look inside the bed . . . dared not! The sight of her blood would have driven me to despair.

And yet—for all my worry—she had *permitted* our union

—in the full knowledge of who I was, she had permitted it? Was that an act of despair? Or of true love? Or a kiss, passed from Margaretta to me, and communicated through the body of our mutual child?

Where was Garri? I couldn't wait about all day. There were only four hours before the first possible moment of the peak!

He arrived as secretively as he had left. He was carrying a package, concealed half by some black fabric and half by his stooped body. He came up to me and placed the item on my bunk.

Without a word he took off the fabric covering. It was a small heat-set and a copper-coloured belt attached to it by a single cord.

He looked at me. I said, "Her message. What was her message?"

"She's going down time," said Garri. "The main concentration of Security men will be policing the up-time nodes."

"How do you know all this?"

Garri smiled, said simply, "She told me."

"Yes, but why? Why you? Who are you, Garri?"

He stared at me for a long time, and gradually the façade of innocence and naïveté dropped away. His eyes grew dark, his mouth solemn. "The trouble is," he said, "one never knows how much a third-millennium person knows. You're a difficult period in history, the only period, really, where there's any substantial editing of information in-put. You know she's your daughter, and you know why, although she doesn't know you know. Part of her message to you was to tell you of her true identity. It's a social custom in our era to lose one's virginity to one's father, but I imagine there was a deeper, more inexplicable motivation for her action, don't you?"

I said nothing. Garri was building up to something.

"We knew each other, of course. She was being studied by the Institute where I work. What she represents, a woman born between two times, a woman perhaps free of the full restrictions of space-mind-time, is what myself and many others have been studying, and trying to achieve. There are many like her, though she was unplanned for. She has great strength of mind, is the best subject we have. I say we," he smiled self-consciously, "I don't mean we. My own work has been on . . . this," he patted the apparatus. "I became very close to Jayameeka, very close. She was severely restricted in the Institute, and I began to feel it was cruel, heartless—I began to revolt against it. After all, I thought, I'm making more progress than my colleagues . . ." again he patted the belt. "So I helped her escape. It's as simple as that. I got her access to this node, but regrettably her illegal presence was discovered, though not my own participation. Her only chance is to beach herself—if it's possible . . ." again his strange smile: he knew full well whether or not it was possible to escape the node-sequence; it was information denied to my own time. "Once beached we hope she will demonstrate her ability to move freely through time; for her sake, for our sake . . . I hope she has developed that ability. If she ever returns, I shall marry her. But my interest is solely in seeing her out of the criminal clutches of my own Institute."

He stopped, then, and picked up the strange apparatus. After a moment, he said, "I really love her, Jaim. I know how you felt, now, leaving Margaretta all that time ago, knowing the wall that would separate you."

I reached out and gripped his shoulder. "I love her too, Garri; more than father to daughter, but not as lover to lover. I just need to be with her for a while, need to talk, to know she is safe. Garri, I must stop her making that run. It's selfish, I know. But I must stop her. Or go with her."

He nodded. "You can't stop her, Jaim. But go with her? With luck. And this is what will get you back."

He held the belt towards me. "What is it?" I asked.

"I imagine something very similar in principle to what is powering the Traveller."

"A time machine?"

"Mechanical. Effective. Well tested, but it takes some real effort of mind. It will never be released, of course; it is the tool of the authority that guards these nodes and prevents unwarranted passing of information. My era developed it from your era's maths. The fifth millennium will begin to apply it to the policing of these frequent nodes of time.

"I told you, Jaim, that yours is a critical time in history. Before now the nodes have been virtually unknown; after now they are a part of life. This era is at the junction . . . denied the results of its own inquisitiveness. But that inquisitiveness will lead to this belt, and to the decision to mate individuals from different times. Until everything was fully tested we ourselves, a millennium hence, didn't know if we *could* develop time travel."

"And you're giving this to me? Out of *friendship?*"

"Out of a desire to see Jayameeka safe, wherever she is."

I was incredulous. I took the belt and the headpiece and turned them over in my fingers. Such power! Such potential in so small a fragment of material. "And no strings . . . no catches. . . .?"

He laughed. "The age of paranoia was in the second millennium. No strings, Jaim. If you like, you are a final test for the belt; a run through time from the age of the Saurians. Trust me, Jaim. There is a recall mechanism—not well tested, I confess—with which I shall return the belt to my own hands within six subjective months. I'm not making a *gift*, merely a convenience!"

He instructed me on its use, a remarkably facile system of safety buttons, and a great deal of brain power. It would, if my own mind failed, be a boost to my projected brain waves to carry me out of the node and into the prehistoric past . . . to "beach" me, hopefully with Jayameeka safely in my arms.

"You understand," said Garri finally, "that you are now no longer a part of your own millennium, that you know too much about the future to live your life without a guardian. . . ."

I accepted what he said, grimly, unhappily.

I obtained breathing apparatus from the depository on the ground floor of my barracks, and strapped the lightweight system over the head-piece of the time machine. As I ran through the streets towards the centre I saw only a few others who had, in this time at least, opted for the legal excursion down-time to the acrid swamps of an era nearly (not quite) at the end of the Traveller's run. Those going into futurity would not need any special equipment since the air, after man's decline, was rich and sweet.

A Security man halted me as I ran, and warned me about going too close to the centre. I acknowledged the warning and took a moment's respite before walking a few paces further and coming into sight of the central area of the node.

Here the crowds were thick and just as monotonous, most staring at the intergalactic enigma (if that were indeed its nature). I searched for Jayameeka but not surprisingly failed to see her.

I jumped through time.

My passage was swift and remarkably easy. The blur of colour and sensation of roaring were more pronounced. I stopped and found myself in stone ruins, with green and wet countryside all around, and just a few travellers like myself walking and exploring. It was a cold day in the dawn of civilized man; beyond the wall of the node I could see un-domesticated sheep. The ruins, chiselled stone and traces of wattle, were long deserted.

Back further and a strong and biting wind howled across the shrub-covered highland; trees were scattered about, and distantly the land was forest covered and impenetrable.

Five travellers, seated, talking together. As I watched, a sixth, from a very distant future time, slipped into sight and out again.

Back further. Motion through time still very easy and natural.

Sun, baking mudflats, lizard life and prowling mammals. They ran from me as I appeared. The topography of the world was changed, and now I was in a valley, and jagged rock hills rose about me. A river had once passed this way.

A shape flickered in and out of vision, a woman, far older than Jayameeka. As I stood in the heat and watched the shimmering air around me I could see the passage of many travellers. Distantly, hidden almost completely by an overhang of rock, was the black shape of the Traveller himself, unaware of his brief stop at the beginning of the Quaternary.

Back. Water.

And further . . . storm clouds and the discharge of lightning. Granitic monoliths rising high above me, shadowy, grey, dimly seen. The heavy movement of animal life, a distant thundering as of water pouring down slopes. White ghosts from the future fading in and out of sight. . . .

A voice, shouting. Lightning flashes. Thunder, the crumble of rock, the roaring of a great beast, white teeth highlit in the electrically tense atmosphere.

Back. Calm, evening, vegetation of many colours. Moisture dripping from broad leaves.

A figure watching me from the jungle.

"Jayameeka!" I cried.

"Go back, Jaim," she shrieked, and the tears were in her voice as well as her eyes. I ran towards her. "You can't follow me," she sobbed.

"Wait . . ."

But she was gone, and I jumped after her, feeling the passage of the centuries measured against the stuttering of my heart. She had seemed surprised, shocked to see me. Had Garri lied to me after all?

Travel became difficult, the passing of the millennia slowed, and I froze, in a time of dinosaurian peak, breathing through my mask and staring into the thick, swampy landscape. The peak of the node had not yet arrived . . . Jayameeka was struggling half in and half out of this time, a ghost form split between now and this location as it had been over a million years ago.

I waded through slush towards her, terrified that I might at any moment sink, or be consumed by some huge reptilian swamp dweller, but nothing occurred, save that the peak approached nearer and suddenly we both slipped a million years back in time.

A huge silver platform stood before me, rising out of the swamp, cutting brilliantly through the hazy, leafy air. All around me, half concealed, looking somehow very dead, were the ruins of a gigantic building, perhaps a station, perhaps a city. It was half submerged, but had lost no fragment of glitter, no ounce of sparkle.

Domes and towers, some of them twisted and bent by time and the impact of weather—great glass panels and the remnants of machines. Jayameeka was running along a buckled metal roadway, her feet leaving slimy imprints on the almost flawless ground beneath her. I waded through the mire and heaved myself up on to a ledge of metal, and dragged my soaking body up the steeply sloping surface until I reached level ground. I raced into a large room, where golden snakes hung coiled around tubular rafters, and climbed through the broken window that looked out upon the roadway. I followed Jayameeka as fast as I could, noticing as I ran the dark shape of the Traveller secure and settled in a pit in the middle of the building (idle thought: what was so special about this Traveller that he had his point of arrival marked by such a monument?). Protected against all ravaging agents, this was his last stop, perhaps, before he returned to his own kind, a single jump further into the past, to a moment that no human could reach, a moment beyond us all.

The seconds were racing past. I called for Jayameeka and saw her struggling against the unseen edge of the node. So close, but this far back the confinement of the node was smaller, tighter. There was dry ground above the swamp, and she was struggling to jump towards it from the overhanging metal roadway, but she seemed unable to pass through. . . .

A figure came into view off to my right. I heard a voice shout, "Stop! Stop or I shoot!"

I could hardly believe what I heard. It was Herok, uniformed and protected, and he was levelling his handgun at the struggling shape of Jayameeka. I could see the tension in his form; the sure sign of a man about to kill. . . .

"NO, HEROK!"

He faltered, glanced at me and realized who I was. "Jaim! What the hell are you . . . STOP!" Still shouting at Jayameeka, about to kill at any moment.

"Don't shoot her, Herok," I begged, and without realizing it my own weapon was in my hands.

"Stay away, Jaim. Stay out of this. . . ."

And without thinking, without bothering to argue any more, I levelled my gun and squeezed the trigger. At the last moment Herok realized what was happening and his mouth opened, his head turned, the gun in his hand fell limply to the roadway and he stared at me. . . .

Too late.

My calm, unhurried shot took his head off at the lower jaw. I shot him as dead as the ruins into which his body tumbled, lost in the darkness of an alien structure and the swamp that was consuming it.

When I looked at Jayameeka she was watching me.

"Come on, Jaim. . . ."

Distantly, all around, other shapes were materializing, some not fading in, some actually coming to rest in this era, anonymous, faceless travellers, each a potential threat.

As I ran towards my daughter she had turned again and was

pushing through the wall. There was a tug at my body and my mind, the sensation of being drawn back up time, but I fought it . . . came closer to Jayameeka when . . . without a flash, without a scream, she was through the node . . . she had escaped the confines of distorted time and was free in the age of the giant reptiles.

Twenty seconds!

If the helmet failed, I had just twenty seconds to try and force my way out of the node. If any thoughts of *why* I should want to beach myself in the Cretaceous period occurred to me, I pushed them aside. To be with Jayameeka was the only thing of importance now—

Less than twenty seconds—

(as I ran three, four strides to the second)

—to achieve that which few men had ever succeeded in achieving.

The edge of the node held me back and I began to push, thinking, mentally urging myself through the wall as hard as I could. And behind me—

"Hold it right there! Stop or we shoot!"

The air became filled with fire, and from each corner of my eye I saw the shapes of Security men bursting through from the future to try and stop my illegal breakout.

Jayameeka appeared before me, shooting calmly and carefully through the edge of the node. The buzz and roar of blaster charges declined. . . .

Two seconds!

I was not going to make it. . . .

One second!

The pressure in front of me vanished and I sprawled upon the dry hard ground, felt the stillness of the air. Jayameeka stopped shooting and crouched beside me, stroking the hair from my face. She was smiling, but shaking her head. We looked into the node and saw the great wall of red and yellow fire spreading in front of us as the frustrated Security men shot towards us, hoping that a solitary charge might escape the confines of time.

Even through the filters the air was acrid. The ground shook with the passage of some beast. Its bass vocality was frightening.

The node faded, and with it the fire and the frustrated men of future ages. Just the swamp and the great metal ruin remained, and the threat of creatures of this time.

"You shouldn't have followed me," said Jayameeka. But she was smiling.

"Garri told me you wanted me to . . ."

"Garri? *He* told you?"

"He said you were friends. . . ."

Jayameeka laughed. "Friends! He helped me escape for his own rotten ends. He's trapped us both in the past, got rid of me and if I can't travel through time as my . . . experimenters, to call them kindly . . . would hope I can do, having tuned my mind in . . . well, you and me both are doomed to a very early grave, Jaim."

I couldn't help smiling at her unintentional pun. I hugged her to me and then showed the belt, and explained its principle.

She gasped, looked incredulous, then stared at me. "You've *really* been suckered, Jaim. That belt has never been tested, not properly." She laughed, then, almost hysterically. "Used to the last. Me, you, used to the last. I'll bet, you know, that my whole escape was intricately planned, that every twist and turn I made trying to survive in the node was monitored and planned for."

The ground shook again, but we took no notice. I fingered the belt controls, feeling dry-mouthed and apprehensive. A test pilot of sorts, I tried to think us three or four days into the future, holding tightly to Jayameeka as I went.

A tingle of electricity on the skin, an abrupt transition from dry day to wet night!

"It works!" I shouted. "Garri *hasn't* let us down!"

Drenched, we hugged. Frozen, we jaunted through the Cretaceous. Laughing, we began the slow journey back to the third millennium after Christ.

We would take our time getting there.

The Touch of a Vanished Hand

Thank God for Gable's hands.

*

A blind man once wrote that in the holding of hands there is an awareness of self existence. The blind man's name was André Goriot and he lived in exile on the seventh world of Sirius.

I set down on Sirius 7 in my youth and found the blind man in his self-contained installation, a small, almost featureless construct, set well in at the base of a cliff. He held my hands and talked of what he had learned about perception and isolation. I was bored and tried to keep my murmurings inaudible, but at the time my throat recorder was new to me and an irritating static sent tingling fingers of skin sensation down my chest. Concentration was difficult to maintain. The blind man was just so much boredom, suffered by my adolescent self only because what he told me would be of use in my level one dissertation.

He held my hands for all the time I was with him and I never recovered from the intimacy of the contact. The very touch of a man's hands thereafter made me shiver and recoil. I wore gloves perpetually, and doggedly declined to shake hands in greeting or at an introduction.

It became so unnerving, the physical revulsion to a hand's

touch that I underwent corrective psychotherapy. It was not a recourse to which I referred myself willingly. The effect of deep space upon fairly ordinary psychoses has been the subject of thousands of level two and three dissertations, yet still the surface has been no more than scratched. An unexpected linkage in my brain resulted in a simple piece of corrective therapy having an effect on my sexuality. Essentially, my drives reversed.

I had no regrets. Why should I have had? With my new motivations and interests I was content; as content as I had been with my old.

Later there was a man called Christopher Gable who had never heard of Goriot. I met him over dinner at the status-B Eurasian club, of which I was a member on nineteen mapspace worlds. Gable had travelled much. In the lines on his face I read of great loss. In the way he talked I saw a certain lacking of identity. Perhaps the two things were related, but I never found out.

Gable was middle-aged and his blond hair was cut above his ears in a very conservative style. He towered over me in height, and yet his clothes hung loose and creased upon his frame, and when he walked he seemed ill at ease with motion.

When I mentioned Northern Europe he was immediately interested and confirmed that he came from Sweden, although that had been more than a decade in his past. I saw, then, the Scandinavian lilt to his interLing. He had already noticed the unshakeable American accent in my own voice, and I spent a while telling him of my brief and pointless participation in the Chino-American war of '78. I had been made prisoner near the beginning of the fracas and had been interned in a small camp that stretched below the ruins of the Bridge Monument in a part of the prison city that had been San Francisco. My Anglo-French status had been denied me, despite my shouting (they weren't prepared to believe that a European would have volunteered so quickly to come into the war: since we only have to do three months military service I thought to get mine over with as quickly as possible. Surely the first three months of a war is safe enough? I didn't understand war) and I had been branded as a North American and interned with several locals who taught me much of American cynicism. We made gravity nets by the waters edge, and some of them chose to drown, but most of us dreamed of far away worlds, and the freedom of space.

That had been a long time in the past, and the hurt and frustration of those sordid years in confinement had long since passed away.

We turned the conversation towards the arts, and towards the scientific arts, and found a common interest in holospan and mobiloforms. Returning to his apartment that same evening I was astonished at the array of original art forms he possessed. Many had been executed by his own hand. The walls were covered with mobiloforms, mostly reconstructions of his earlier life; I saw people and places that fired my imagination, all moving through their ten second cycles with never tiring repetitiveness.

Over the days our friendship developed and we began to shirk work to be together, to talk over common ground and enjoy the emotions and pleasures of each other's company.

Over the weeks our relationship developed into something more than friendship, and the essential absence of women in the city became an irrelevancy, and Gable wondered why he had ever brooded and pined for female companionship. There was nothing we wanted or desired that we could not both supply for each other.

All this was on Rigel Nine, an oxygen-nitrogen world, so distant from its primary that the sky was never blue in any terran sense, and the surface was always cold. The underground city of Voronezh basked in homeostasis, but shuddered too often for our likings to the cracking and movement of the

Niner's crust as it moved before forces within our comprehension but beyond our capability to control.

The time comes to leave Rigel Nine and we go out onto the surface. The landscape of the planet has been terraformed in as much as it has been flattened. We gaze at miles of flatness, the granite-like rocks ground to sand which has blown away. The deep blue sky is star speckled, as it always is. Immensely tall conoids reach into the sky at regular intervals, black in colour, splitting the wind into confused patterns of flow. These are the power houses of Voronezh and they harness the powers of wind and sun.

The roadways wind between the towers and we walk along one to where another intersects. A hundred yards away, small and opaquely white, is the landing and despatching block; we step upon it and reach out to hold hands.

This is the way of travel and there is nothing particularly intimate in the touch. Our suits coded for our destination, the block transmits us through space in extended seconds. As we move to our goal, the third world of Bianco's Star, we feel the passage of suns and worlds and spread thin to conserve our identity. It is a sensation of disembodiment, time slows, and I know little save the touch of Gable's hands upon my own, and the excitement of our next few months together. The cerebro-tactile linkage keeps us in contact and we travel through the void as a unit. Until.

I come out of space on the third world of Bianco's Star, on the heat-seared equator of the world; I stand upon the cool, white landing block and the gaping maw of a subterranean tunnel opens wide so I might move into the equable temperature of the terran installation below.

I feel Gable's hands clasping my own and turn to him— without thinking that I should be seeing him, without realizing that the grasp should have ceased to be as we landed and separated . . . as we appear to have done.

Gable holds my hands and he is nowhere to be seen. I have

a feeling that I shall never see him again, and as I go below, shocked and weak, I know—because I have heard of these things happening before—that he has been lost and will remain lost forever.

We had come to Bianco's Star to offer our artistic talents to the major art industry of the world—crystal sculpture. I sat in my small apartment for many days, harnessed to the projection headpiece, shattering a seven pound crystal in carefully directed ways, and producing nothing. My thoughts were cloudy, my emotions unpredictable but predominantly blue. The crystal lost weight, the dust filled the air, the shape changed from linear to abstract, to various meaningless forms, to a perfect feather that found some small numbers of admirers and earned me the credit-status to move to Earth.

Gable's touch was on my hands all the time, and I never knew if he was with me in awareness or not.

On Earth I revisited England and found peace of mind, for a while, in the roaring city of London. I hid away in Highgate, in a shack built of red brick and ordinary steel, that stood below the great Northern Flyover. The whole region was a shanty town, a lake of ruins, fire-blackened houses and cracked tarmacadam roadways. The City rose five hundred storeys above the ancient Thames and at night the lights from those roaring megaliths made the shanty town a jungle of harsh concreted walls, and intense shadows.

This was all a vision of San Francisco, a curious reflection and reconstruction of my fears and frustrations in the months following my release from internment. I relived in agonizing dreams and extended periods of unshakeable reminiscence, the exhausting trek across the continent of America, following the straggling columns of Americans all searching their homes and families. And I, with an ocean separating me from my own security, living in dread of death before I could touch the land at Cobh, or Plymouth.

The feeling of wrongness within the city grew, and with each passing day I became more uncomfortable. I talked to virtually no one and lived a hermitic existence, eking out my resources as much as was possible. I became more and more thankful for the continual pressure of Gable's hands upon my own, but attempts to communicate with him failed.

After three weeks in London I could take the isolation no longer, and travelled to Sweden where I found Gable's birthplace. I traced his life through school and three cities, through a broken marriage and a finished career: he had taught emotive art at the University of Uppsala, but his drug commitments and adolescent behaviour (he had created obscene designs out of the vone booths on the university campus) finished him as a lecturer. That had been in the early days of powerthought design, and Uppsala had been the home of many of the earlier models of the projection apparatus that would later become almost a household possession. He had abused his privileged status and he had been sacked.

From the mobiloforms of Gable that I saw there, from the expression on his face, the spring in his step, I decided that the disasters of his early life had not particularly bothered him.

His wife had left him shortly before he would have thrown her out. Their contract was nearly expired anyway, and would not have been renewed because of artistic and culinary incompatibility, the most mundane of reasons for divorce in those days. Gable had moved to Stockholm and opened a breeding contract with a middle-aged Norwegian. I found his seventeen-year-old son living in the lake district of Jutland. He rode an air horse across the marshy ground of his inherited farm and dropped from the seat even before the sleek machine had stopped. He stared at me across a patch of reeds before turning to skim flattened pebbles across the still waters of the lake. I saw Gable in his hair, in his eyes, in the arrogance of his bearing.

"I was not very fond of my father. Nor he of me."

His voice was Gable's voice. I wanted to listen to him talk for hours, but he fell silent.

"Why did your father leave? Why did he become so depressed?"

"Why?" He laughed. He kicked at some mechanism hidden in the reeds and his lake erupted into turbulence. He stripped off his clothes and walked to the water's edge. Gable in every way. I felt my stomach knot and suppressed the desire I felt. He stepped into the waves and shouted, "I was greater than him. In every way." He began to swim and he turned on his back and there was a smile of horrifying coldness upon his face. "I took his soul. I drained him. I became Him . . . and more."

The pressure on my hands increased. Was Gable listening? I squeezed the unseen hands and felt the despair of the trapped man. I wondered in what hell Gable was existing. Was his son interested in knowing his father's fate? Should I tell him?

Gable's son did not reappear. The turbulence of the lake died quite suddenly and I assumed that the youth had come ashore out of my sight. I sat by the water's edge and after a few hours the lake seemed to shrink and the freshness of the landscape became submerged in an aura of stagnation. I searched for the son and found only ruin . . . a ruined farmhouse, an overgrown road, a rusty air horse, unused for many years.

A sudden terrible fear came over me and I ran from the farm, screaming. But when I reached the mainway all was normal again.

In the darkness of the night train to Boulogne, confused and cold, I felt every finger's pressure on my own, imagined I could sense the ooze of sweat in Gable's palms, as he screamed in his emptiness, threshed and struggled to regain his material existence. I sobbed, felt sick.

Under the channel, the red lights hypnotized me as the monorail glided silently through the submarine world. Then Dover, and the smell of the continent I had just left. In Dover, by the hovercraft docks, I knew the pleasures of flesh, immersed myself in the body of a dockside bord, and slept the night dreaming of Gable. His hands clutched desperately at my own and I awoke several times during the night to find my arms outstretched and the fingers clenching and unclenching, the bisexual figure beside me watching in consternation.

There was a moment, some little while later, when I felt my hands touch warm, smooth flesh, and yet I sat alone on the platform of a monorail station, waiting to journey north.

I sat in the lounge of the station and closed my eyes, and it seemed my hands ran across the belly of a small but shapely woman, explored navel and pubis, and stroked the outside of her thighs for an interminable time. I sat in the dimmed light and stared at my palms, and I felt the fullness of a breast, and my finger tips touched the hard button of a nipple and then wandered again in a drunkard's walk towards the feminine apex.

Opening my awareness to the station I found it in ruins, the rails warped and useless, the station tumbledown and filled with the litter of ages, cans and the bodies of air cars. The viscera of a nation, decaying through time.

Leaving Earth, with its frightening transmutations, I jumped to Mars, but found I could not land. I moved on, dispersing through space in the direction of Centaurus. Gable's grip played a bolero on each hand and I squeezed back, reassuring him, always reassuring him. I could not make contact at Centaurus and journeyed on, dispersing even more, and I noticed that the stars were thinning, and as I came in close to Sirius its glowing disc faded and became black, and Gable seemed to hesitate, as if aware of my shock.

The Universe about me was gone in a second and I recalled the events of a moment before, of standing at the platform on Rigel Nine, of holding hands with Gable, of jumping.

And the dream in that drawn-out moment of time between worlds, the events and shock of Gable's loss, in fact, just a sublimation of my own failure to transmit correctly.

And now Gable, on a world somewhere, alive and dreaming every night of his past and his future, and feeling me gripping his hands as I drift through a curious non-existence, wondering whether a day or a million years passes.

*

Thank God for Gable's touch.

The Graveyard Cross

He had been the first to go, but he knew he would not be the first to return. He would not be a hero, but he had no need of that; after twenty years in space he wanted nothing but home.

It would not be his home, either. There would be none of the old gang, the happy group who had watched him leave, nearly three centuries before. But that was not important. There would be greenness beneath his feet and coolness on his face, and his past would be there, inscribed in the very genes of the people whom he would get to know.

He would have lost very little.

He switched on the transceiver with a rising sense of excitement.

"This is Deep Space Probe Orion. Commander Summerson . . ."

And after a few moments: "Welcome, Summerson. It's been a long time."

It was the first human voice he had heard in twenty years. He requested landing permission on Earth, asked for the correct co-ordinates for touchdown.

"This is Littrow City—on the Moon. You'll have to land at Serenitatis Base, Commander Summerson. You'll have to check in here before anything."

"No thank you, Littrow—I've waited twenty years for a sight of Earth and I can't wait a second longer. I want to go straight down."

"Impossible. I repeat, impossible. Commander Summerson,

you must *not* attempt to make any such landing. Please bring your ship down at Serenitatis."

Argument was useless. He complied, reluctantly, complaining all the time that since he had never left the ship in the whole of his mission, there could be no possibility of his having acquired a strange disease. Why did he need quarantine?

"It isn't quarantine, Commander. But you've been gone three centuries and things have changed on Earth. You may not want to go. . . ."

"Oh I'll want to go! And nothing is going to stop me."

He snapped off the transceiver, and swallowed his disappointment, but he landed at the huge unmanned base in the Mare Serenitatis, and waited to be picked up.

Decontamination. Then de-robing.

Summerson was small, less than five feet five inches, and his body was thin. To look at him was to think: emaciation. But he was very fit. And something within him drove him towards Earth, something irrational, perhaps, but something strong.

Debriefing, and an account of stars and worlds that set alight the minds of those who listened. Those sessions were quiet indeed save for the voice of Summerson as he told of *Cyberon* and *Vax Sinester*, of worlds passing silently below, searched and then ignored as he went deeper into the deep, watching for a second Earth that he would never find.

When the sessions were finished Summerson packed his belongings together and went to Base Commander Wolfe to say goodbye. His job was done; now at last he could go back to Earth.

Wolfe said No, and Summerson sat quietly and watched the younger man.

"Explain that." Icy.

"Earth has changed."

"Of course. I'm expecting to be the alone-est man on Earth

for a while. But the things I want most of all won't have changed."

"Everything has changed," said Wolfe. "Everything down to the smallest leaf. Summerson, that isn't Earth any more. Earth died a long time ago; after you left, before I was born. It died of a cancer that had begun hundreds of years ago. Small and unnoticed in those days, it eventually took hold and Earth died. It's a different planet, Summerson. Totally."

Summerson shook his head and his fists clenched. "War? Are you telling me that there was—"

Wolfe laughed. "Not war, never war. War maims—it never destroys. Let me rephrase what I said. Earth *evolved*."

"Let me ask some questions," said Summerson, and inside he was breaking up because there was something wrong, something very wrong, and it was going to stop him; he knew it and he could not face it.

"Are there humans on Earth?" Wolfe smiled, nodded his head. "Are there two sexes of humans? Do they have arms and legs, a single head and a heart on the left side of their chest cavities?" All affirmative.

"Is there air on Earth? Is there water? Is there food? Life? Cities?"

"Certainly there are."

"Can I live on Earth?"

"You can. You can live there like any of us could live there. It wouldn't be much of a life—at the outside probably a day. Long enough to see a few sights before you choke up so much blood you drown, and find yourself being consumed before you've fully died."

Summerson stared at Wolfe and shook his head.

"Your Earth is dead, Summerson. Face the facts."

"Not dead," cried Summerson. "Only hidden. It's there, beneath, disguised, distorted perhaps, but there just the same. I must see it."

"Fine. We'll fly you across it. As many times as you like."

"I must *stand* on it."

"Wear a suit and we'll take you to the desert areas."

"Oh Christ, Wolfe, don't you understand? I must *be* there, I must feel it in my body like it was in my body twenty years ago!"

"Three hundred years ago!" shouted Wolfe, and they glared at each other, softened and fell back into sullen silence.

"You can't go back," said Wolfe.

"I'm going back," said Summerson.

"You won't survive."

"I'm going back at any cost. You can't stop me, Wolfe, not you, not anyone. I'm going back at any cost."

"The cost will be very great."

"I'm a rich man. My investments at the time I left were—"

"Not the money cost. You'll never need money at Littrow, or Tycho, or Clavius, or Mars . . . you are a lifelong guest if you care to stay."

"I don't. I don't care to stay, I care to go. What cost?"

Lafayette, in white, with deep-set brown eyes that never seemed capable of meeting Summerson's gaze, fixed him down on a bed of steel, and began to push electrodes. He worked with an intensity that negated conversation and Summerson was glad because he was thinking of Oxford Street and a park (with a lake) that was called Hyde Park and had vanished a long time ago, Wolfe had said.

The electrodes aggravated and there were so many of them, and a computer burbled self-indulgently and planned and plotted Summerson's body and designed the frame that could be built upon the frame he already had.

Lafayette, talking with a slightly French accent (he was from French Imbrium where the French tradition was maintained) told Summerson that he was to sleep now, and he would wake in twenty hours. Nothing would have changed, but over the weeks he would grow.

Summerson grew, and from five feet five he reached six six, and that was where he stopped because the computer said to stop. His long bones had lengthened and widened, his ribs had expanded, his shoulders broadened, the overall calcium content of his frame was increased (with no noticeable effect on his increased weight) and a para-parathyroid stopped his body correcting the fault. He was skeletal to look at and his head was small, but only because his body was so large.

He looked at himself in the mirror and felt sick. But it would get him back to earth.

He was fed, and nourished, and the skeletal display vanished and thick muscle appeared at a noticeable rate and eventually he was heavy set and a monstrous-looking man, and only two months had passed since he had insisted on the treatment.

Wolfe came to see him.

"How does it feel to be tall?"

"Why did they do it? Why is it necessary?"

They sat facing each other and Wolfe grinned. "It gives you a competitive advantage. Or put it this way, it deletes the competitive *dis*advantage of your short height."

"And there's more? Yes, I can see there's more."

"It was your choice."

It had been his choice and there was no denying it. To get back to Earth he would have to adapt to Earth. So Summerson tried to forget about being six foot six when he had lived a lifetime as a short man among men, and he tried to think of Earth, which was easy to do.

Wolfe sent him a woman and when he didn't express absolute delight, he sent a second, and a third. Summerson rejected them all.

Wolfe was upset and made the fact plain in no uncertain terms. Summerson accepted the anger and when Wolfe was calm again he pointed out that blind dates went out with the Ark.

"We could make your life on the Moon—or Mars—one long, lingering holiday. Summerson, I appeal to you. Don't risk your life, don't waste your experience by going down to Earth. If you want work, there is masses of it. Anywhere in the System,

Summerson, anywhere. Name it and you'll go there and you'll never want, never need."

Summerson clenched his fists. "You don't—you *won't*—understand. Sure, in a year, maybe two, I'll come back, I might *beg* you to take me back. But only after I've been Home, Wolfe. I must go home first. I must survive and I must feel Earth again. *Then* send me beautiful women and the keys to the Solar System. . . ."

Wolf sighed. "Earth will chew you up and spit you out, even with the changes we can make in you. Once down you'll never find peace, you'll never be able to return. Think, Summerson, think man. The Solar System is buzzing with life. It's all new, it's all fresh, clean. It's frontier work, the sort of work a man like you would find second nature. You're a leader, Summerson, a man to place on a pedestal. Think about it."

"I've thought all I need. Earth, Wolfe, Earth is where I'm going, and *then* I'll think about your offers."

He was a frantic scrambling shape, sending up clouds of dust as he flailed across the crater bed beneath bigger and heavier loads: Earth watched.

In time he could move as fluently as a sprinter in track gear, and he could dodge and duck, and reverse direction on a thin and unexpected line. All this on Luna, and when they placed him in the IG simulator he did as well. He became fast and powerful; he could run. He could escape.

Lafayette began to thicken his skin.

"Why?" said Summerson. And Lafayette just smiled. "Your choice," he said.

"You sound like Wolfe. Why? Why thicken my skin?"

"Radiation," said Lafayette. "There's less oxygen on Earth, now, but more supersonic air vessels. The ozone layer has been reduced to an ozone smear. The UV reaching the surface would fry you in a week."

"My God," said Summerson as his skin thickened across the days. "The effect on evolution!" He sat up. Already his brain was learning to cope with new surface sensations. Heat he never felt. He could blister himself before he felt the pain. But his body was aware of heat and his reflexes remained fast. Pain came slowly. Damage was less likely because of his almost chitinous pelt.

"Exactly," said Lafayette, "what exactly will happen is anybody's guess. Over the next few generations we should start to see an effect."

They tanned him then, and he emerged as brown as oak. "Is everybody this colour?"

"Getting that way," said Lafayette.

There was a day when they took out his lungs and placed them in a machine. The machine cycled its strange body fluids through the veins and arteries of Summerson's gas-bags, and the walls, the linings of the air sacs, thickened. They became more resistant as the chemicals in the machine blood stimulated them and coaxed them. The mucous glands multiplied and spread about, and the cilia tracts in the bronchi became as dense as forests.

For several days the lungs wheezed on the machine and Summerson breathed not at all, his blood cycling through the body of a volunteer who lay, with Summerson, in a coma, breathing high oxy atmosphere and keeping their resting bodies alive and nourished.

The lungs found their way back to the body, and then there was his heart, which they removed and enlarged, made it into a three times as powerful squeeze-bag of muscle and sinew, and the bundle of *His* was removed and replaced with an artificial cable that was ten times as fast and twenty times as efficient, and would remain so for a thousand years thanks to the way that Lafayette had designed it.

One day Summerson awoke after sleeping for twenty days and found himself hung like Goliath. "Why? For whose benefit?"

"Sexual prowess is very important. It can save your neck."

"To impress women?"

"To quiesce dominant males."

"How bloody stupid."

"Earth has changed," said Wolfe simply. "Oh my God," said Summerson, and crept away to hide.

They strengthened his fingers and thickened his nails until he carried five spears at the end of each arm, and could dent hardboard with a single prod. They toughened the edge of each hand until the nerve endings had gone and the horny layer was thick and strong as iron.

As Summerson slept Lafayette removed the scalp and the skin around his eyes; down to his mouth the living bone was exposed and for twenty days a grinning skull watched as Lafayette softened the bone, and then thickened it, and as the calcium and phosphate lay down in crystal lattices so he inserted a criss-cross of non-irritating steel rods, and Summerson's skull became as strong as a helmet, and the brain below it was not the least affected.

Lafayette built a new cornea and fixed it to Summerson's so that the join could not be seen. The new cornea was a biological material that joined at the edge of the eye with the old cornea and formed a tough and deflective barrier against a normally blinding stab.

When Summerson looked into a mirror he could no longer see himself. But since he knew he was there he could take the shock and sublimate it into mere uneasiness.

If Summerson ever had doubts he walked to the edge of the enclosed city; there, standing dark and unreal, he would stare at the planet Earth. When the planet was in full bloom he felt something inside him stir and cry, and he knew that whatever was happening to him, he was right to go through with it, for it meant survival on that beautiful world.

When the Earth was in quarter phase then, as the months went by, he would feel uncertainty. He would look at himself and remember how he had been, and only the knowledge that no one down there was going to recognize him anyway kept him from screaming to Lafayette to "take it all off".

Monitoring his frustration, Wolfe arranged for a visit by Roz Steele.

There was a time when Summerson would have gasped. Women as large as Roz were circus exhibits, not lovers. And yet, standing inches taller than her, he found her magnificent.

She was black skinned and when he touched her she hardly felt the touch, and when he kissed her she hardly felt the kiss, and when he took her hand he found the callouses and stiffened fingers and he knew, then, that . . .

Roz said, "Don't look so surprised. You knew that other starmen had been arriving back before you."

"And you wanted to go to Earth . . . and this is what they did to you."

Roz nodded. "I'm a damn sight better looking than I was when I left."

"And you went back to Earth."

"No. I never made it. I gave up wanting to go down towards the end of my adaptation. I've lived the fullest life possible since then."

For a moment Summerson found himself nodding, then he realized. "Wolfe sent you to work on me."

"He sent me to lie with you. As simple as that. You will work on yourself. I hope you *do* go down to Earth. You'll be the first one that did."

"And the others?"

"Scattered through the solar system, mostly on Mars. That's a world and a half. I spent ten years there. I'm going back soon. Why don't you come with me?"

Summerson smiled. "How do you know we'll get along?"

She reached over and unbuttoned his tunic. Summerson stood motionless with his heart hammering and the excitement of the moment causing him to rise to his full gargantuan extent. When he was naked she unbuttoned her own robe and let it slip from her shoulders.

It was a passion that Summerson might never have known, for he was not, in his original form, a passionate man. An attitude to love depends largely on confidence in one's physical appearance, and now Summerson felt powerful, and he was a powerful lover.

Lafayette, seeming to relish his task, called for Summerson for one last time and while Summerson slept he made him into a high-tension man. He altered the threshold level of the feedback loop that governed the adrenalin flow into Summerson's vascular system, and when Summerson emerged he found that the slightest sensation of unease precipitated him into a state of complete mental and physical alertness. He began to bristle, he began to twist and turn as he walked as if some shadow haunted him and, should it creep up on him, would overcome him.

Likewise his temper suffered and he snapped and jumped, and his eyes became the eyes of a searching man, never still, always restive.

Except when they gazed at Earth.

Roz took her leave and Summerson watched her go with regret. She shipped for Mars and inside him Summerson knew that should he ever leave Earth he would head after her.

He had lost his taste for food and Lafayette explained that his stomach was changed. It would now break down alcohol in a matter of seconds. No hang-overs for Summerson. At the slightest sign of poison or infected food the stomach would void its contents and flush the chamber with acid which would also be voided. Much of the food on Earth was unfit to eat because of high phosphorous and chlorine contamination. It would be poison to Summerson. A tiny bio-sensor in the wall of his stomach was his guardian.

"Food is not so important to you now," said Lafayette. "You're a walking storehouse of all the vital amino-acids, vitamins and elements you need. Only a few weeks' supply, of course, but no doubt you *will* eat and these are just back-ups.

There are bio-monitors in the hepatic portal and right brachial veins and they're reading your blood composition all the time. Any ingredient falling below the necessary level you can rectify at once. Prolonged deficit will be made known to you by a skin itch over your right arm. A timing mechanism—a unit of monkey liver cells actually, designed to accumulate whatever your stores are secreting; critical level reached— reflex loop to histamine-loaded cells in your skin, and you are warned."

"Monkey cells," said Summerson, almost in disbelief.

"Your body thinks they're you. We tagged them with your identity factor. Settling in nicely I should imagine.

"We've done much the same thing to some highly educated lymphocytes—they've been exposed to every disease organism we know about. They'll be your watch-dogs. Instead of the delay to produce primary immunity, during which time you'd die of many of these diseases, you can now react with secondary immunity which appears very fast."

"And I won't reject the cells?"

"Not if I've done my job properly. Those, by the way, are human lymphocytes, but like the monkey cells they've been tagged with your own identity-factor. You'll greet them like friends. They're also very long-lived cells—just a lysosome stabilizing gimmick that was developed about a hundred years ago."

"When I die my white cells will live on, is that it? Roaming the wastelands of Earth searching for a host."

For a few hours, as Summerson basked in Earthlight on the rim of a small crater, south-west of the colony at Littrow, he imagined that the preparations were finished. His body had been rebuilt and he could no longer call himself Summerson with quite the same meaning as before.

But now it seemed worthwhile, the waiting, the delaying, the endless sleeps while Lafayette had probed and changed and strengthened and destroyed.

Lafayette had enjoyed his task. He was the Base surgeon but the few travellers who returned and who needed the engineering job for their return to Earth were his real interest.

And yet, when it was finished, none ever returned. It was as if their changed bodies caused their minds to change, made them find Earth as repulsive as Wolfe found it.

Summerson felt no such repulsion. He was a hideous being by his own standards, and if he reflected the needs of Earth, then Earth was probably a hideous world. But beauty, as the saying went, is only skin deep. Summerson was interested in a deeper level of Earth. And the longing was still with him; the desire to return, whilst not now voiced as often as it had been voiced by his newly returned (shorter, whiter, less perfect) self, was just as strong.

He returned to Littrow and to his solex, and though Roz was gone and the room was cold and empty, he found comfort there.

And D'Quiss.

"I'm Felix D'Quiss," he said, rising from the couch. A tall, thin man; sparse blond hair over a nordic head; eyes blue, quite intense. A firm shake of ugly hands, the big meeting the grotesquely big. Smart, in a white protex suit, the telltale signs of medical status scattered across the pockets—a watch, a pen, a probe, a contact unit unobtrusively lodged behind his ear.

"Summerson," said Summerson. "Mark II."

"I know. You have taken the changes with remarkable complacency."

"I want to get down to Earth. I'd change anything for that."

"I'm glad to hear it."

Summerson shivered and crossed to the ice-box. He fetched out two mash cans and proffered one to D'Quiss who declined it. Summerson opened his own and sipped the drink. "Let me guess," he said, crossing to the wall window and watching as Earth seemed to twist away again, just out of reach. "My mind."

"Yes."

"You're going to change it. You're going to remove Summerson from my head like you removed him from my body."

"Part of the sacrifice," said D'Quiss, smiling. "You said when they started on you that no cost was too great. You will have to have meant it if you want to get to Earth."

"I certainly want to do that!" Summerson said loudly. "With the emphasis on the *I*. If you alter my mind out of all proportion, if you take the little Summerson in my skull and change him into a para-Summerson, then it isn't *me* any longer. The man who goes down to Earth might not give a damn about the planet. . . . Is that what you want? Is that what happened to Roz and the others? After all this anatomical change you then 'make' us not want to return? Because in fact you've been adapting us to conditions on Mars. . . ? Well, I'm sorry to disappoint you, Mr D'Quiss, but I've taken all the change I intend to take. And I *still* intend to go down to Earth."

D'Quiss nodded, smiling in a self-assured way. "Is this the rational and calm Summerson that came to Littrow?"

"I'm losing my identity, D'Quiss. That's enough to make any man jumpy."

"You're not losing your identity, merely your appearance, your inadequacies."

"I've lost all the inadequacies I intend to lose. Tell Wolfe I'm leaving right now."

D'Quiss sat quietly and stared at Summerson. He told him, then, that there would be no more change. That the adaptation by engineering was over, finished. The mind, however, was a delicate organ, dependent for its function on environment, both social and physical, and Summerson's mind could not tolerate the environment, both social and physical, of Earth.

"So you want to change it. Like I said, chop here, replace there, Mark III Summerson, grinning idiot, oblivious, non-existent."

Nothing of the sort, said D'Quiss. A few emplacements to help Summerson fight the mental pressures.

"Look at it this way. You've already manifested several neuroses."

"For example?"

"Your shame, embarrassment when Lafayette expanded your sex organ."

"Oh . . . that."

"Yes, that. A small enough point on its own, but on Earth do you realize how destructive any sort of sexual embarrassment is? You would not survive to walk down the street. But we can mask, condition, certain facets of your personality that might be embarrassing to you."

"No. Positively no."

"Or we can place artificial connections between several areas of your brain that will allow you to see exactly when a dangerous mood, feeling, response is approaching, and you can then say to yourself, *careful, Summerson, pretend* . . . you see? It will give you the ability to conquer your mental inadequacies without losing the power of choice. Well?"

Summerson was silent.

D'Quiss went on. "Let me put it this way. Earth is totally hostile. Not hostile by its own standards—it has the same range from extreme to extreme within the population with the bulk of the population filling the centre of the curve. But in the three hundred years you have been away that curve has shifted towards the hostile extreme. What was extreme in your day is now matter of fact. Violence, death, attitude to privacy, of body and home, all these things are set within different parameters. You wouldn't last five minutes."

"So you keep telling me. So Wolfe and Lafayette keep telling me."

"All right, so it's a figurative expression. You might survive a week, a month, a year, but it would be fighting all the time, a terrible struggle for survival."

D'Quiss was watching him very intently, but his face showed complete calm, unlike Wolfe who had seemed almost exasperated by Summerson's doggedness. "And with a few electrodes in my head I would find it easier to survive. Is that what you're saying?"

D'Quiss nodded. "The most essential thing is that you keep your wits about you, that you remain even-tempered. Stable. When your heart breaks your mind has got to be oblivious to it; when your heart sings, the same thing goes. When your temper flares you can calm at a moment's thought, but the cause of your anger will not be obliterated so you can still act on it."

"A few electrodes . . . no invisible conditioning, no twisting of a paranoia here and moving it slightly so I can't feel persecuted?"

"Not unless you want it."

"I don't want it! I want Summerson—me!—to see Earth as he saw it when he left. I want to see the change, feel the difference, seek out the unchanged elements. I want to feel the sadness or the horror as Summerson, *this* Summerson, would have felt it three hundred years ago." He turned to stare up at the Crescent Earth. "When I was twenty years younger," he said softly.

D'Quiss watched him impassively. After a while Summerson moved from the window and sprawled out in an armchair, staring at the other man.

D'Quiss showed no discomfiture. "Why do you want to go back? What's the real reason?"

Summerson laughed. "Does there have to be a *real* reason? Isn't it possible that I was telling the truth?" D'Quiss said nothing. After a moment Summerson went on, his eyes focused nowhere in particular. "It's funny you know. I can remember standing on the ramp at Southend, looking at the shuttle. Such a tiny ship. I wanted nothing else but to get away from Earth. Since I was a kid I wanted to be a probepilot. My parents did everything they could to discourage me, but I was too determined. They came to Southend when I was launched and watched me leave, and I didn't even say goodbye to them. Twenty years in space and I couldn't stop thinking about them. I really came to understand them, to love them. Can you imagine that? Twenty years, and no way back. . . ."

"It must be an intolerable thought."

"Thanks," said Summerson dully. "But no, nothing is intolerable. It's just . . . the emptiness."

"The emptiness of space?"

"Of everything. A man is much more than just a mind in a body. That's just a small part of him. He's everything that relates to him and which he relates to in turn, and that part of me has gone and I feel just . . . just a shard. There's only one place I know where I can come to terms with that emptiness."

"Earth?"

"Earth."

"What do you plan on doing once you get there?"

"Oh, explore. Remember. Write. Talk to people."

"What if they regard you as a freak?"

"Why should they?"

"Why shouldn't they? An off-worlder, *the* off-worlder to many of them. You will be the first to set foot on Earth for more than two generations. They will react to you, I'm sure of that, but that reaction could well be hostile; and if not hostile to begin with, then later certainly. When the novelty wears off. . . ."

"Will they leave me alone? Will they let me search for the things I want to search for?"

"I don't know," said D'Quiss. "You'll have to find yourself employment which could be difficult. And if you feel that you might want to leave for the Moon, then we'll have to arrange a method of communication so we can come and pick you up."

"You'd do that? After I've declined your every offer for help whilst I was here?"

"We're not barbarians," said D'Quiss.

Summerson slept.

After five days he awoke looking the same, (feeling the

same, but weighing slightly more—the weight of the bio-lam electrodes and miniature power pack embedded partly in his skull and partly in the substance of his brain.

They tried a simple test involving the arousal of his anger and he became angry. They explained that he had merely to think about *not* getting angry and it would pass. They tried the test again and he felt anger rise in him, and then he thought it away and he saw the test for what it was. He tried to think away the remorse at losing Roz, but he couldn't.

It only worked for the future. And when he eventually left Earth he would be able to lose the electrodes, the power pack and the influence of D'Quiss.

He packed his bags and, almost fatalistically, walked towards Wolfe's office. Wolfe was there, and Lafayette. And D'Quiss sitting relaxedly in a corner and smoking a non-inhalant cigarette.

"Are you ready to go?"

"You mean no more changes? I can hardly believe it."

Wolfe smiled. "You'll survive unless there's something we've overlooked, something important."

"Which we don't know about," said Lafayette, almost as if he were justifying a certain failure.

"But which we will know about after your decline," said D'Quiss from the side of the room.

Now at last Summerson took his grateful leave and went to the base airlock. A bus took him to Serenitatis, to a small ship, now long disused, that would take him down to Earth.

He had been on the Moon for over a year. And as he walked across the metal ramp to the waiting ship he suddenly felt all the excitement at going home he had felt as he had arrived in the Solar System, all those months before.

With a yell and a laugh he jumped high in the vacuum and bounded to the ship, to take his place (the only passenger) in the small cabin. Wolfe was a black shape in the brightly lit bus, parked half a mile from the ramp.

The sea, the ocean, heaving, white flecked (but somehow . . . duller than he remembered), Summerson's eyes trying to leave his head to see down to the Earth. Asia, drifting below, and China, and the China Sea, scattered islands, the buzz of high-flying planes, eyes peering at the ship as it glided slowly round the world.

The coast of California sliding below like some huge projection—more buzzing, a swarm of high-flying sightseers, klaxon blasts rending the high atmosphere, the swarms dropping away in front to reassemble behind.

The Atlantic, darker, more sombre than the Pacific, and England, then, and down.

Home.

He was an island. There was dust and shadows. There was no moon. The sun shone through clouds. There was movement, and the cries of the dying. There was dying, and the roar of movement. There was the barking of dogs and the straying of cats.

He was an island and he stopped in the middle of the world and there was nothing to see but the shadows that moved by, and the walls that enclosed him, brick fingers pointing to the sky. He went to where he had once lived.

It was now a slag tip, the waste of centuries poured across an area of several square miles. Bomb waste, desolation, with driverless machines calmly chewing their way through the sea of junk.

There was a girder twisted into the shape of a cross, a single cross, a graveyard cross. He walked through ghosts and filth and picked up a handful of ash and stared at it for a long time.

He saw no people, just dark, hard faces. He heard them, he touched them physically, but they moved so fast, they lived so distant. He tried to move fast to match velocities, but they changed direction and he could never keep up. He drifted through streets, cities, towns, breathing the dust, choking up his food, waking up with his face a bloody mess, registering the attack of screaming gangs, feeling the delayed pain, conscious of his own ferocity . . . everything moved around him, never with him. Everything seemed so fast. He spoke words and the words were heard, and he heard words back, but there was never any . . .

Communication.

There was no communication. He was a perfectly adapted man, but they could not have known about communication. They had prepared him for poison, fumes, attack and flight, but they had not prepared him for the indifference.

He died a hundred times—hit, spin, shattered—left naked to die and he crept away and found himself and . . .

Hit, spin, slugged, and woman's laughter, and an insane and blind achievement of sexual satisfaction and . . .

Crawled away.

There was the filth of alleyways, the smell of faeces, the pain of broken bones that healed so quickly. . . .

The fierceness of dogs, the fastness of movement, the stench of air, the burning of sun, the coldness of children, the emptiness of thought. Confusion, starvation of emotion.

No communication.

He could not identify. He was planes apart, worlds away, points out of focus, miles off target. He was so alien that he hardly registered, and his body was a fragment of litter and it blew away. . . .

Something went wrong and his anger became uncontrollable. He was hit on the head and something dislodged, and he lost control. And there were armed men and he was hustled away at right angles to the human flow, and he found himself:

In peace. There was peace. A small room, a barred window, the distant grating of metal locks. A filthy pit in the floor, a hard bed. Rats, roaches, sweat, tears. . . . Light from the window—sounds so distant they were almost familiar. Peace —and Earth.

He had found Earth again.

Sitting in the stillness he knew he was home at last.

Mythago Wood

When, in 1944, I was called away to the war, I felt so resentful of my father's barely expressed disappointment that, on the eve of my departure, I walked quietly to his desk and tore a page out of his notebook, the diary in which his silent, obsessive work was recorded. The fragment was dated simply "August 34", and I read it many times, appalled at its incomprehensibility, but content that I had stolen at least a tiny part of his life with which to support myself through those painful, lonely times.

Following a short, and very bitter comment on the distractions in his life—the running of Oak Lodge, our family home, the demands of his two sons, and of his wife (by then, I remember, desperately ill and close to the end of her life)— was a passage quite memorable for its incoherence:

A letter from Watkins—agrees with me that at certain times of the year the aura around the woodland could reach as far as the house. Must think through the implications of this. He is keen to know the power of the oak vortex that I have measured. What to tell him? Certainly not of the first mythago. Have noticed too that the enrichment of the pre-mythago zone is more persistent, but concomitant with this, am distinctly losing my sense of time.

I treasured this piece of paper for many reasons, for the moment or two of my father's passionate interest that it represented—and for the way it locked me out of its understanding, as he had locked me out at home. Everything he loved, everything I hated.

I was wounded in early 1945, and in a military hospital met a young Frenchman, and became close friends with him. I managed to avoid evacuation to England, and when the war finished I stayed in France, travelling south to convalesce in the hills behind Marseilles; it was a hot, dry place, very still, very slow; I lived with my young friend's parents, and quickly became a part of the tiny community.

Letters from my brother Christian, who had returned to Oak Lodge after the war, arrived every month throughout the long year of 1946. They were chatty, informative letters, but there was an increasing note of tension in them, and it was clear that Christian's relationship with his father was deteriorating rapidly. I never heard a word from the old man himself, but then I never expected to; I had long since resigned myself to the fact that, even at best, he regarded me with total indifference. All his family had been an intrusion in his work, and his guilt at neglecting us, and especially at driving his wife to taking her own life, had blossomed rapidly, during the early years of the war, into an hysterical madness that could be truly frightening. Which is not to say that he was perpetually shouting; on the contrary, most of his life was spent in silent, absorbed contemplation of the oak woodland that bordered our home. At first infuriating, because of the distance it put between him and his family, soon those long periods of quiet became blessed, earnestly welcomed.

He died in November 1946, of the illness that had afflicted him for years. When I heard the news I was torn between my unwillingness to return to Oak Lodge, at the edge of the Knaresthorpe estate in Herefordshire, and Christian's obvious distress. He was alone, now, in the house where we had lived through our childhood together; I could imagine him prowling through the empty rooms, perhaps sitting in father's dank and unwholesome study and remembering the hours of denial, the smell of wood and compost that the old man had trudged in through the glass-panelled doors after his week-long sorties into the deep woodlands. The forest had spread into that room as if my father could not bear to be away from the rank undergrowth, and cool, moist oak-glades even when making token acknowledgement of his family. He made that acknow-ledgement in the only way he knew: by telling us—and mainly telling my brother—stories of the ancient forestlands beyond the house, the primary woodland of oak and ash in whose dark interior (he once said) wild boar could still be heard, and smelled, and tracked by their spoor.

I doubt if he had ever seen such a creature, but I vividly recalled (in that evening as I sat in my room, overlooking the tiny village in the hills, Christian's letter a crushed ball still held in my hand) how I had listened to the muffled grunting of some woodland animal, and heard the heavy, unhurried crashing of something bulky moving inwards, towards the winding pathway that we called Deep Track, a route that led spirally towards the very heartwoods of the forest.

I knew I would have to go home, and yet I delayed my departure for nearly another year. During that time Christian's letters ceased abruptly. In his last letter, dated April 10th, he wrote of Guiwenneth, of his unusual marriage, and hinted that I would be surprised by the lovely girl to whom he had lost his "heart, mind, soul, reason, cooking ability and just about everything else, old boy". I wrote to congratulate him, of course, but there was no further communication between us for months.

Eventually I wrote to say I was coming home, that I would stay at Oak Lodge for a few weeks, and then find accommoda-tion in one of the nearby towns. I said goodbye to France, and to the community that had become so much a part of my life, and travelled to England by bus and train, by ferry, and then by train again. And on August 20th, hardly able to believe what was happening to me, I arrived by pony and trap at the disused railway line that skirted the edge of the extensive

Knaresthorpe estate. Oak Lodge lay on the far side of the grounds, four miles further round the road, but accessible via the right of way through the estate's fields and woodlands. I intended to take an intermediate route and so, lugging my single, crammed suitcase as best I could, I began to walk along the grass-covered railway track, peering, on occasion, over the high, red-brick wall that marked the limit of the estate, trying to see through the gloom of the pungent pine-woods. Soon this woodland, and the wall, vanished, and the land opened into tight, tree-bordered fields, to which I gained access across a rickety wooden stile, almost lost beneath briar and full-fruited blackberry bushes. I had to trample my way out of the public domain and so onto the south trackway that wound, skirting patchy woodland and the stream called "sticklebrook", up to the ivy-covered house that was my home.

It was late morning, and very hot, as I came in distant sight of Oak Lodge. Somewhere off to my left I could hear the drone of a tractor. I thought of old Alphonse Jeffries, the estate's farm supervisor, and with memory of his weather-tanned, smiling face came images of the mill-pond, and fishing for pike from his tiny rowing boat.

Memory of the mill-pond was as tranquil as its surface, and I moved away from the south track, through waist high nettles and a tangle of ash and hawthorn scrub until I came out close to the bank of the wide, shadowy pool, its full size hidden by the gloom of the dense stand of oak woodland that began on its far side. Almost hidden among the rushes that crowded the nearer edge of the pond was the shallow boat from which we had fished, years before; its white paint was flaked away almost entirely now, and although the craft looked watertight, I doubted if it would take the weight of a full grown man. I didn't disturb it but walked around the bank and sat down on the rough concrete steps of the crumbling boat-house; from here I watched the surface of the pool rippling with the darting motions of insects, and the occasional passage of a fish, just below.

"A couple of sticks and a bit of string . . . that's all it takes."

Christian's voice startled me. He must have walked along a beaten track from the lodge, hidden from my view by the shed. Delighted, I jumped to my feet and turned to face him. The shock of his appearance was like a physical blow to me, and I think he noticed the fact, even though I threw my arms about him and gave him a powerful brotherly bear-hug.

"I had to see this place again," I said.

"I know what you mean," he said, as we broke our embrace. "I often walk here myself." There was a moment's awkward silence as we stared at each other. I felt, distinctly, that he was not particularly pleased to see me. "You're looking brown and drawn, old boy," he said. "Healthy and ill together. . . ."

"Mediterranean sun, grape-picking, and shrapnel. I'm still not one hundred percent." I smiled. "But it *is* good to be back, to see you again."

"Yes," he said dully. "I'm glad you've come, Steve. Very glad. Really. I'm afraid the place . . . well, a bit of a mess. I only got your letter yesterday and I haven't had a chance to do anything. Things have changed quite a bit, you'll find."

And he more than anything. I could hardly believe that this was the chipper, perky young man who had left with his army unit in 1944. He had aged incredibly, his hair quite streaked with grey, more noticeable for his having allowed it to grow long and untidy at the back and sides. He reminded me very much of father, the same distant, distracted look, the same hollow cheeks and deeply wrinkled face. But it was his whole demeanour that had shocked me. He had always been a stocky, muscular chap; now he was like the proverbial scarecrow, wiry, ungainly, on edge all the time. His eyes darted about, but never seemed to focus upon me. And he smelled. Of moth-balls, as if the crisp white shirt and grey flannels that he wore had been dragged out of storage; and another smell beyond the naptha . . . the hint of woodland and grass. There was dirt under his fingernails, and in his hair, and his teeth were yellowing.

He seemed to relax slightly as the minutes ticked by. We sparred a bit, laughed a bit, and walked around the pond, whacking at the rushes with sticks. I could not shake off the feeling that I had arrived home at a bad time.

"Was it difficult . . . with the old man, I mean? The last days."

He shook his head. "There was a nurse here for the final two weeks or so. I can't exactly say that he went peacefully, but she managed to stop him damaging himself . . . or me, for that matter."

"Your letters certainly suggested a growing hostility. To understate the case."

Christian smiled quite grimly, and glanced at me with a curious expression, somewhere between agreement and suspicion. "You got that from my letters, did you? Well, yes. He became quite crazed soon after I came back from the war. You should have seen the place, Steve. You should have seen him. I don't think he'd washed for months. I wondered what he'd been eating . . . certainly nothing as simple as eggs and meat. In all honesty I think, for a few months at any rate, he'd been eating wood and leaves. He was in a wretched state. Although he let me help him with his work, he quickly began to resent me. He tried to kill me on several occasions, Steve. And I mean that, really desperate attempts on my life. There was a reason for it, I suppose. . . ."

I was astonished by what Christian was telling me. The image of my father had changed from that of a cold, resentful man into a crazed figure, ranting at Christian and beating at him with his fists.

"I always thought that, for you at least, he had a touch of affection; he always told *you* the stories of the wood; I listened, but it was you who sat on his knee. Why would he try to kill you?"

"I became too involved," was all Christian said. He was keeping something back, something of critical importance. I could tell from his tone, from his sullen, almost resentful expression. Did I push the point or not? It was hard to make the decision. I had never before felt so distant from my own brother. I wondered if his behaviour was having an effect on Guiwenneth, the girl he had married. I wondered what sort of atmosphere she was living in up at Oak Lodge.

Tentatively, I broached the subject of the girl.

Christian struck angrily at the rushes by the pond. "Guiwenneth's gone," he said simply, and I stopped, startled.

"What does that mean, Chris? Gone where?"

"She's just gone, Steve," he snapped, angry and cornered. "She was father's girl, and she's gone, and that's all there is to it."

"I don't understand what you mean. Where's she gone *to*? In your letter you sounded so happy. . . ."

"I shouldn't have written about her. That was a mistake. Now let it drop, will you?"

After that outburst, my unease with Christian grew stronger by the minute. There was something very wrong with him indeed, and clearly Guiwenneth's leaving had contributed greatly to the terrible change I could see; but I sensed there was something more. Unless he spoke about it, however, there was no way through to him. I could find only the words, "I'm sorry."

"Don't be."

We walked on, almost to the woods, where the ground became marshy and unsafe for a few yards before vanishing into a musty deepness of stone and root and rotting wood. It was cool, here, the sun being behind us now, and beyond the thickly foliaged trees. The dense stands of rush moved in the breeze and I watched the rotting boat as it shifted slightly on its mooring.

Christian followed my gaze, but he was not looking at the boat or the pond; he was lost, somewhere in his own thoughts. For a brief moment I experienced a jarring sadness at the sight of so fine a young man so ruined in appearance and attitude. I wanted desperately to touch his arm, to hug him, and I could hardly bear the knowledge that I was afraid to do so.

Quite quietly I asked him, "What on earth has happened to you, Chris? Are you ill?"

He didn't answer for a moment, then said, "I'm not ill," and struck hard at a puffball, which shattered and spread on the breeze. He looked at me, something of resignation in his haunted face. "I've been going through a few changes, that's all. I've been picking up on the old man's work. Perhaps a bit of his reclusiveness is rubbing off on me, a bit of his detachment."

"If that's true, then perhaps you should give up for a while. The old man's obsession with the oak forest eventually killed him, and from the look of you, you're going the same way."

Christian smiled thinly and chucked his reedwhacker out into the pond, where it made a dull splash and floated in a patch of scummy green algae. "It might even be worth dying to achieve what he tried to achieve . . . and failed."

I didn't understand the dramatic overtone in Christian's statement. The work that had so obsessed our father had been concerned with mapping the woodland, and searching for evidence of old forest settlements. He had clearly invented a whole new jargon for himself, and effectively isolated me from any deeper understanding of his work. I said this to Christian, and added, "Which is all very interesting, but hardly *that* interesting."

"He was doing much more than that, much more than just mapping. But do you remember those maps, Steve? Incredibly detailed . . ."

I could remember one quite clearly, the largest map, showing carefully marked trackways and easy routes through the tangle of trees and stony outcrops; it showed clearings drawn with almost obsessive precision, each glade numbered and identified, and the whole forest divided into zones, and given names. We had made a camp in one of the clearings close to the woodland edge. "We often tried to get deeper into the heart-woods, remember those expeditions, Chris? But the deep track just ends, and we always managed to get lost, I seem to recall, and very scared."

"That's true," Christian said quietly, looking at me quizzically; and added, "What if I told you the forest had *stopped* us entering? Would you believe me?"

I peered into the tangle of brush, tree and gloom, to where a sunlit clearing was visible. "In a way I suppose it did," I said. "It stopped us penetrating very deeply because it made us scared, because there are few trackways through, and the ground is choked with stone and briar . . . very difficult walking. Is that what you meant? Or did you mean something a little more sinister?"

"Sinister isn't the word I'd use," said Christian, but added nothing more for a moment; he reached up to pluck a leaf from a small, immature oak, and rubbed it between thumb and forefinger before crushing it in his palm. All the time he stared into the deep woods. "This is primary oak woodland, Steve, untouched forest from when all of the country was covered with deciduous forests of oak and ash and elder and rowan and hawthorn . . ."

"And all the rest," I said with a smile. "I remember the old man listing them for us."

"That's right, he did. And there's more than eight square miles of such forest stretching from here to well beyond Grimley, eight square miles of original, post-Ice Age forestland. Untouched, uninvaded for thousands of years." He broke off and looked at me hard, before adding, "Resistant to change."

I said, "He always thought there were boars alive in there. I remember hearing something one night, and he convinced me that it was a great big old bull boar, skirting the edge of the woods, looking for a mate."

Christian led the way back towards the boathouse. "He was probably right. If boars *had* survived from mediaeval times, this is just the sort of woodland they'd be found in."

With my mind opened to those events of years ago, memory inched back, images of childhood—the burning touch of sun on bramble-grazed skin; fishing trips to the mill-pond; tree camps, games, explorations . . . and instantly I recalled the Twigling.

As we walked back to the beaten pathway that led up to the lodge, we discussed the sighting. I had been about nine or ten years old. On our way to the sticklebrook to fish we had decided to test out our stick and string rods on the mill-pond, in the vain hope of snaring one of the predatory fish that lived there. As we crouched by the water (we only ever dared go out in the boat with Alphonse) we saw movement in the trees, across on the other bank. It was a bewildering vision that held us enthralled for the next few moments, and not a little terrified : standing watching us was a man in brown, leathery clothes, with a wide, gleaming belt around his waist, and a spiky, orange beard that reached to his chest; on his head he wore twigs, held to his crown by a leather band. He watched us for a moment only, before slipping back into the darkness. We heard nothing in all this time, no sound of approach, no sound of departure.

Running back to the house we had soon calmed down. Christian decided, eventually, that it must have been old Alphonse, playing tricks on us. But when I mentioned what we'd seen to my father he reacted almost angrily (although Christian recalls him as having been excited, and bellowing for that reason, and not because he was angry with our having been near the forbidden pool). It was father who referred to the vision as "the Twigling", and soon after we had spoken to him he vanished into the woodland for nearly two weeks.

"That was when he came back hurt, remember?" We had reached the grounds of Oak Lodge, and Christian held the gate open for me as he spoke.

"The arrow wound. The gypsy arrow. My God, that was a bad day."

"The first of many."

I noticed that most of the ivy had been cleared from the walls of the house; it was a grey place now, small, curtainless windows set in the dark brick, the slate roof, with its three tall chimney stacks, partially hidden behind the branches of a big old beech tree. The yard and gardens were untidy and un-kempt, the empty chicken coops and animal shelters ram-shackle and decaying. Christian had really let the place slip. But when I stepped across the threshold, it was as if I had never been away. The house smelled of stale food and chlorine, and I could almost see the thin figure of my mother, working away at the immense pinewood table in the kitchen, cats stretched out around her on the red-brick floor.

Christian had grown tense again, staring at me in that fidgety way that marked his unease. I imagined he was still unsure whether to be glad or angry that I had come home like this. For a moment I felt like an intruder. He said, "Why don't you unpack and freshen up. You can use your old room. It's a bit stuffy, I expect, but it'll soon air. Then come down and we'll have some late lunch. We've got all the time in the world to chat, as long as we're finished by tea." He smiled, and I thought this was some slight attempt at humour. But he went on quickly, staring at me in a cold, hard way, "Because if you're going to stay at home for a while, then you'd better know what's going on here. I don't want you interfering with it, Steve, or with what I'm doing."

"I wouldn't interfere with your life, Chris—"

"Wouldn't you? We'll see. I'm not going to deny that I'm nervous of you being here. But since you are . . ." he trailed off, and for a second looked almost embarrassed. "Well, we'll have a chat later on."

Intrigued by what Christian had said, and worried by his apprehension of me, I nonetheless restrained my curiosity and spent an hour exploring the house again, from top to bottom, inside and out, everywhere save father's study, the contempla-tion of which chilled me more than Christian's behaviour had done. Nothing had changed, except that it was untidy, and untenanted. Christian had employed a part-time cleaner and

cook, a good soul from a nearby village who cycled to the
Lodge every week and prepared a pie or stew that would last
the man three days. Christian did not go short of farm produce,
so much so that he rarely bothered to use his ration book. He
seemed to get all he needed, including sugar and tea, from the
Knaresthorpe estate, which had always been good to my
family.

My own room was dust free, but quite stale. I opened the
window wide and lay down on the bed for a few minutes,
staring out and up into the hazy, late summer sky, past the
waving branches of the gigantic beech that grew so close to
the Lodge. Several times, in the years before my teens, I had
climbed from window to tree, and made a secret camp among
the thick branches; by moonlight I had shivered in my under-
pants, crouched in that private place, imagining the dark
doings of night creatures below.

Lunch, in mid-afternoon, was a substantial feast of cold
pork, chicken and hard-boiled eggs, in quantities that, after
two years in France on strict rations, I had never thought to
see again. We were, of course, eating his food supply for
several days, but the fact seemed irrelevant to Christian, who
at any rate only picked at his meal.

Afterwards we talked for a couple of hours, and Christian
relaxed quite noticeably, although he never referred to
Guiwenneth, or to father's work, and I never broached either
subject. We were sprawled in the uncomfortable armchairs
that had belonged to my grandparents, surrounded by the time-
faded mementoes of our family . . . photographs, a noisy rosewood clock, horrible pictures of exotic Spain, all framed in
cracked mock-gilded wood, and all pressed hard against the
same floral wallpaper that had hugged the walls of the sitting-
room since a time before my birth. But it was home, and
Christian was home, and the smell, and the faded surrounds,
all were home to me. I knew, within two hours of arriving, that
I would have to stay. It was not so much that I belonged here—
although I certainly felt that—but simply that the place

belonged to me, not in any mercenary sense of ownership, more in the way that the house and the land around the house shared a common life with me; we were part of the same evolution; even in France, even as far as Greece, where I had been in action, I had not been separated from that evolution, merely stretched to an extreme.

As the heavy old rosewood clock began to whirr and click, preceding its laboured chiming of the hour of five, Christian abruptly rose from his chair and tossed his half-smoked cigarette into the empty fire grate.

"Let's go to the study," he said, and I rose without speaking and followed him through the house to the small room where our father had worked. "You're scared of this room, aren't you?" he said as he opened the door and walked inside, crossing to the heavy oak desk and pulling out a large leather-bound book from one of the drawers.

I hesitated outside the study, watching Christian, almost unable to move my legs to carry myself into the room. I recognized the book he held, my father's notebook. I touched my back pocket, the wallet I carried there, and thought of the fragment of that notebook that was hidden inside the thin leather. I wondered if anyone, my father or Christian, had ever noticed that a page was missing. Christian was watching me, his eyes bright with excitement now, his hands trembling as he placed the book on the desk top.

"He's dead, Steve. He's gone from this room, from the house. There's no need to be afraid any more."

"Isn't there?"

But I found the sudden strength to move, and stepped across the threshold. The moment I entered the musty room I felt totally subdued, deeply affected by the coolness of the place, the stark, haunted atmosphere that hugged the walls and carpets and windows. It smelled slightly of leather, here, and dust too, with just a distant hint of polish, as if Christian made a token effort to keep this stifling room clean. It was not a crowded room, not a library as my father would have perhaps liked it to be. There were books on zoology and botany, on history and archaeology, but these were not rare copies, merely the cheapest copies he could find at the time. There were more paperbacks than stiff-covered books, and the exquisite binding of his notes, and the deeply varnished desk, had an air of Victorian elegance about them that belied the otherwise shabby studio.

On the walls, between the cases of books, were his glass-framed specimens, pieces of wood, collections of leaves, crude sketches of animal and plant life made during the first years of his fascination with the forest. And almost hidden away among the cases and the shelves was the patterned shaft of the arrow that had struck him fifteen years before, its flights twisted and useless, the broken shaft glued together, the iron head dulled with corrosion, but a lethal-looking weapon nonetheless.

I stared at that arrow for several seconds, reliving the man's agony, and the tears that Christian and I had wept for him as we had helped him back from the woodlands, that cold autumn afternoon, convinced that he would die.

How quickly things had changed after that strange, and never fully explained incident. If the arrow linked me with an earlier day, when some semblance of concern and love had remained in my father's mind, the rest of the study radiated only coldness.

I could still see the greying figure, bent over his desk writing furiously. I could hear the troubled breathing, the lung disorder that finally killed him; I could hear his caught breath, the vocalized sound of irritation as he grew aware of my presence, and waved me away with a half-irritated gesture, as if he begrudged even that split second of acknowledgement.

How like him Christian looked, now, standing there all dishevelled and sickly looking, and yet with the mark of absolute confidence about him, his hands in the pockets of his flannels, shoulders drooped, his whole body visibly shaking.

He had waited quietly as I adjusted to the room, and let the memories and atmosphere play through me. As I stepped up to the desk, my mind back on the moment at hand, he said, "Steve, you should read the notes. They'll make a lot of things clear to you, and help you understand what it is I'm doing as well."

I turned the notebook towards me, scanning the sprawling, untidy handwriting, picking out words and phrases, reading through the years of my father's life in a few scant seconds. The words were as meaningless, on the whole, as those on my purloined sheet. To read them brought back a memory of anger and of danger, and of fear. The life in the notes had sustained me through nearly a year of war and had come to mean something outside of their proper context. I felt reluctant to dispel that powerful association with the past.

"I intend to read them, Chris. From beginning to end, and that's a promise. But not for the moment."

I closed the book, noticing as I did that my hands were clammy and trembling. I was not yet ready to be so close to my father again, and Christian saw this, and accepted it.

Conversation died quite early that night, as my energy expired, and the tensions of the long journey finally made themselves known to me. Christian came up with me and stood in the doorway of my room, watching as I turned back the sheets and pottered about, picking up bits and pieces of my past life, laughing, shaking my head and trying to evoke a last moment's tired nostalgia. "Remember making camp out in the beech?" I said, watching the grey of branch and leaf against the still bright evening sky. "Yes," said Christian with a smile. "Yes, I remember very clearly."

But it was as fatigued as that, and Christian took the hint and said, "Sleep well, old chap. I'll see you in the morning."

If I slept at all, it was for the first two or three hours after putting head to pillow. I woke sharply, and brightly, in the dead of night, one or two o'clock, perhaps; the sky was very dark now, and it was quite windy outside. I lay and stared at the window, wondering how my body could feel so fresh, so alert. There was movement downstairs, and I guessed that Christian was doing some tidying, restlessly walking through the house, trying to adjust to the idea of me moving in.

The sheets smelled of mothballs and old cotton; the bed creaked in a metallic way when I shifted on it, and when I lay still the whole room clicked and shuffled, as if adapting itself to its first company in so many years. I lay awake for ages, but must have drifted to sleep again before first light, because suddenly Christian was bending over me, shaking my shoulder gently.

I started with surprise, awake at once, and propped up on my elbows, looking around. It was dawn. "What is it, Chris?"

"I've got to go, old boy. I'm sorry, but I have to."

I realized he was wearing a heavy oilskin cape, and had thick-soled walking boots on his feet. "Go? What d'you mean, go?"

"I'm sorry, Steve. There's nothing I can do about it." He spoke softly, as if there were someone else in the house who might be woken by raised voices. He looked more drawn than ever in this pale light, and his eyes were narrowed, I thought with pain, or anxiety. "I have to go away for a few days. You'll be all right. I've left a list of instructions downstairs, where to get bread, eggs, all that sort of thing. I'm sure you'll be able to use my ration book until yours comes. I shan't be long, just a few days. That's a promise. . . ."

He rose from his crouch and walked out of the door. "For God's sake Chris, where are you going?"

"Inwards," was all he said, before I heard him clump heavily down the stairs. I remained motionless for a moment or two, trying to clear my thoughts, then rose, put on my dressing-gown and followed him down to the kitchen. He had already left the house. I went back up to the landing window and saw him skirting the edge of the yard and walking swiftly down towards the south track. He was wearing a wide-brimmed hat, and carrying a long, black staff; on his back he had a small rucksack, slung uncomfortably over one shoulder.

"Where's inwards, Chris?" I said to his vanishing figure, and watched long after he had disappeared from view. "What's going on inside your head?" I asked of his empty bedroom as I wandered restlessly through the house; Guiwenneth, I decided in my wisdom, her loss, her leaving . . . how little one could interpret from the words "she's gone". And in all our chat of the evening before he had never alluded to the girl again. I had come home to England expecting to find a cheerful young couple, and instead had found a haunted, wasting brother living in the derelict shadow of our family home.

By the afternoon I had resigned myself to a period of solitary living, for wherever Christian had gone (and I had a fairly good idea) he had hinted clearly that he would be gone for some time. There was a lot to do about the house, and the yard, and there seemed no better way to spend my time than in beginning to rebuild the personality of the house. I made a list of essential repairs, and the following day walked into the nearest town to order what materials I could, mostly wood and paint, which I found in reasonable supply.

I renewed my acquaintance with the Knaresthorpe family, and with many of the local families with whom I had once been friendly. I terminated the services of the part-time cook; I could look after myself quite well enough. And I visited the cemetery; a single, brief visit, coldly accomplished.

The month of August turned to September, and I noticed a definite crispness in the air by evening, and early in the morning. It was a season I loved, the turn from summer to autumn, although it bore with it association of return to school after the long vacation, and that was a memory I didn't cherish. I soon grew used to being on my own in the house, and although I took long walks around the deep woodlands, watching the road and the railway track for Christian's return, I had ceased to feel anxious about him by the end of my first week home, and had settled comfortably into a daily routine of building in the yard, painting the exterior woodwork of the house ready for the onslaught of winter, and digging over the large, untended garden.

It was during the evening of my eleventh day at home that this domestic routine was disturbed by a circumstance of such peculiarity that afterwards I could not sleep for thinking about it.

I had been in the town of Hobbhurst for most of the afternoon, and after a light evening meal was sitting reading the newspaper; towards nine o'clock, as I began to feel ready for an evening stroll, I thought I heard a dog, not so much barking as howling. My first thought was that Christian was coming back, my second that there were no dogs in this immediate area at all.

I went out into the yard; it was after dusk, but still quite bright, although the oakwoods were melded together into a grey-green blur. I called for Christian, but there was no response. I was about to return to my paper when a man stepped out of the distant woodland, and began to trot towards me; on a short, leather leash he was holding the most enormous hound I have ever seen.

At the gate to our private grounds he stopped, and the dog began to growl; it placed its forepaws on the fence, and in so doing rose almost to the height of its master. I felt nervous at once, keeping my attention balanced between the gaping, panting mouth of that dark beast, and the strange man who held it in check.

It was difficult to make him out clearly, for his face was painted with dark patterns and his moustaches drooped to well below his chin; his hair was plastered thickly about his scalp; he wore a dark woollen shirt, with a leather jerkin over the top, and tight, check-patterned breeches that reached to just below his knees. When he stepped cautiously through the gate I could see his rough and ready sandals. Across his shoulder he carried a crude-looking bow, and a bundle of arrows, held together with a simple thong and tied to his belt. He, like Christian, carried a staff.

Inside the gate he hesitated, watching me. The hound was restless beside him, licking its mouth and growling softly. I had never seen a dog such as this, shaggy and dark-furred, with the narrow pointed face of an Alsatian, but the body, it seemed to me, of a bear; except that its legs were long and thin, an animal made for chasing, for hunting.

The man spoke to me, and although I felt familiar with the words, they meant nothing. I didn't know what to do, so I shook my head and said that I didn't understand. The man hesitated just a moment before repeating what he had said, this time with a distinct edge of anger in his voice. And he started to walk towards me, tugging at the hound to prevent it straining at the leash. The light was draining from the sky, and he seemed to grow in stature in the greyness as he approached. The beast watched me, hungrily.

"What do you want?" I called, and tried to sound firm when I would rather have run inside the house. The man was ten paces away from me. He stopped, spoke again and this time made eating motions with the hand that held his staff. *Now* I understood. I nodded vigorously. "Wait here," I said, and went back to the house to fetch the cold joint of pork that was to last me four more days. It was not large, but it seemed an hospitable thing to do. I took this, half a granary loaf, and a jug of bottled beer out into the yard. The stranger was crouched, now, the hound lying down beside him, rather reluctantly, it seemed to me. As I tried to approach them, the dog roared in a way that set my heart racing, and nearly made me drop my gifts. The man shouted at the beast, and said something to me. I placed the food where I stood and backed away. The gruesome pair approached and again squatted down to eat.

As he picked up the joint I saw the scars on his arm, running down and across the bunched muscles. I also smelled him, a raw, rancid odour, sweat and urine mixed with the fetid aroma of rotting meat. I nearly gagged but held my ground watching as the stranger tore at the pork with his teeth, swallowing hard and fast. The hound watched me.

After a few minutes the man stopped eating, looked at me, and with his gaze fixed on mine, almost challenging me to react, passed the rest of the meat to the dog, which growled loudly and snapped at the joint. The hound chewed, cracked and gulped the entire piece of pork in less than four minutes, while the stranger cautiously—and without much apparent pleasure—drank beer, and chewed on a large mouthful of bread.

Finally this bizarre feast was over. The man rose to his feet and jerked the hound away from where it was licking the ground noisily. He said a word I intuitively recognized as "thankyou". He was about to turn when the hound scented something; it uttered a high-pitched keen, followed by a raucous bark, and snatched itself away from its master's restraining grip, racing across the yard to a spot between the ramshackle chicken houses. Here it sniffed and scratched until its master reached it, grabbed the leather leash, and shouted angrily and lengthily at his charge. The hound moved with him, padding silently and monstrously into the gloom beyond the yard. The last I saw of them they were running at full speed, around the edge of the woodland, towards the farmlands around the village of Grimley.

In the morning the place where man and beast had rested *still* smelled rank. I skirted the area quickly as I walked to the woods and found the place where my strange visitors had exited from the trees; it was trampled and broken, and I followed the line of their passage for some yards into the shade before stopping and turning back.

Where on earth had they come from? Had the war had such an effect on men in England that some had returned to the wild, using bow and arrow and hunting dog for survival?

Not until midday did I think to look between the chicken huts, at the ground so deeply scored by that brief moment's digging. What had the beast scented, I wondered, and a sudden chill clawed at my heart. I left the place at a run, unwilling, for the moment, to confirm my worst fears.

How I knew I cannot say; intuition, or perhaps something that my subconscious had detected in Christian's words and mannerisms the week or so before, during our brief encounter. In any event, late in the afternoon that same day I took a spade to the chicken huts, and within a few minutes of digging had proved my instinct right.

It took me half an hour of sitting on the back doorstep of the house, staring across the yard at the grave, to find the courage to uncover the woman's body totally. I was dizzy, slightly sick, but most of all I was shaking; an uncontrollable, unwelcome shaking of arms and legs, so pronounced that I could hardly pull on a pair of gloves. But eventually I knelt by the hole and brushed the rest of the dirt from the girl's body.

Christian had buried her three feet deep, face down; her hair was long and red; her body was still clad in a strange green garment, a patterned tunic that was laced at the sides and, though it was crushed up almost to her waist now, would have reached to her calves. A staff was buried with her. I turned the head, holding my breath against the almost intolerable smell of putrefaction, and with a little effort could gaze upon the withering face. I saw then how she had died, for the head and stump of the arrow were still embedded in her eye. Had Christian tried to withdraw the weapon and succeeded only in breaking it? There was enough of the shaft left for me to notice that it had the same carved markings as the arrow in my father's study.

Poor Guiwenneth, I thought, and let the corpse drop back to its resting place. I filled in the dirt again. When I reached the house I was cold with sweat, and in no doubt that I was about to be violently sick.

Two days later, when I came down in the morning, I found the kitchen littered with Christian's clothes and effects, the floor covered with mud and leaf litter, the whole place smelling unpleasant. I crept upstairs to his room and stared at his semi-naked body; he was belly down on the bed, face turned towards me, sleeping soundly and noisily, and I imagined that he was sleeping enough for a week. The state of his body, though, gave me cause for concern. He was scratched and scarred from neck to ankle, and filthy, and malodorous to an extreme. His hair was matted with dirt. And yet, about him there was something hardened and strong, a tangible physical change from the hollow-faced, rather skeletal young man who had greeted me nearly two weeks before.

He slept for most of the day, emerging at six in the evening wearing a loose-fitting grey shirt and flannels, torn off just above the knee. He had half-heartedly washed his face, but still reeked of sweat and vegetation, as if he had spent the days away buried in compost.

I fed him, and he drank the entire contents of a pot of tea as I sat watching him; he kept darting glances at me, suspicious little looks as if he were nervous of some sudden move or surprise attack upon him. The muscles of his arms and wrists were pronounced. This was almost a different man.

"Where have you been, Chris?" I asked after a while, and was not at all surprised when he answered, "In the woods, old boy. Deep in the woods." He stuffed more meat into his mouth and chewed noisily. As he swallowed he found a moment to say, "I'm quite fit. Bruised and scratched by the damned brambles, but quite fit."

In the woods. Deep in the woods. What in heaven's name could he have been doing there? As I watched him wolf down his food I saw again the stranger, crouching like an animal in my yard, chewing on meat as if he were some wild beast. Christian reminded me of that man. There was the same air of the primitive about him.

"You need a bath rather badly," I said, and he grinned and made a sound of affirmation. "What have you been doing, Chris? In the woods. Have you been camping?"

He swallowed noisily, and drank half a cup of tea before shaking his head. "I have a camp there, but I've been searching, walking as deep as I could get. But I still can't get beyond . . ." he broke off, and glanced at me, a questioning look in his eyes. "Did you read the old man's notebook?"

I said that I hadn't. In truth, I had been so surprised by his abrupt departure, and so committed to getting the house back into some sort of shape, that I had forgotten all about father's notes on his work. And even as I said this I wondered if the truth of the matter was that I had put father, his work and his notes, as far from my mind as possible, as if they were spectres whose haunting would reduce my resolve to go forward.

Christian wiped his hand across his mouth and stared at his empty plate. He suddenly sniffed himself and laughed. "By the Gods, I do stink. You'd better boil me up some water, Steve. I'll wash right now."

But I didn't move. Instead I stared across the wooden table at him; he caught my gaze and frowned. "What is it? What's on your mind?"

"I found her, Chris. I found her body. Guiwenneth. I found where you buried her."

I don't know what reaction I expected from Christian. Anger, perhaps, or panic, or a sudden babbling burst of explanation. I half hoped he would react with puzzlement, that the corpse in the yard would turn out not to be the remains of his wife, and that he had no involvement with its burial. But Christian knew about the body. He stared at me blankly, and a heavy, sweaty silence made me grow uncomfortable.

Suddenly I realized that Christian was crying, his gaze unwavering from my own, but moistened, now, by the great flood of tears through the remaining grime on his face. And yet he made no sound, and his face never changed its expression from that of bland, almost blind contemplation.

"Who shot her, Chris?" I asked quietly. "Did you?"

"Not me," he said, and with the words his tears stopped, and his gaze dropped to the table. "She was shot by a mythago. There was nothing I could do about it."

Mythago? The meaning was alien to me, although I recognized the word from the scrap of my father's notebook that I carried. I queried it and Chris rose from the table, but rested his hands upon it as he watched me. "A mythago," he repeated. "It's still in the woods . . . they all are. That's where I've been, seeking among them. I tried to save her, Steve. She was alive when I found her, and she might have stayed alive, but I brought her out of the woods . . . in a way, I did kill her. I took her away from the vortex, and she died quite quickly. I panicked, then. I didn't know what to do. I buried her because it seemed the easiest way out. . . ."

"Did you tell the police? Did you report her death?"

Christian grinned, but it was not with any morbid humour. It was a knowing grin, a response to some secret that he had not yet shared; and yet the grin was merely a defence, for it faded rapidly. "Not necessary Steve . . . the police would not have been interested."

I rose angrily from the table. It seemed to me that Christian was behaving, and had behaved, with appalling irresponsibility. "Her family, Chris . . . her parents! They have a right to know."

And Christian laughed.

I felt the blood rise in my face. "I don't see anything to laugh at."

He sobered instantly, looked at me almost abashed. "You're right. I'm sorry. You don't understand, and it's time you did. Steve, she had no parents because she had no life, no real life. She's lived a thousand times, and she's never lived at all. But I still fell in love with her . . . and I shall find her again in the woods; she's in there somewhere. . . ."

Had he gone mad? His words were the unreasoned babblings of one insane, and yet something about his eyes, something about his demeanour, told me that it was not so much insanity as obsession. But obsession with what?

"You *must* read the old man's notes, Steve. Don't put it off any longer. They will tell you about the wood, about what's going on in there. I mean it. I'm neither mad nor callous. I'm just trapped, and before I go away again, I'd like you to know why, and how, and where I'm going. Perhaps you'll be able to help me. Who knows? Read the book. And then we'll talk. And when you know what our dear departed father managed to do, then I'm afraid I have to take my leave of you again."

There is one entry in my father's notebook that seems to mark a turning point in his research, and in his life. It is a longer entry than the rest of that particular time, and follows an absence of seven months from the pages. While his entries are detailed, he could not be described as having been a dedicated diarist, and the style varies from clipped notes to fluent description. (I discovered, too, that he himself had torn many pages from the thick book, thus concealing my minor crime quite effectively. Christian had never noticed the missing page.) On the whole, he seems to have used the notebook, and the quiet hours of recording, as a way of conversing with himself —a means of clarification of his own thoughts.

The entry in question is dated September 1933, and was written shortly after our encounter with the Twigling. After reading the entry for the first time I thought back to that year and realized I had been just nine years old.

Wynne-Jones arrived after dawn. Walked together along the south track, checking the flux-drains for signs of mythago activity. Back to the house quite shortly after— no-one about, which suited my mood. A crisp, dry autumn day. Like last year, images of the Urscumug are strongest as the season changes. Perhaps he senses autumn, the dying of the green. He comes forward, and the oakwoods whisper to him. He must be close to genesis. Wynne-Jones thinks a further time of isolation needed, and it must be done. Jennifer already concerned and distraught by my absences. I feel helpless—can't speak to her. Must do what is needed.

Yesterday the boys glimpsed the Twigling. I had thought him resorbed—clearly the resonance stronger than we had believed. He seems to frequent woodland edge, which is to be expected. I have seen him along the track several times, but not for a year or so. The persistence is worrying. Both boys clearly disturbed by the sighting; Christian less emotional. I suspect it meant little to him, a poacher perhaps, or local man taking short cut to Grimley. Wynne-Jones suggests we go back into woods and call the Twigling deep, perhaps to the hogback glade where he might remain in strong oak-vortex and eventually fade. But I know that penetrating into deep woodland will involve more than a week's absence, and poor Jennifer already deeply depressed by my behaviour. Cannot explain it to her, though I dearly want to. Do not want the children involved in this, and it worries me that they have now twice seen a mythago. I have invented magic forest creatures—stories for them. Hope they will associate what they see with products of their own imaginations. But must be careful. Until it is resolved, until the Urscumug mythago forms must not let any but Wynne-Jones know of what I have discovered. The completeness of the resurrection essential. The Urscumug is the most powerful because he is the primary. I know for certain that the oakwoods will contain him, but others might be frightened of the power they would certainly be able to feel, and end it for everyone. Dread to think what would happen if these forests were destroyed, and yet they cannot survive for ever.

Today's training with Wynne-Jones: test pattern 26: iii, shallow hypnosis, green light environment. As the frontal bridge reached sixty volts, despite the pain the flow across my skull was the most powerful I have ever known. Am now totally convinced that each half of the brain functions in a slightly different way, and that the hidden awareness is located on the right hand side. It has been lost for so long! The Wynne-Jones bridge enables a superficial communion between the fields around each hemisphere, and the zone of the pre-mythago is excited accordingly. If only there were some way of exploring the living brain to find exactly where the site of this occult presence lies.

The forms of the mythagos cluster in my peripheral vision, still. Why never in fore-vision? These unreal images are mere reflections, after all. The form of Hood was subtly different—more brown than green, the face less friendly, more haunted, drawn. This is certainly because earlier images (even the Hood mythago that actually formed in the woodland, two years ago) were affected by my own confused childhood images of the greenwood, and the merry band. But now, evocation of the pre-mythago is more powerful, reaches to the basic form, without interference. The Arthur form was more real as well, and I glimpsed the various marshland forms from the latter part of the first millennium A.D. Wynne-Jones would love me to explore these folk heroes, unrecorded and unknown, but I am anxious to find the primary image.

The Urscumug formed in my mind in the clearest form I have ever seen him. Hints of the Twigling in shape, but he is much more ancient, far bigger. Decks himself with wood and leaves, on top of animal hides. Face seems smeared with white clay, forming a mask upon the exaggerated features below; but it is hard to see the face clearly. A mask upon a mask? The hair a mass of stiff and spiky points; gnarled hawthorn branches are driven up through the matted hair, giving a most bizarre appearance. I believe he carries a spear, with a wide, stone blade ... an angry-looking weapon, but again, hard to see, always just out of focus. He is so old, this primary image, that he is fading from the human mind, and in any event is touched with confusion, the over-assertion of later cultural interpretation of his appearance . . . a hint of bronze particularly, mostly about the arms (torques). I suspect that the legend of the Urscumug was powerful enough to carry through all the neolithic and on into the second millennium B.C., perhaps even later. Wynne-Jones thinks the Urscumug may pre-date even the neolithic.

Essential, now, to spend time in the forest, to allow the vortex to interact with me and form the mythago. I intend to leave the house within the next week.

Without commenting on the strange, confusing passage that I had read, I turned the pages of the diary and read entries here and there. I could clearly recall that autumn in 1933, the time when my father had packed a large rucksack and wandered into the woods, walking swiftly away from my mother's hysterical shouting, flanked by his diminutive scientist friend (a sour-faced man who never acknowledged anyone but my father, and who seemed embarrassed to be in the house when he came to visit). Mother had not spoken for the rest of the day, and she did nothing but sit in her bedroom and occasionally weep. Christian and I had become so distraught by her behaviour that in the late afternoon we had penetrated the oakwoods as deeply as we dared, calling for our father, and finally panicking at the gloomy silence, and the loud, sudden sounds that disturbed it. He had returned weeks later, dishevelled and stinking like a tramp. The entry in his notebook, a few days later, is a short and bitter account of failure. Nothing had happened. A single, rather rambling paragraph caught my attention.

The mythogenetic process is not only complex, it is reluctant. My mind is not at rest and as Wynne-Jones has explained, it is likely that my human consideration, my worries, form an effective barrier between the two mythopoetic energy flows in my cortex—the *form* from the right brain, the *reality* from the left. The pre-mythago zone is not sufficiently enriched by my own life force for it to interact in the oak vortex. I fear too that the natural disappearance of so much life from the forest is affecting the interface. The boars are there, I'm sure. But perhaps the life number is critical. I estimate no more than forty, moving within the spiral vortex bounded by the ashwood intrusions into the oak circle. There are no deer, no wolves, although the most important animal, the hare, frequents the woodland edge in profusion. But perhaps the absence of so much that had once lived here has thrown the balance of the formula. And yet, through the primary existence of these woods, life was changing. By the thirteenth century there was much botanical life that was alien to the *ley matrix* in places where the mythagos still formed. The form of the myth men changes, adapts, and it is the later forms that generate easiest. Hood is back—like all the Jack-in-the-Greens, is a nuisance, and several times moved into the ridge-zone around the hogback glade. He shot at me, and this is becoming a cause of great concern! But I cannot enrich the oak vortex sufficiently with the pre-mythago of the Urscumug. What is the answer? Perhaps the memory is too far gone, too deep in the silent zones of the brain, now, to touch the trees.

Christian saw me frown as I read through this tumble of words and images. Hood? Robin Hood? And someone—this Hood—shooting at my father in the woods? I glanced around the study and saw the iron-tipped arrow in its long, narrow glass case, mounted above the display of woodland butterflies. Christian was turning the pages of the notebook, having watched me read in silence for the better part of an hour. He was perched on the desk; I sat in father's chair.

"What's all this about, Chris? It reads as if he were actually trying to create copies of storybook heroes."

"Not copies, Steve. The real thing. There. Last bit of reading for the moment, then I'll go through it with you in layman's terms."

It was an earlier entry, not dated by year, only by day and month, although it was clearly from some years before the 1933 recording.

I call those particular times "cultural interfaces"; they form zones, bounded in space, of course, by the limits of the country, but bounded also in time, a few years, a decade or so, when the two cultures—that of the invaded and the invader—are in a highly anguished state. The mythagos grow from the power of hate, and fear, and form in the natural woodlands from which they can either emerge—such as the Arthur, or Artorius form, the bear-like man with his charismatic leadership—or remain in the natural land-scape, establishing a hidden focus of hope—the Robin Hood form, perhaps Hereward, and of course the hero-form I call the Twigling, harassing the Romans in so many parts of the country. I imagine that it is the combined emotion of the two races that draws out the mythago, but it clearly sides with that culture whose roots are longest established in what I agree could be a sort of *ley matrix*; thus, Arthur forms and helps the Britons against the Saxons, but later Hood is created to help the Saxons against the Norman invader.

I drew back from the book, shaking my head. The expressions were confusing, bemusing. Christian grinned as he took the notebook and weighed it in his hands. "Years of his life, Steve, but his concern with keeping detailed records was not everything it might have been. He records nothing for years, then writes every day for a month."

"I need a drink of something. And a few definitions."

We walked from the study, Christian carrying the note-book. As we passed the framed arrow I peered closely at it. "Is he saying that the real Robin Hood shot that into him? And killed Guiwenneth too?"

"It depends," said Christian thoughtfully, "on what you

mean by real. Hood came to that oak forest, and may still be there. I think he is. As you have obviously noticed, he was there four months ago when he shot Guiwenneth. But there were many Robin Hoods, and all were as real or unreal as each other, created by the Saxon peasants during their time of repression by the Norman invader."

"I don't comprehend this at all, Chris—but what's a 'ley matrix'? What's an 'oak vortex'? Does it mean anything?"

As we sipped scotch and water in the sitting room, watching the dusk draw closer, the yard beyond the window greying into a place of featureless shapes, Christian explained how a man called Alfred Watkins had visited our father on several occasions and shown him on a map of the country how straight lines connected places of spiritual or ancient power— the barrows, stones and churches of three different cultures. These lines he called leys, and believed that they existed as a form of earth energy running below the ground, but influencing that which stood upon it. My father had thought about leys, and apparently tried to measure the energy in the ground below the forest, but without success. And yet he had measured *something* in the oakwoods—an energy associated with all the life that grew there. He had found a spiral vortex around each tree, a sort of aura, and those spirals bounded not just trees, but whole stands of trees, and glades. Over the years he had mapped the forest. Christian brought out that map of the woodland area, and I looked at it, again, but from a different point of view, beginning to understand the marks made upon it by the man who had spent so much time within the territories it depicted. Circles within circles were marked, crossed and skirted by straight lines, some of which were associated with the two pathways we called south and deep track. The letters HB in the middle of the vast acreage of forest were clearly meant to refer to the "hogback" glade that existed there, a clearing that neither Christian nor I had ever been able to find. There were zones marked out as "spiral oak", "dead ash zone" and "oscillating traverse".

"The old man believed that all life is surrounded by an energetic aura—you can see the human aura as a faint glow in certain light. In these ancient woodlands, *primary* woodlands, the combined aura forms something far more powerful, a sort of creative field that can interact with our unconscious. And it's in that unconscious that we carry what he calls the pre-mythago—that's *myth imago*, the image of the idealized form of a myth creature. This takes on substance in a natural environment, solid flesh, blood, clothing, and—as you saw—weaponry. The form of the idealized myth, the hero figure, alters with cultural changes, assuming the identity and technology of the time. When one culture invades another—according to father's theory—the heroes are made manifest, and not just in one location! Historians and legend seekers argue about where Arthur of the Britons, and Robin Hood *really* lived and fought, and don't realize that they lived in *many* sites. And another important fact to remember is that when the pre-mythago forms it forms in the *whole* population . . . and when it is no longer needed, it remains in our collective unconscious, and is transmitted through the generations."

"And the changing forms of the mythago," I said, to see if I had understood my sketchy reading of father's notes, "is based on an archetype, an archaic primary image which father called the Urscumug, and from which all later forms come. And he tried to raise the Urscumug from his own unconscious mind. . . ."

"And failed to do so," said Christian, "although not for want of trying. The effort killed him. It weakened him so much that his body couldn't take the pace. But he certainly seems to have created several of the more recent adaptations of the Urscumug."

There were so many questions, so many areas that begged for clarification. One above all: "But a thousand years ago, if I understand the notes correctly, there was a country-wide *need* of the hero, the legendary figure, acting for the side of Right. How can one man capture such a passionate mood?

How did he *power* the interaction? Surely not from the simple family anguish he caused among us, and in his own head. As he said, that created an unsettled mind and he couldn't function properly."

"If there's an answer," said Christian calmly, "it's to be found in the woodland area, perhaps in the hogback glade. The old man wrote in his notes of the need for a period of solitary existence, a period of meditation. For a year, now, I've been following his example directly. He invented a sort of electrical bridge which seems to *fuse* elements from each half of the brain. I've used his equipment a great deal, with and without him. But I already find images—the pre-mythagos —forming in my peripheral vision *without* the complicated programme that he used. He was the pioneer; his own interaction with the wood has made it easier for those who come after. He achieved a certain success; I intend to complete his work, eventually. I shall raise the Urscumug, this hero of the first men."

"To what end, Chris?" I asked quietly, and in all truth could not see a reason for so tampering with the ancient forces that inhabited both woodland and human spirit. Christian was clearly obsessed with the idea of raising these dead forms, of finishing something the old man had begun. But in my reading of his notebook, and in my conversation with Christian, I had not heard a single word that explained *why* so bizarre a state of nature should be so important to the ones who studied it.

Christian had an answer. And as he spoke to me his voice was hollow, the mark of his uncertainty, the stigma of his lacking conviction in the truth of what he said. "Why, to study the earliest times of man, Steve. From these mythagos we can learn so much of how it was, and how it was hoped to be. The aspirations, the visions, the cultural identity of a time so far gone that even its stone monuments are incomprehensible to us. To learn. To communicate through those persistent images of our past that are locked in each and every one of us."

He stopped speaking, and there was the briefest of silences, interrupted only by the heavy rhythmic sound of the clock. I said, "I'm not convinced, Chris." For a moment I thought he would shout his anger; his face flushed, his whole body tensed up, furious with my calm dismissal of his script. But the fire softened, and he frowned, staring at me almost helplessly. "What does that mean?"

"Nice-sounding words; no conviction."

After a second he seemed to acknowledge some truth in what I said. "Perhaps my conviction has gone, then, buried beneath . . . beneath the other thing. Guiwenneth. She's become my main reason for going back now."

I remembered his callous words of a while ago, about how she had no life yet a thousand lives. I understood instantly, and wondered how so obvious a fact could have remained so doggedly elusive to me. "She was a mythago herself," I said. "I understand now."

"She was my father's mythago, a girl from Roman times, a manifestation of the Earth Goddess, the young warrior princess who can unite the tribes. I can find no recorded legends about her, but she is associated with the oral tradition, with the Celtic tradition of keeping a name silent. She was a powerful woman, and led—in all her appearances—a powerful resistance to the Romans. . . ."

"Like Queen Boadicea."

"Before and after that uprising. Legends of Guiwenneth inspired many tribes to take offensive action against the invader." His gaze became distant for a moment. "And then she was formed in this wood, and I found her and came to love her. She was not violent, perhaps because the old man himself could not think of a woman being violent. He imposed a structure on her, disarming her, leaving her quite helpless in the forest."

"How long did you know her?" I asked, and he shrugged.

"I can't tell, Steve. How long have I been away?"

"Twelve days or so."

"As long as that?" He seemed surprised. "I thought no more than three. Perhaps I knew her for many months, then, but it seems no time at all. I lived in the forest with her, trying to understand her language, trying to teach her mine, speaking with signs and yet always able to talk quite deeply. But the old man pursued us right to the heartwoods, right to the end. He wouldn't let up—she was *his* girl, and he had been as struck by her as had I. I found him, one day, exhausted and terrified, half buried by leaves at the forest edge. I took him home and he was dead within the month. That's what I meant by his having had a reason for attacking me. I took Guiwenneth from him."

"And then she was taken from you. Shot dead."

"A few months later, yes. I became a little too happy, a little too content. I wrote to you because I had to tell *someone* about her . . . clearly that was too much for fate. Two days later I found her in a glade, dying. She might have lived if I could have got help to her in the forest, and left her there. I carried her out of the wood, though, and she died." He stared at me and the expression of sadness hardened to one of resolve. "But when I'm back in the wood, her myth image in my own subconscious has a chance of being formed . . . she might be a little tougher than my father's version, but I can find her again, Steve, if I look hard, if I can find that energy you asked about, if I can get into the deepest part of the wood, to that central vortex. . . ."

I looked at the map again, at the spiral field around the hog-back glade. "What's the problem? Can't you find it?"

"It's well defended. I get near it, but I can't ever get beyond the field that's about two hundred yards around it. I find myself walking in elaborate circles even though I'm convinced I've walked straight. I can't get in, and whatever's in there can't get out. All the mythagos are tied to their genesis zones, although the Twigling, and Guiwenneth too, could get to the very edge of the forest, down by the pool."

But that wasn't true! And I'd spent a shaky night to prove

it. I said, "One of the mythagos has come out of the wood . . . a tall man with the most unbelievably terrifying hound. He came into the yard and ate a leg of pork."

Christian looked stunned. "A mythago? Are you sure?"

"Well, no. I had no idea at all what he was until now. But he stank, was filthy, had obviously lived in the woods for months, spoke a strange language, carried a bow and arrows. . . ."

"And ran with a hunting dog. Yes, of course. It's a late bronze age, early iron age image, very wide-spread. The Irish have taken him to their own with Cuchulainn, made a big hero out of him, but he's one of the most powerful of the myth images, recognizable all across Europe." Christian frowned, then. "I don't understand . . . a year ago I saw him, and avoided him, but he was fading fast, decaying . . . it happens to them after a while. Something must have fed the mythago, strengthened it. . . ."

"Some *one*, Chris."

"But who?" It dawned on him, then, and his eyes widened slightly. "My God. Me. From my own mind. It took the old man years, and I thought it would take me a lot longer, many more months in the woodlands, much more isolation. But it's started already, my own interaction with the vortex. . . ."

He had gone quite pale, and he walked to where his staff was propped against the wall, picked it up and weighed it in his hands. He stared at it, touched the markings upon it.

"You know what this means," he said quietly, and before I could answer went on, "She'll form. She'll come back, my Guiwenneth. She may be back already."

"Don't go rushing off again, Chris. Wait a while; rest."

He placed his staff against the wall again. "I don't dare. If she has formed by now, she's in danger. I have to go back." He looked at me and smiled thinly, apologetically. "Sorry brother. Not much of a homecoming for you."

As quickly as this, after the briefest of reunions, I had lost

Christian again. He was in no mood to talk, too distracted by the thought of Guiwenneth alone and trapped in the forest to allow me much of an insight into his plans, and into his hopes and fears for some resolution to their impossible love affair.

I wandered through the kitchen and the rest of the house as he gathered his provisions together. Again and again he assured me that he would be gone for no more than a week, perhaps two. If she was in the wood he would have found her by that time; if not, then he would return and wait a while before going back to the deep zones and trying to form her mythago. In a year, he said, many of the more hostile mythagos would have faded into non-existence, and she would be safer. His thoughts were confused, his plan that he would strengthen her to allow her the same freedom as the man and the hound did not seem supportable on the evidence from our father's notes; but Christian was a determined man. If one mythago could escape, then so could the one he loved.

One idea that appealed to him was that I should come with him as far as the glade where we had made camp as children, and pitch a tent there. This could be a regular rendezvous for us, he said, and it would keep his time sense on the right track. And if I spent time in the forest I might encounter other mythagos, and could report on their state. The glade he had in mind was at the edge of the wood, and quite safe.

When I expressed concern that my own mind would begin to produce mythagos, he assured me that it would take months for the first pre-mythago activity to show up as a haunting presence at the edge of my vision. He was equally blunt in saying that, if I stayed in the area for too long, I would certainly start to relate to the woodland, whose aura—he thought —had spread more towards the house in the last few years.

Late the following morning we set off along the south track. A pale yellow sun hung high above the forest. It was a cool, bright day, the air full of the scent of smoke, drifting from the distant farm where the stubbly remains of the summer harvest were being burned. We walked in silence until we came to the mill-pond; I had assumed Christian would enter the oak woodland here, but wisely he decided against it; not so much because of the strange movements we had seen there as children, but because of the marshy conditions. Instead, we walked on until the woodland bordering the track thinned. Here Christian turned off the path.

I followed him inwards, seeking the easiest route between tangles of bracken and nettles, enjoying the heavy stillness. The trees were small, here at the edge, but within a hundred yards they began to show their real age, great gnarled oak-wood trunks, hollow and half-dead, twisting up from the ground, almost groaning beneath the weight of their branches. The ground rose slightly, and the tangled undergrowth was broken by weathered, lichen-covered stubs of grey limestone; we passed over the crest and the earth dipped sharply down, and a subtle change came over the woodland; it seemed darker, somehow, more alive, and I noticed that the shrill September bird-sound of the forest edge was replaced, here, by a more sporadic, mournful song.

Christian beat his way through bramble thickets, and I trudged wearily after, and we soon came to the large glade where, years before, we had made our camp. One particularly large oak tree dominated the surrounds, and we laughed as we traced the faded initials we had once carved there. In its branches we had made out look-out tower, but we had seen very little from that leafy vantage point.

"Do I look the part?" asked Christian, holding his arms out, and I grinned as I surveyed his caped figure, the rune-inscribed staff looking less odd, now, more functional.

"You look like something. Quite what I don't know."

He glanced around the clearing. "I'll do my best to get back here as often as I can. If anything goes wrong, I'll try and leave a message if I can't find you, some mark to let you know. . . ."

"Nothing's going to go wrong," I said with a smile. It was clear that he didn't wish me to accompany him beyond this glade, and that suited me. I felt a chill, an odd tingle, a sense of being watched. Christian noticed my discomfort and admitted that he felt it too, the presence of the wood, the gentle breathing of the trees.

We shook hands, then embraced awkwardly, and he turned on his heels and paced off into the gloom. I watched him go, then listened, and only when all sound had gone did I set about pitching the small tent.

For most of September the weather remained cool and dry, a dull sort of month, that enabled me to drift through the days in a very low-key state. I worked on the house, read some more of father's notebook (but quickly tired of the repetitive images and thoughts) and with decreasing frequency walked into the woodlands and sat near, or in the tent, listening for Christian, cursing the midges that haunted the place, and watching for any hint of movement.

With October came rain and the abrupt, almost startling realization that Christian had been gone for nearly a month. The time had slipped by, and instead of feeling concerned for him I had merely assumed that he knew what he was doing, and would return when he was quite ready. But he had been absent for weeks without even the slightest sign. He could surely have come back to the glade once, and left some mark of his passing.

Now I began to feel more concern for his safety than perhaps was warranted. As soon as the rain stopped I trudged back through the forest and waited out the rest of the day in the miserable, leaking canvas shelter. I saw hares, and a wood owl, and heard distant movements that did not respond to my cries of "Christian? Is that you?"

It got colder. I spent more time in the tent, creating a sleeping bag out of blankets and some tattered oilskins I found in the cellar of Oak Lodge. I repaired the splits in the tent, and stocked it with food and beer, and dry wood for fires. By the middle of October I noticed that I could not spend more than an hour at the house before becoming restless, an unease that could only be dispelled by returning to the glade and taking up my watching post, seated cross-legged just inside the tent, watching the gloom a few yards away. On several occasions I took long, rather nervous sorties further into the forest, but I disliked the sensation of stillness and the tingling of my skin that seemed to repeatedly say that I was being watched. All imagination, of course, or an extremely sensitive response to woodland animals, for on one occasion, when I ran screaming and yelling at the thicket wherein I imagined the voyeur was crouched, I saw nothing but a red squirrel go scampering in panic up into the crossed and confused branches of its home oak.

Where *was* Christian? I tacked paper messages as deep in the wood, and in as many locations, as I could. But I found that wherever I walked too far into the great dip that seemed to be swallowing the forest down, I would, at some point within the span of a few hours, find myself approaching the glade, and the tent again. Uncanny yes, and infuriating too; but I began to get an idea of Christian's own frustration at not being able to maintain a straight line in the dense oakwood. Perhaps, after all, there *was* some sort of field of force, complex and convoluted, that channelled intruders back onto an outward track.

And November came, and it was very cold indeed. The rain was sporadic and icy, but the wind reached down through the dense, browning foliage of the forest and seemed to find its way through clothes and oilskin and flesh to the cooling bones beneath. I was miserable, and my searches for Christian grew more angry, more frustrated. My voice was often hoarse with shouting, my skin blistered and scratched from climbing trees. I lost track of time, realizing on more than one occasion, and with some shock, that I had been two, or perhaps three days in the forest without returning to the house. Oak Lodge grew stale and deserted. I used it to wash, to feed, to rest, but as soon as the worst ravages to my body were corrected, thoughts of Christian, anxiety about him, grew in my mind and pulled me back to the glade, as surely as if I were a metal filing tugged to a magnet.

I began to suspect that something terrible had happened to him; or perhaps not terrible, just natural: if there really were boars in the wood, he might have been gored by one, and be either dead or dragging himself from the heartwoods to the edge, unable to cry for help. Or perhaps he had fallen from a tree, or quite simply gone to sleep in the cold and wet and failed to revive in the morning.

I searched for any sign of his body, or his having passed by, and I found absolutely nothing, although I discovered the spoor of some large beast, and marks on the lower trunks of several oaks that looked like nothing else than the scratchings of a tusked animal.

But my mood of depression passed, and by mid-November I was quite confident again that Christian was alive. My feelings, now, were that he had somehow become trapped in this autumnal forest.

For the first time in two weeks I went into the village, and after obtaining food supplies, I picked up the papers that had been accumulating at the tiny newsagents. Skimming the front pages of the weekly local, I noticed an item concerning the decaying bodies of a man and an Irish wolfhound, discovered in a ditch on farmland near Grimley. Foul play was not suspected. I felt no emotion, apart from a curious coldness, a sense of sympathy for Christian, whose dream of freedom for Guiwenneth was surely no more than that, a fervent hope, a desire doomed to frustration.

As for mythagos, I had only two encounters, neither of them of much note; the first was with a shadowy man-form that skirted the clearing, watching me, and finally ran into the darkness, striking at the trunks of trees with a short, wooden stick. The second meeting was with the Twigling, whose shape I followed stealthily as he walked to the mill-pond and stood in the trees, staring across at the boat-house. I felt no real fear of these manifestations, merely a slight apprehension. But it was only after the second meeting that I began to realize how alien was the wood to the mythagos, and how alien were the mythagos to the wood. These were creatures created far away from their natural age, echoes of the past given substance, equipped with a life, a language and a certain ferocity that was quite inappropriate to the war-scarred world of 1947. No wonder the aura of the woodland was so charged with a sense of solitude, an infectious loneliness that had come to inhabit the body of my father, and then Christian, and which was even now crawling through my own tissues, and would trap me if I allowed it.

It was at this time, too, that I began to hallucinate. Notably at dusk, as I stared into the woodlands, I saw movement at the edge of my vision. As first I put this down to tiredness, or imagination, but I remembered clearly the passage from my father's notebook in which he described how the pre-mythagos, the initial images, always appeared at his peripheral vision. I was frightened at first, unwilling to acknowledge that such creatures could be resident in my own mind, and that my own interaction with the woodland had begun far earlier than Christian had thought; but after a while I sat and tried to see details of them. I failed to do so. I could sense movement, and the occasional manlike shape, but whatever field was inducing their appearance was not yet strong enough to pull them into full view; either that, or my mind could not yet control their emergence.

On the 24th of November I went back to the house and spent a few hours resting and listening to the radio. A thunderstorm passed overhead and I watched the rain and the darkness, feeling quite wretched and cold. But as soon as the air cleared, and the clouds brightened, I draped my oilskin about my shoulders and headed back to the glade. I had not expected to find anything different, and so what should have been a surprise was more of a shock.

The tent had been demolished, its contents strewn and trampled into the sodden turf of the clearing. Part of the guy rope dangled from the higher branches of the large oak, and the ground hereabouts was churned as if there had been a fight. As I walked into the space I noticed that the ground was pitted by strange footprints, round and cleft, like hooves, I thought. Whatever the beast had been it had quite effectively torn the canvas shelter to tatters.

I noticed then how silent the forest was, as if holding its breath and watching. Every hair on my body stood on end, and my heartbeat was so powerful that I thought my chest would burst. I stood by the ruined tent for just a second or two and the panic hit me, making my head spin and the forest seem to lean towards me. I fled from the glade, crashing into the sopping undergrowth between two thick oak trunks. I ran through the gloom for several yards before realizing I was running *away* from the woodland edge. I think I cried out, and turned and began to run back.

A spear thudded heavily into the tree beside me and I had run into the black wood shaft before I could stop; a hand gripped my shoulder and flung me against the tree. I shouted out in fear, staring into the mud-smeared, gnarled face of my attacker. He shouted back at me:

"Shut up, Steve! For God's sake, shut up!"

My panic quietened, my voice dropped to a whimper and I peered hard at the angry man who held me. It was Christian, I realized, and my relief was so intense that I laughed, and for long moments failed to notice what a total change had come about him.

He was looking back towards the glade. "You've got to get out of here," he said, and before I could respond he had wrenched me into a run, and was practically dragging me back to the tent.

In the clearing he hesitated and looked at me. There was no smile from behind the mask of mud and browning leaves. His eyes shone, but they were narrowed and lined. His hair was slick and spikey. He was naked but for a breechclout and a ragged skin jacket that could not have supplied much warmth.

He carried three viciously pointed spears. Gone was the skeletal thinness of summer. He was muscular and hard, deep-chested and heavy-limbed. He was a man made for fighting.

"You've got to get out of the wood, Steve; and for God's sake don't come back."

"What's happened to you, Chris . . . ?" I stuttered, but he shook his head and pulled me across the clearing and into the woods again, towards the south track.

Immediately he stopped, staring into gloom, holding me back. "What is it, Chris?" And then I heard it too, a heavy crashing sound, something picking its way through the bracken and the trees towards us. Following Christian's gaze I saw a monstrous shape, twice as high as a man, but man-shaped and stooped, black as night save for the great white splash of its face, still indistinct in the distance and greyness.

"God, it's broken out!" said Chris. "It's got between us and the edge."

"What is it? A mythago?"

"*The* mythago," said Chris quickly, and turned and fled back across the clearing. I followed, all tiredness suddenly gone from my body.

"The Urscumug? That's *it*? But it's not human . . . it's animal. No human was ever that tall."

Looking back as I ran, I saw it enter the glade and move across the open space so fast I thought I was watching a speeded up film. It plunged into the wood behind us and was lost in darkness again, but it was running now, weaving between trees as it pursued us, closing the distance with incredible speed.

Quite suddenly the ground went out from under me. I fell heavily into a depression in the ground, to be steadied, as I tumbled, by Christian, who moved a bramble covering across us and put a finger to his lips. I could barely make him out in this dark hidey hole, but I heard the sound of the Urscumug die away, and queried what was happening.

"Has it moved off?"

"Almost certainly not," said Christian. "It's waiting, listening. It's been pursuing me for two days, out of the deep zones of the forest. It won't let up until I'm gone."

"But why, Chris? Why is it trying to kill you?"

"It's the old man's mythago," he said. "He brought it into being in the heartwoods, but it was weak and trapped until I came along and gave it more power to draw on. But it was the old man's mythago, and he shaped it slightly from his own mind, his own ego. Oh God, Steve, how he must have hated, and hated us, to have imposed such terror onto the thing."

"And Guiwenneth . . ." I said.

"Yes . . . Guiwenneth . . ." Christian echoed, speaking softly now. "He'll revenge himself on me for that. If I give him half a chance."

He stretched up to peer through the bramble covering. I could hear a distant, restless movement, and thought I caught the sound of some animal grumbling deep in its throat.

"I thought he'd failed to create the primary mythago."

Christian said, "He died believing that. What would he have done, I wonder, if he'd seen how successful he'd been." He crouched back down in the ditch. "It's like a boar. Half boar, half man; it walks upright, but can run like the wind. It paints its face white in the semblance of a human face. Whatever age it lived in, one thing's for sure, it lived a long time before man as we understand 'man' existed; this thing comes from a time when man and nature were so close that they were indistinguishable."

He touched me, then, on the arm, a hesitant touch, as if he were half afraid to make this contact with one from whom he had grown so distant.

"When you run," he said, "run for the edge. Don't stop. And when you get out of the wood, don't come back. There is no way out for me, now. I'm trapped in this wood by something in my own mind as surely as if I were a mythago myself. Don't come back here, Steve. Not for a long, long time."

"Chris—" I began, but too late. He had thrown back the

covering of the hole and was running from me. Moments later the most enormous shape passed over-head, one huge, black foot landing just inches from my frozen body. It passed by in a split second, but as I scrambled from the hole and began to run I glanced back and the creature, hearing me, glanced back too, and for that instant of mutual contemplation, as we both moved apart in the forest, I saw the face that had been painted across the blackened features of the boar.

The Urscumug opened its mouth to roar, and my father seemed to leer at me.

CODA

One morning, in early spring, I found a brace of hare hanging from one of the pot-hooks in the kitchen; below them, scratched in the yellow paintwork on the wall, was the letter C. The gift was repeated about two months later, but then nothing, and a year has passed.

I have not been back to the wood.

I have read my father's diary ten times if I have read it once, steeping myself in the mystery of his life as much as he had steeped himself in the mystery of his own unconscious links with the primeval woodland. I find, in his erratic recordings, much that tells of his sense of danger, of what—just once —he calls "ego's mythological ideal", the involvement of the creator's mind which he feared would influence the shape and behaviour of the mythago forms. He had known of the danger, then, but I wonder if Christian had fully comprehended this most subtle of the occult processes occurring in the forest. From the darkness and pain of my father's mind a single thread of gentleness and love had emerged in the fashioning of a girl in a green tunic, dooming her to a helplessness in the forest that was contrary to her natural form. But if she were to emerge again it would be with Christian's mind controlling her, and Christian had no such pre-conceived ideas about a woman's strength or weakness. It would not be the same encounter.

It is summer now. The trees are full-leaved, the forest at its most impenetrable. I stay in the house, out of range, although I've noticed that, at dusk especially, shapes and figures begin to cluster in my peripheral vision. The aura of the woodland has reached the front of the house. Only in the back room, among the books and specimens, can I find a temporary escape from the encroaching dark.